MW00977671

BLACKBIRCH PRESS, INC.
WOODBRIDGE, CONNECTICUT

How to Use These Books

The Blackbirch Encyclopedia of Science & Invention not only informs readers with entries on key developments, concepts, and people in science, it also presents a "snapshot" background and classification for each topic. To get the most from these books, readers may want to know the purpose of the infographic material that accompanies an entry.

The names and concepts following the idea light bulb list the people, theories, and discoveries that have contributed significantly to that entry's scientific development. Words or names that appear on the lists in **CAPITAL LETTERS** have a separate entry in the encyclopedia. Likewise, any words or names that appear in **boldface** in the text appear as separate entries in the encyclopedia.

The icons that precede the text of each entry classify it within the scientific world. Here are the fields to which each icon refers.

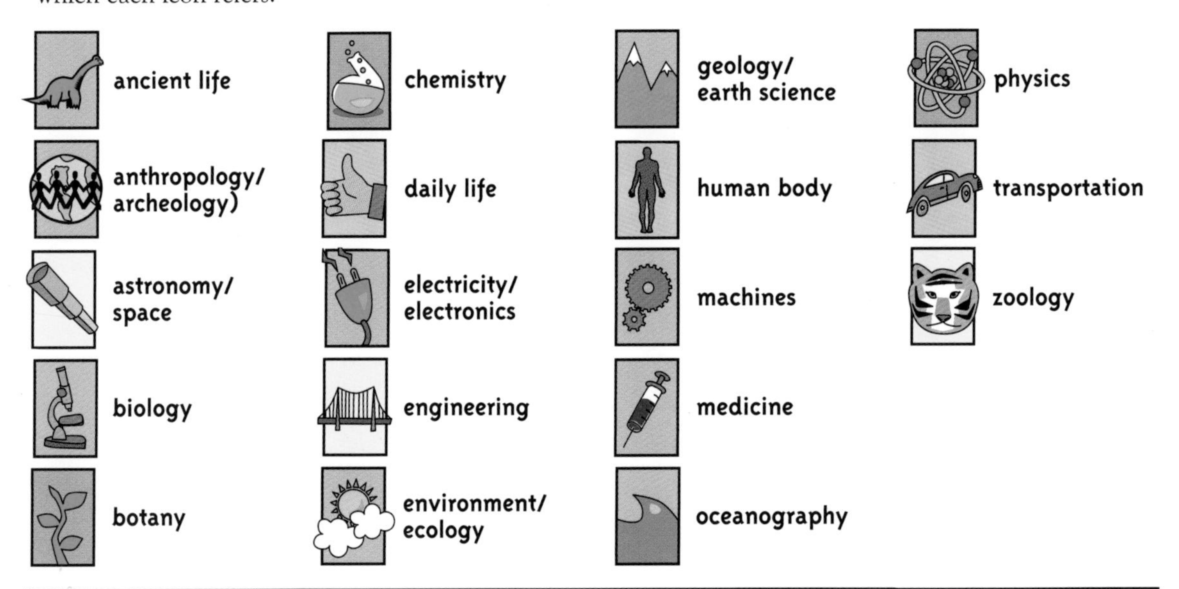

Published by Blackbirch Press, Inc.
260 Amity Road
Woodbridge, CT 06525
Web site: www.blackbirch.com
e-mail: staff@blackbirch.com

First Edition

Printed in the United States.

10 9 8 7 6 5 4 3 2 1

Library of Congress Cataloging-in-Publication Data

Tesar, Jenny E.
The Blackbirch encyclopedia of science and invention / by Jenny Tesar and Bryan Bunch
p. cm. —
Includes index.
ISBN 1-56711-577-2 (hardcover: alk. paper)
1. Science—Encyclopedias, Juvenile. 2. Technology—Encyclopedias, Juvenile. [1. Science—Encyclopedias. 2. Technology—Encyclopedias.] I. Bunch, Bryan H. II. Title

Q121.T47 2001
503—dc21

2001001134

Laënnec, René

Physician: invented the stethoscope
Born: February 17, 1781, Quimper, France
Died: August 13, 1826, Kerlouanec, France

Doctors used to listen to a patient's heart by putting an ear to the chest. But Laënnec called this impractical and "hardly suitable where most women were concerned." One day in 1816, facing a woman complaining of heart problems, he remembered a trick he learned as a child: when a person hits one end of a log, the sound travels through the log and can be heard by someone at the other end.

Laënnec rolled sheets of paper into a tube. He placed one end of the tube to his ear and the other end on the woman's chest. The sounds of her beating heart came through loud and clear. Laënnec called his invention a stethoscope, from Greek words meaning "to study the chest." His first permanent stethoscope was a wooden tube about 9 inches (23 cm) long.

René Laënnec

Stethoscope

Laënnec used the stethoscope to study chest sounds and correlate them with autopsy findings. For instance, he described normal breathing sounds, abnormal heartbeats, and murmurs resulting from diseased heart valves. Following publication of his work in 1819, the stethoscope became widely used by doctors.

RESOURCES

- Duffin, Jacalyn. *To See with a Better Eye: A Life of R. T. H. Laennec.* Princeton, NJ: Princeton University, 1998.
- THE MONAURAL STETHOSCOPE. **http://www.cybernurse.com/antiques/Tour/index.html**

Lagrange, Joseph-Louis

Mathematician: discovered special orbit points
Born: January 25, 1736, Turin, Italy
Died: April 10, 1813, Paris, France

In addition to numerous brilliant contributions to mathematics, Lagrange produced important work in astronomy and mechanics. He discovered five special positions near any two orbiting masses in the solar system, such as Earth and the Moon or Earth and the Sun. At these Lagrangian points, the gravitational pull of the two masses is such that a third, smaller mass can orbit in a fixed position. Groups of asteroids occupy the Lagrangian points of Jupiter's orbit; after the first was

The Earth-Moon system has 5 Lagrangian points.

found in 1906, astronomers remembered that Lagrange had predicted this in 1772. Space scientists applied Lagrangian points in 1995, launching the international satellite SOHO (Solar and Heliospheric Observatory) into a Lagrangian point of the Earth-Sun system. There, it has an uninterrupted view of the Sun. When earlier solar observatories orbited Earth, their observations were interrupted whenever Earth moved between their position and the Sun.

Lagrange's monumental *Mécanique Analytique* [Analytic Mechanics], published in 1788, summarized all the work done in mechanics (the science of how forces affect objects) since **Isaac Newton**. His use of formulas and equations to explain mechanical systems changed mechanics into a branch of mathematical analysis.

In 1793, the French government put Lagrange in charge of establishing a new system of **measurement**, the metric system. Lagrange was largely responsible for making it a decimal system, with all units differing from each other by multiples of 10.

RESOURCES

- CLASSICAL MECHANICS. **http://www.gsu.edu/other/timeline/mech.html**
- DEVELOPMENT OF MECHANICS. **http://www.chembio.uoguelph.ca/educmat/chm386/rudiment/tourclas/tourclas.htm**

Lamarck, Jean-Baptiste

Biologist: classified invertebrates, developed theory of evolution
Born: August 1, 1744, Bazantin, France
Died: December 18, 1829, Paris, France

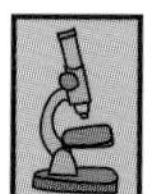

As Lamarck studied invertebrates at the National Museum of Natural History in Paris, he became increasingly disenchanted with the **classification** system proposed by **Carolus Linnaeus**. "The celebrated Linnaeus, and almost all other naturalists up to now, have divided the entire series of invertebrate animals into only two classes: insects and worms. As a consequence, anything that could not be called an insect must belong, without exception, to the class of worms."

Beginning in the 1790s, Lamarck revised invertebrate classification, adding new categories such as mollusks, echinoderms, polyps (jellyfish and corals), crustaceans, and arachnids (spiders and scorpions). His system is the basis of modern classification of these organisms.

Lamarck also was interested in **fossils**, wondering if they might be ancestors of

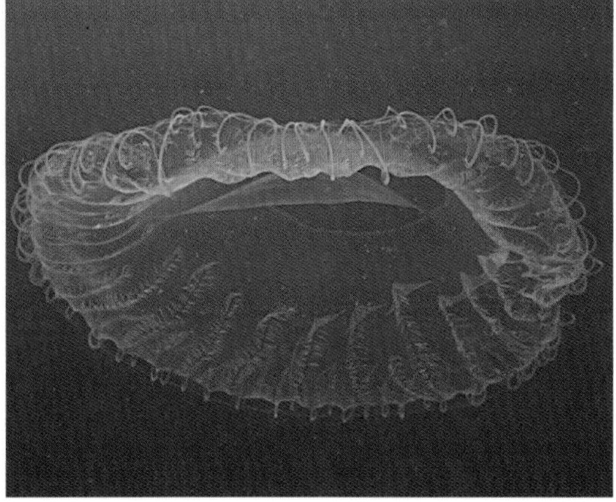

Lamarck created new classification categories for arachnids (spiders and scorpions) and polyps (jellyfish).

living species. This led to the first comprehensive theory of **evolution**, presented by Lamarck in 1809. According to Lamarck's theory, characteristics acquired during an organism's life can be inherited by its offspring. He argued, for example, that as a giraffe stretches to reach tree leaves, its neck lengthens. The longer neck is passed on to the next generation, which continues the habit of stretching. In this manner, over many generations a short-necked animal evolves into a long-necked giraffe.

Lamarck's theory has been disproved by modern genetics, which has shown that acquired characteristics do not affect **genes** and cannot be inherited.

- More about Jean-Baptiste Lamarck.

  http://curbar.clarehall.cam.ac.uk/userpages/djhc2/biogs/lamrck_2.htm

  http://www.ucmp.berkeley.edu/history/lamarck.html

Land, Edwin Herbert

Inventor: created instant photography
Born: May 7, 1909, Bridgeport, Connecticut
Died: March 1, 1991, Cambridge, Massachusetts

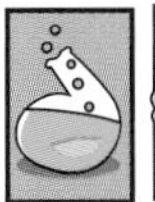

As a student at Harvard University in the late 1920s, Land invented the first modern filters to produce polarized light—a

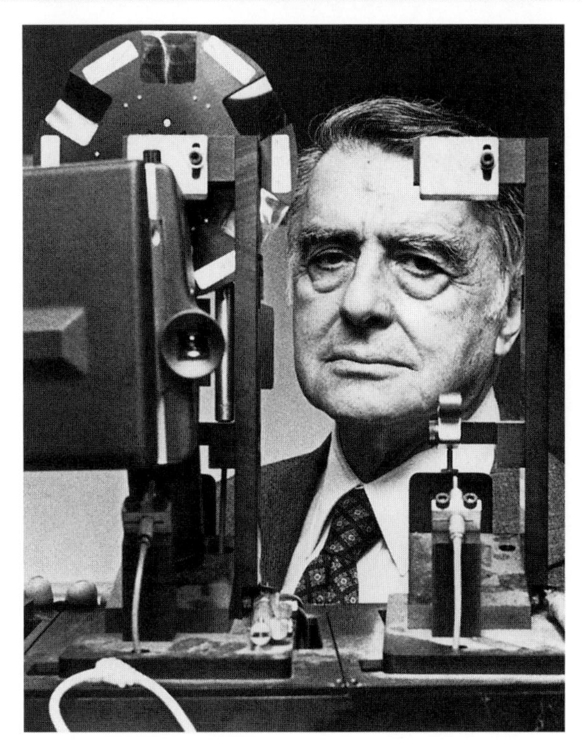

Edwin Herbert Land

light in which all waves are aligned in the same plane. With additional experimentation, he developed filters in which a polarizing material is sandwiched between two layers of plastic or glass. He called the devices Polaroid sheets and envisioned how they could reduce glare in items such as sunglasses, car headlights, and camera filters. In 1937, he formed the Polaroid Corporation to develop optical products.

One day in 1944, Land's young daughter asked why she couldn't see a photograph he had just taken. Land later recalled that he "undertook the task of solving the puzzle she had set me. Within the hour, the camera, the film, and the physical chemistry became so clear to me."

Several years of hard work were needed before Land perfected the camera and special film needed for instant **photography**. First marketed in 1948 as the Polaroid Land Instant Camera, the product quickly became a great success. In 1977, Land introduced an instant movie camera. It was superseded, however, by magnetic video tape recording.

RESOURCES

- More about Edwin Herbert Land.
  http://www.rowland.org/land/land.html
  http://web.mit.edu/invent/www/inventorsI-Q/land.html

Landsteiner, Karl

Immunologist: discovered blood types
Born: June 14, 1868, Vienna, Austria
Died: June 26, 1943, New York, New York

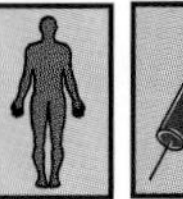
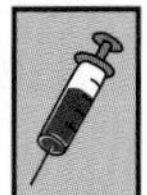

Landsteiner demonstrated that when blood from two people is mixed, the red blood cells sometimes clump together. In 1901 he

Blood must be tested to determine blood group.

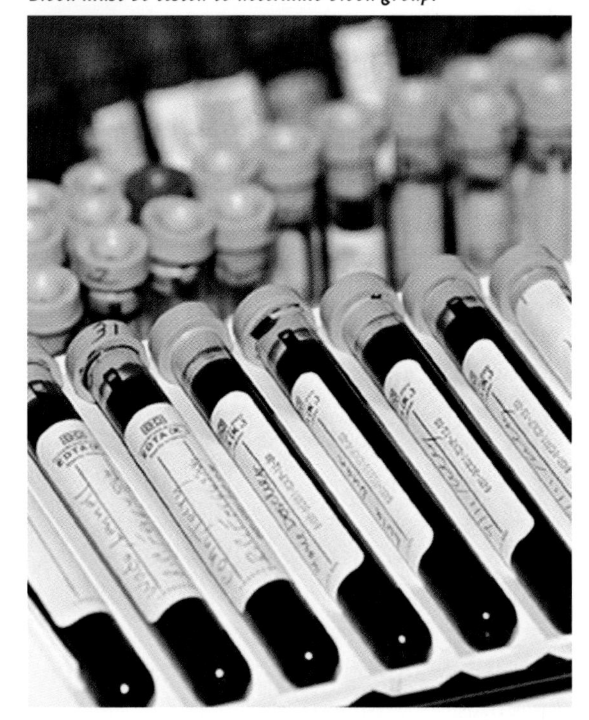

Karl Landsteiner

identified three blood groups, which were labeled A, B, and O. The following year two colleagues added a fourth group, AB. Discovery of these blood groups led to techniques for typing blood, which opened the way to safe transfusions.

Nobel Prize 1930

Landsteiner received the Nobel Prize in physiology or medicine "for his discovery of human blood groups."

During the following decades, Landsteiner studied allergic reactions and **immunity**, and discovered the blood groups M, N, and P. In 1940, he discovered a blood factor in Rhesus monkeys, which was named the Rhesus, or Rh, factor. The Rh factor also occurs in humans; people with it are said to be Rh-positive and those without, Rh-negative. If an Rh-negative person receives Rh-positive blood, red blood cells form clumps that can clog capillaries and impede oxygen transport.

How It Works

Blood groups are based on substances on red blood cells called antigens and substances in blood plasma called antibodies. For example, type A blood has A antigens and anti-B antibodies. People with type A blood can safely receive A and O blood. But if given B or AB blood, the A blood's anti-B antibodies attack and clump together the "invading" red blood cells.

Resources

- More about Karl Landsteiner.

  http://www.nobel.se/medicine/laureates/1930/landsteiner-bio.html

  http://www.nobel.se/medicine/laureates/1930/press.html

- History of Transfusion Medicine.

  http://www.aabb.org/All_About_Blood/FAQs/aabb_faqs.htm#highlights

  http://www.arcbs.redcross.org.au/educ/history.htm

Langmuir, Irving

Chemist: invented gas-filled lamp
Born: January 31, 1881, Brooklyn, New York
Died: August 16, 1957, Falmouth, Massachusetts

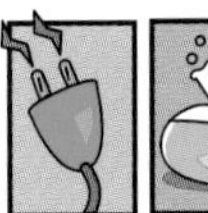

Langmuir's first significant achievement was improving the light bulb, saving Americans millions of dollars in electric

Irving Langmuir

bills. He showed that a light bulb's tungsten filament would last longer if the bulb's vacuum were replaced by nitrogen gas. He later found that tungsten filaments work

NOBEL PRIZE 1932

The Nobel Prize in chemistry was awarded to Langmuir "for his discoveries and investigations in surface chemistry."

best when coated with an extremely thin layer of thoria, an oxide of thorium.

Langmuir's experiments with thin films of oil floating on water laid the foundations of modern surface chemistry. He

YEARBOOK: 1913

- The gas-filled light bulb is introduced.
- The first home refrigerator goes on sale.
- The first true **assembly line** is introduced by Henry Ford [American: 1863–1947].

explained the chemical forces that bond together a single layer of molecules and reasons that chemical reactions occur between adjacent substances. He coined the terms *electrovalence* and *covalence*. Electrovalence refers to the transfer of electrons from atoms of one element to atoms of another. Covalence describes the sharing of a pair of electrons by two atoms.

Langmuir improved light bulbs.

In the 1940s, Langmuir collaborated with **Vincent J. Schaeffer** on improving smokescreens and creating artificial rain.

RESOURCES

- MORE ABOUT IRVING LANGMUIR.

  http://www.nobel.se/chemistry/laureates/1932/langmuir-bio.html

  http://www.ge.com/ibhisil.htm

Lasers

EINSTEIN (proposed mechanism to explain stimulated emission of light) ➤ **TOWNES/SCHAWLOW/Gould** (conceived laser) ➤ **MAIMAN** (first working laser) ➤ Development of lasers based on semiconductors ➤ Development of lasers based on carbon dioxide ➤ Development of free electron lasers

People once imagined laser beams cutting through spaceship walls, but today lasers have more practical uses such as burning

Cutting steel with a laser

CDs, decoding DVD movies, carrying conversations on **fiber optic** cables, and "welding" parts of human eyes. In less than a hundred years, lasers have gone from an obscure theory of **Albert Einstein** to a common part of everyday life.

In 1917, Einstein combined his own studies of **light** with the **quantum theory** of the atom to predict that light falling on excited atoms stimulates production of more light. The word *laser* is an acronym of "light amplification by stimulated emission of radiation." In 1953, **Charles Townes** applied Einstein's idea to **microwaves** and in 1958, with **Arthur Leonard Schawlow**, described how to

How It Works

Part of the energy in an atom or molecule is in the electrons. Changing the energy level of an electron occurs in distinct steps. In a laser, visible light or electric current is first used to raise the energy of billions of atoms from one step to the next, which is called pumping. Then photons of light of just the right energy are used to cause electrons to drop down one step. When an electron falls back to a lower step, it releases the extra energy as another photon, so there are two photons of the same energy instead of one. These encounter more electrons, creating a cascade of photons, all with exactly the same energy. Lasers trap these photons between mirrors, but one mirror also allows some photons out of the trap, where they emerge as a beam of light of one wavelength, or color, with matching peaks and valleys for the waves.

obtain similar results with visible light. A student, Gordon Gould [American: 1920–], had independently conceived the laser in 1957 and obtained a patent,

Lasers use a medium to emit photons of light.

but had little influence otherwise. The invention of the laser is usually attributed to **Theodore Harold Maiman**, who built the first working laser in 1960.

Since 1960, many different types of lasers have been invented to handle specific needs. Lasers based on semiconductors were introduced in 1962, and practical semiconductor lasers for telephone communications developed in 1970. Semiconductor lasers change electric current directly into light. Also developed in 1970 were powerful lasers based on carbon dioxide gas, capable of cutting or welding metals. In 1977, the first free electron lasers were invented—lasers in which the electrons are not confined to atoms. By 1984, some lasers produced X rays and other extremely short bursts of light.

Today, lasers have innumerable uses. At the exotic end, tight laser beams create artificial stars that astronomers use to compensate for viewing problems caused by atmospheric twinkling. On the familiar side, speedy office printers are also laser-based.

RESOURCES

- Taylor, Nick. *Laser: The Inventor, the Nobel Laureate, and the Thirty-year Patent War*. New York: Simon & Schuster, 2000.
- Townes, Charles H. *How the Laser Happened: Adventures of a Scientist*. New York: Oxford University, 1999.
- MORE ABOUT LASERS.

  http://library.thinkquest.org/16468/lasers.htm

  http://www.colorado.edu/physics/2000/lasers/

  http://www.howstuffworks.com/laser.htm

  http://www4.nas.edu/beyond/beyonddiscovery.nsf/web/laser10?OpenDocument

Lathes

A lathe is a tool used to hold and shape materials by cutting, a process called machining. The material to be machined is rotated while the cutting blade removes varying amounts one layer at a time. The simplest operation with a lathe is to create a uniform cylinder, but by varying the number of layers removed at different locations, complex three-dimensional objects can be machined. The lathe is the most basic of machine tools, which are devices most often used to make parts of other machines or parts of useful objects in general. A lathe is named for the material it machines. For example, chair legs are usually produced on wood lathes while camshafts are made on metal lathes.

The earliest evidence for use of a lathe is a sculpture from about 500 B.C.E. showing a king on a chair made with a wood lathe. Lathes were gradually improved with devices to adjust cutting edges and to manipulate rotation to make more complex patterns. By the 1500s, lathes could make wooden screws, for example. By 1701, a lathe that cut iron had been developed.

A primitive wood lathe

Unknown inventors added most improvements to lathes, but in 1797, Henry Maudslay [English: 1771–1831] made one of the greatest advances. Called a slide rest, Maudslay's invention holds and guides the cutting tool as the lathe turns. Before the slide rest, operators held the cutting tool in their hands.

RESOURCES

- Conover, Ernie. *The Lathe Book: A Complete Guide for the Wood Craftsman*. Newtown, CT: Taunton, 1993.

Laveran, Charles Louis Alphonse

Medical researcher: discovered malaria parasite
Born: June 18, 1845, Paris, France
Died: May 18, 1922, Paris, France

Malaria, a **disease** characterized by periodic chills and fevers, has afflicted people since ancient times. It wasn't until the 1870s, however, when the germ theory of disease was formulated, that researchers began to look to microorganisms as the cause of malaria.

NOBEL PRIZE 1902

Ross received the Nobel Prize for physiology or medicine "for his work on malaria."

NOBEL PRIZE 1907

Laveran received the Nobel Prize for physiology or medicine for "his work on the role played by protozoa in causing diseases."

Charles Louis Alphonse Laveran

Laveran initially studied malaria at a hospital in Algeria in 1879 to learn the role of tiny black particles found in the blood of malaria patients. As he examined malarial blood under a microscope, he discovered cysts as well as particles, and suspected the cysts might be formed by a parasite. On November 6, 1880, he saw organisms released from a cyst swim through the blood. He identified them as a previously unknown type of protozoan, later classified in the genus *Plasmodium*. He also showed that *Plasmodium* destroys red blood cells and changes their red pigment into black-pigmented particles.

Laveran was the first to show that protozoans can cause human disease. He wondered how *Plasmodium* enter the human body but was unable to find these parasites in air, soil, or water. Ronald Ross [English: 1857–1932], working in India, proved in 1898 that *Anopheles* mosquitoes carry the *Plasmodium* and transmit them to humans.

RESOURCES

- Desowitz, Robert S. *The Malaria Capers: More Tales of Parasites and People, Research and Reality*. New York: W.W. Norton, 1991.
- MORE ABOUT CHARLES LOUIS ALPHONSE LAVERAN.
  http://www.nobel.se/medicine/laureates/1907/laveran-bio.html
  http://www.nobel.se/medicine/laureates/1907/press.html
- MALARIA.
  http://www-micro.msb.le.ac.uk/224/Malaria.html

Lavoisier, Antoine Laurent

Chemist: explained combustion
Born: August 26, 1743, Paris, France
Died: May 8, 1794, Paris, France

Chemists of the 18th century believed that objects lose a weightless substance called phlogiston during combustion (burning). Lavoisier questioned this, for he found that some materials gain weight during combustion. In 1774, **Joseph Priestley** told Lavoisier that he had discovered a previously unknown gas that seemed to aid combustion. Priestley initially called the gas “dephlogisticated air;” Lavoisier later named it “oxygen.” Lavoisier disproved the phlogiston theory by demonstrating that oxygen is needed for combustion, and that combustion is a reaction in which oxygen combines with other elements.

Lavoisier showed that respiration is a process of slow combustion. He explained that oxygen is picked up by blood in the lungs, then used inside the body to burn food. He also showed that people breathe in more oxygen when they are active than at rest.

Antione Laurent Lavoisier

Lavoisier was the first to list the known elements, and he worked out a system for naming compounds based on the elements they contain. Then, in 1789, revolution against the king broke out in France. Lavoisier, a member of the agency that collected taxes for the king, was arrested and guillotined. Said mathematician **Joseph-Louis Lagrange**, “It required only a moment to sever that head, and perhaps a century will not be sufficient to produce another like it.”

RESOURCES

- McKie, Douglas. *Antoine Lavoisier.* New York: Da Capo, 1990. Reprint.
- Poirier, Jean-Pierre. *Lavoisier: Chemist, Biologist, Economist.* Philadelphia: University of Pennsylvania, 1998.
- Yount, Lisa. *Antoine Lavoisier, Founder of Modern Chemistry.* Springfield, NJ: Enslow, 1997. (JUV/YA)

Lawrence, Ernest Orlando

Physicist: invented the cyclotron
Born: August 8, 1901, Canton, South Dakota
Died: August 27, 1958, Palo Alto, California

The first **particle accelerator**, a device for breaking apart atomic nuclei, was a linear device whose development was announced in 1929. That same year Lawrence conceived the idea of a circular particle accelerator. In this device, called the cyclotron, pulsing magnetic fields accelerate ions (electrically charged particles) to successively higher energy levels as they orbit thousands or millions of times in a circular path. A fast-moving particle is then aimed at a nucleus, smashing it.

Ernest Orlando Lawrence

NOBEL PRIZE 1939

Lawrence received the Nobel Prize in physics for inventing the cyclotron.

Lawrence's first cyclotron, built in 1930, was an unimpressive-looking device with an accelerating chamber only 5 inches (12.7 cm) in diameter. The device boosted the energy of hydrogen ions to 80,000 electron volts, however, proving the effectiveness of Lawrence's concept.

YEARBOOK: 1939

- Lawrence's cyclotron with a 60-inch (152-cm) accelerating chamber begins operations, accelerating particles to 16 million electron volts.
- Philip H. Abelson [American: 1919–] identifies the products created when a uranium atom is split.
- **Irène and Frédéric Joliot-Curie** demonstrate that splitting uranium atoms can cause a chain reaction.

Over the next three decades, Lawrence built increasingly powerful cyclotrons that ushered in a new age of experimentation, led to the discovery of numerous **subatomic particles**, produced new elements heavier than uranium, and created artificially radioactive substances for use in medicine and research.

RESOURCES

- BIOGRAPHY OF ERNEST ORLANDO LAWRENCE.
  http://www.nobel.se/physics/laureates/1939/lawrence-bio.html
- CYCLOTRON: INVENTION FOR THE AGES.
  http://www.lbl.gov/Science-Articles/Archive/early-years.html

Leakey Family

Paleoanthropologists: discovered remains of early humans
Louis **Born:** August 7, 1903, Kabete, Kenya
Died: October 3, 1972, London, England
Mary **Born:** February 6, 1913, London, England
Died: December 9, 1996, Nairobi, Kenya
Richard **Born:** December 19, 1944, Nairobi, Kenya

The Leakeys were pioneers in paleoanthropology—a branch of anthropology that deals with the ancestors of modern humans (*Homo sapiens*). Working in Africa, they made pivotal discoveries that contributed greatly to the understanding of human **evolution**.

Louis discovered the Oldowan tool industry in eastern Africa—the world's earliest known manufacture of stone tools, dating from about 2.4 million to 1.5 million years ago. He also described *Homo habilis*, the earliest known member of the genus *Homo*, living in Africa during the same period.

In 1959, Mary, Louis's wife, unearthed remains of the first fossil of an early human relative, now called *Paranthropus boisei*. In 1978, she led a team of specialists that found trails of footprints left by *Australopithecus afarensis*, human ancestors over 3 million years old. The footprints showed that upright posture—an important human characteristic—evolved much earlier than had been believed.

In 1984, Richard, the son of Louis and Mary, found the first fossil of *Homo ergaster*, a human ancestor that lived about 1.5 million to 200,000 years ago. Richard's wife, Maeve, also has made notable finds, including the 1998 discovery of a 3.5-million-year-old skull of what appeared to be a new genus of early humans.

RESOURCES

- Morrell, Virginia. *Ancestral Passions: The Leakey Family and the Quest for Humankind's Beginnings*. New York: Simon & Schuster, 1996.
- Poynter, Margaret. *The Leakeys: Uncovering the Origins of Humankind*. Springfield, NJ: Enslow, 1997. (JUV/YA)
- THE LEAKEY FAMILY.
  http://www.time.com/time/time100/scientist/profile/leakey.html

Leavitt, Henrietta

Astronomer: developed method to measure distances to stars
Born: July 4, 1868, Lancaster, Massachusetts
Died: December 12, 1921, Cambridge, Massachusetts

Working at the Harvard College Observatory in the early 1900s, Leavitt was given the task of cataloging **stars** that go through cycles of brightness and darkness, known as variable stars. While studying the Magellanic Clouds—**galaxies** that she established are beyond our Milky Way galaxy—she discovered and cataloged 1,777 previously unknown variable stars.

Leavitt noticed that a certain type of variable star named Cepheid variables

Leavitt developed a method to measure the distance to stars.

have cycles of brightness and darkness that are inversely proportional to the stars' absolute magnitude (brightness). That is, the brighter on average the star, the slower its cycle. She used this information to invent a way to measure distances to stars. Leavitt's method helped **Edwin Hubble** and other astronomers map the **universe** and make additional discoveries.

RESOURCES

- MORE ABOUT HENRIETTA LEAVITT.

  http://web.mit.edu/invent/www/inventorsI-Q/leavitt.html

  http://www.hno.harvard.edu/gazette/1998/03.19/ReachingfortheS.html

Lederberg, Joshua

Geneticist: discovered genetic recombination
Born: May 23, 1925, Montclair, New Jersey

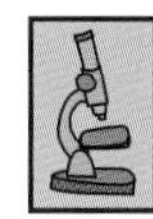

In the early 1940s, most biologists believed that **bacteria** reproduce asexually by splitting in two, with descendants inheriting identical genes. In 1946, Lederberg and Edward L. Tatum [American: 1909–1975] announced their discovery that bacteria also have a type of sexual reproduction termed genetic recombination. They mixed together two different strains of **Escherichia coli** bacteria, creating offspring that had a new combination of genes. This recombination demonstrated

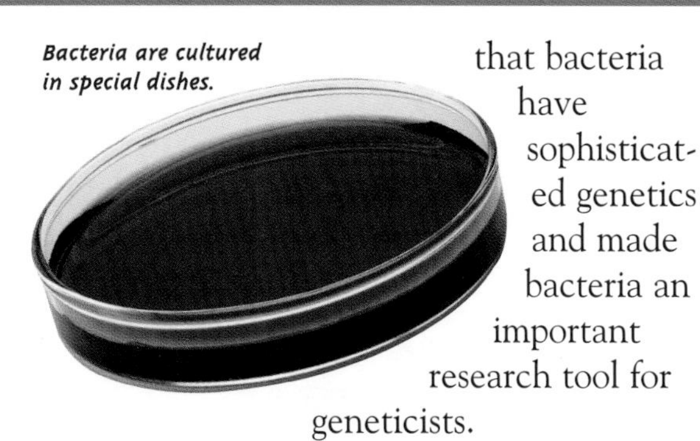
Bacteria are cultured in special dishes.

that bacteria have sophisticated genetics and made bacteria an important research tool for geneticists.

In 1952, Lederberg and his student Norton Zinder [American: 1928–] discovered a process they named transduction. Transduction is another type of genetic recombination, in which certain viruses carry bacterial genes from one bacterium to another. The latter bacterium incorporates the transferred genes into its own DNA and, when it reproduces, passes them on to its descendants.

Nobel Prize 1958

Lederberg was awarded the Nobel Prize in physiology or medicine "for his discoveries concerning genetic recombination and the organization of the genetic material of bacteria." He shared the prize with Tatum and George Wells Beadle [American: 1903–1989], who were honored "for their discovery that genes act by regulating definite chemical events."

Lederberg's experiments were the first to manipulate the genetic material of any organism, and paved the road to **genetic engineering**.

RESOURCES

• Biography of Joshua Lederberg.
http://www.nobel.se/medicine/laureates/1958/lederberg-bio.html

Leeuwenhoek, Antoni van

Microscopist: discovered many microscopic organisms and structures
Born: October 24, 1632, Delft, Netherlands
Died: August 26, 1723, Delft, Netherlands

Leeuwenhoek was a shopkeeper who sold linens, but he is remembered for his hobby. Using **microscopes** he constructed himself, he discovered a world invisible to the unaided eye. Each of Leeuwenhoek's microscopes had a single, biconvex lens that he ground himself. He was so expert at grinding that his single-lens microscopes were better than any compound microscopes then available.

The lens was mounted between two thin metal plates. By holding this instrument close to his eye, Leeuwenhoek

Antoni van Leeuwenhoek

looked at an object held on the tip of a needle on the other side of the lens, which could be adjusted to improve the focus. Liquid specimens were placed in thin glass tubes for viewing.

Notable Quotable

"My efforts are ever striving toward no other end than, as far as in me lieth, to set the truth before my eyes, to embrace it, and to lay out to good account the small talent that I've received: in order to draw the world away from its old heathenish superstition, to go over to the truth, and to cleave unto it."

—Antoni van Leeuwenhoek

Leeuwenhoek was the first person to see **bacteria** and ciliated protists (one-celled organisms that move by means of hairlike cilia). He also discovered small invertebrates such as hydras and rotifers. He was the first to accurately describe red blood cells and the lens of the eye.

Leeuwenhoek described his discoveries in letters to the Royal Society in London beginning in 1673. "Whenever I found out anything remarkable, I have thought it my duty to put down my discovery on paper, so that all ingenious people might be informed thereof," he once wrote.

RESOURCES

- Ruestow, E.G. *The Microscope in the Dutch Republic: The Shaping of Discovery.* New York: Cambridge University, 1996.
- Yount, Lisa. *Antoni Van Leeuwenhoek, First to See Microscopic Life.* Springfield, NJ: Enslow, 1996. (JUV/YA)
- More about Antoni van Leeuwenhoek. **http://www.ucmp.berkeley.edu/history/leeuwenhoek.html**

Leondardo da Vinci

Artist, scientist, inventor: Renaissance thinker
Born: April 15, 1452, Vinci, Italy
Died: May 2, 1519, Amboise, France

More than anyone else, Leonardo exemplified the "Renaissance man"—an expert in many fields, with wide interests and great creativity. His works of art, such as *Mona Lisa* and *The Last Supper*, are painting masterpieces celebrated around the world. As proven by his meticulously illustrated notebooks, he also was an

An anatomical drawing by da Vinci

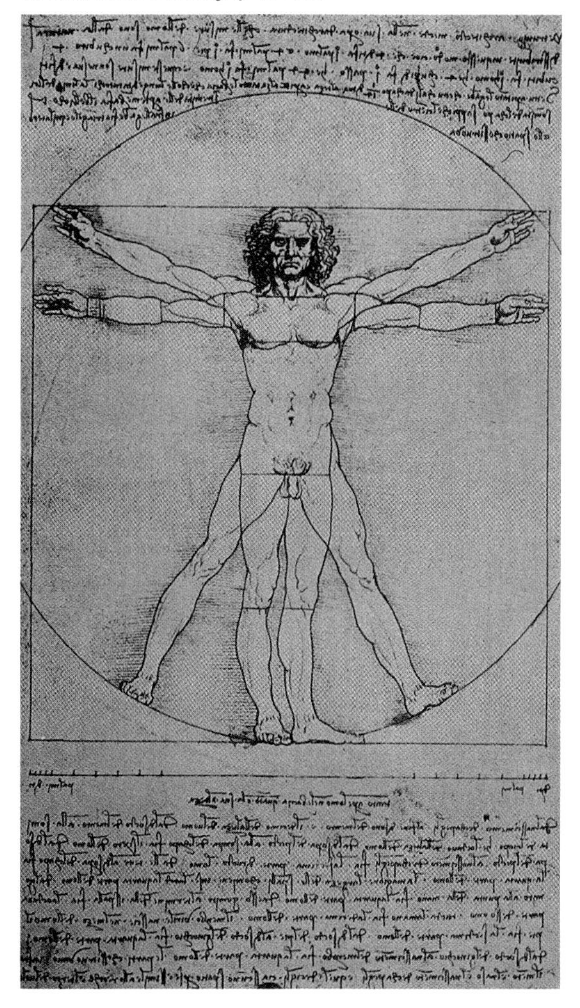

Leonardo da Vinci

outstanding anatomist, architect, engineer, and inventor.

Like other artists of the Renaissance (1400—1600), Leonardo studied the human body and carried out dissections to better understand **anatomy** and **physiology**. He used his artistic skills to create accurate drawings of bones, muscles, the heart, and other human and animal organs. He correctly concluded, contrary to the teachings of **Claudius Galen**, that air in the lungs does not come in direct contact with blood, and that vessels do not carry air to the heart.

Leonardo's engineering achievements included design of an improved canal **lock**, the basis of most locks used today. He designed cathedrals and fortresses, a tank, and other vehicles and weapons of war. He also invented instruments that measured the force of winds and the speed of ships. Many of his drawings showed concepts, such as parachutes and helicopters, that weren't invented until centuries later. The drawings were so exact that modern engineers have been able to build working models of Leonardo's concepts.

Notable Quotable

Experiment is the sole interpreter of the artifices of Nature.

—Leonardo da Vinci

At canal building sites, Leonardo found **fossils**. He reasoned that fossil shells of marine animals found on mountains weren't placed there by the biblical flood of Genesis, since "things heavier than water cannot float upon its surface but remain at the bottom and are not removed from there except by pressure from the waves." Rather, he envisioned Earth as undergoing transformations that cause areas once submerged under water to become exposed.

RESOURCES

- Herbert, Janis. *Leonardo Da Vinci for Kids: His Life and Ideas.* Chicago: Chicago Review, 1998. (JUV/YA)
- Leonardo Da Vinci. *The Notebooks of Leonardo da Vinci.* Mineola, NY: Dover, 1975.
- Nuland, Sherwin B. *Leonardo Da Vinci.* New York: Viking, 2000.
- LEONARDO DA VINCI: SCIENTIST, INVENTOR, ARTIST. **http://www.mos.org/leonardo/**

Leopold, Aldo

Ecologist: founded wildlife ecology
Born: January 11, 1886, Burlington, Iowa
Died: April 21,1948, near Baraboo, Wisconsin

After receiving a master's degree in forestry in 1909, Leopold joined the U.S. Forest Service. He soon began to focus on **conservation** of natural resources; for example, he campaigned against overgrazing by cattle, which had caused extensive erosion in the American Southwest. By 1915, he was contradicting contemporary thinking that conservation is important solely for economic reasons; he argued that conservation also is important for ethical and aesthetic reasons.

In 1933, Leopold published *Game Management*. The first major book on wildlife ecology, it describes the management and restoration of wildlife populations. The book also stresses the importance of biological communities and the interconnections of organisms within communities.

Aldo Leopold

Notable Quotable

Keeping records enhances the pleasure of the search and the chance of finding order and meaning in these events.

—Aldo Leopold

Beginning in 1934, Leopold made the first systematic attempts to restore ecosystems, replacing abandoned farmland with communities of native plants and animals.

Another influential book, *A Sand County Almanac*, is a collection of Leopold's observations published poshumously in 1949. It presents Leopold's philosophy that humans are morally obligated to respect and protect the natural world. "A thing is right when it tends to preserve the integrity, stability, and beauty of the biotic community. It is wrong when it tends otherwise," he wrote.

RESOURCES

- Anderson, Peter. *Aldo Leopold, American Ecologist.* Danbury, CT: Franklin Watts, 1996. (JUV/YA)
- Leopold, Aldo. *The Essential Aldo Leopold, Quotations and Commentaries.* Madison, WI: University of Wisconsin, 1999.
- Lorbiecki, Marybeth. *Aldo Leopold, A Fierce Green Fire*. New York: Oxford University, 1999.
- Excerpts from the Works of Aldo Leopold.
  http://gargravarr.cc.utexas.edu/chrisj/leopold-quotes.html

Lesseps, Ferdinand de

Diplomat: developer of the Suez Canal
Born: November 19, 1805, Versailles, France
Died: December 7, 1894, La Chenaie, France

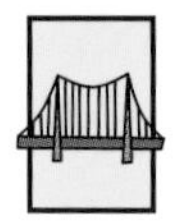

The Isthmus of Suez in Egypt connects the Mediterranean and Red seas. A **canal** across it eliminates a long voyage around Africa when traveling between Europe and Asia. Ancient civilizations recognized this shortcut and dug shallow canals that eventually filled with sand and were lost. Completion of the Suez Canal in 1869 was a great achievement and Lesseps, the person responsible for its construction, became famous for it.

While working as a diplomat in Egypt in the 1830s, Lesseps came across a report written in 1798 by J.B. Le Père [French: 1761–1844] that reviewed the feasibility of building a Suez canal. Fascinated, Lesseps hoped that he might one day carry out the idea. He was given the necessary authority by the Turkish governor of Egypt in 1854.

Surveyors drew up a plan and construction began in 1859. The Suez Canal formally opened on November 17, 1869.

In 1879, Lesseps formed a company to build a Panama canal in Central America linking the Atlantic and Pacific oceans. He encountered unexpected difficulties. His plan to build a canal without **locks** proved unworkable in the mountainous terrain. The rocky soil was harder to dig than the sandy soil at Suez. Yellow fever and intense heat took their toll. By 1889 the project was bankrupt and work stopped. Work resumed under another company in 1894, and the Panama Canal opened in 1914.

The Suez Canal connects the Mediterranean and Red seas.

RESOURCES

- History of Ferdinand de Lesseps and the Panama Canal.
  http://www.ared.com/history.htm
- November 17th, 1869; The Inauguration of the Suez Canal.
  http://www.sis.gov.eg/calendar/html/cl171196.htm

Levi-Montalcini, Rita

Biologist: identified first growth factor
Born: April 22, 1909, Turin, Italy

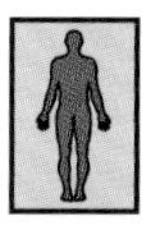

Growth factors are **proteins** in the bodies of vertebrates that play important roles in cell division, development, and survival. In the 1950s, working at Washington University in St. Louis, Missouri, Levi-Montalcini discovered the first such protein. Since the protein stimulates the growth of nerve cells, she named it nerve growth factor (NGF). She and Stanley Cohen [American: 1922–] isolated NGF from the salivary glands of mice and Cohen determined its chemical structure. As an outgrowth of this work Cohen discovered epidermal (skin) growth factor. Other growth factors have since been found, proving Levi-Montalcini's belief that different growth factors influence development of different types of cells.

Nobel Prize 1986

The Nobel Prize in physiology or medicine was awarded to Levi-Montalcini and Cohen for their discoveries of growth factors.

Levi-Montalcini discovered NGF in malignant mouse tumors. It has since been shown that in normal cells, production of growth factor is regulated. In cancerous cells, however, there is no regulation, leading to rapid cell division.

Rita Levi-Montalcini

Levi-Montalcini's early research on nerve cells in Italy during the 1930s and 1940s was hampered by anti-Semitic laws and by World War II. Nonetheless, in a simple laboratory in her home, she made important observations on how nerve cells differentiate, develop, and spread in chicken embryos.

RESOURCES

- McGrayne, Sharon Bertsch. *Nobel Prize Women in Science: Their Lives, Struggles, and Momentous Discoveries*. Secaucus, NJ: Carol, 1993.
- Autobiography of Rita Levi-Montalcini.

http://www.nobel.se/medicine/laureates/1986/levi-montalcini-autobio.html

Libby, Willard

Chemist: developed carbon-14 dating
Born: December 17, 1908, Grand Valley, Colorado
Died: September 8, 1980, Los Angeles, California

In 1939, scientists discovered that some neutrons produced by cosmic rays entering Earth's atmosphere are absorbed by nitrogen atoms. The nitrogen decays into a radioactive isotope of carbon, carbon-14. Libby hypothesized that the carbon-14 combines with oxygen to form carbon dioxide. Since plants absorb carbon dioxide to make carbon-containing foods, and animals eat plants and use the carbon for growth and energy, Libby believed that organisms contain small amounts of carbon-14.

It also was known that a radioactive element decays, or changes into a more stable element, at a specific rate, called its half-life. Carbon-14's half-life is about 5,700 years. In 5,700 years, half the carbon-14 atoms break down into other atoms. In another 5,700 years, half of the remaining carbon-14 atoms break down, and so on.

Libby correctly assumed that all living things have the same ratio of carbon-14 to non-radioactive isotopes of carbon. But when an organism dies, it stops taking in carbon; therefore carbon-14 that decays is not replaced. Libby reasoned that by comparing the amount of carbon-14 in

Nobel Prize 1960

The Nobel Prize in chemistry was awarded to Libby for development of the carbon-14 dating technique.

Libby designed equipment for dating ancient remains of trees and other organisms.

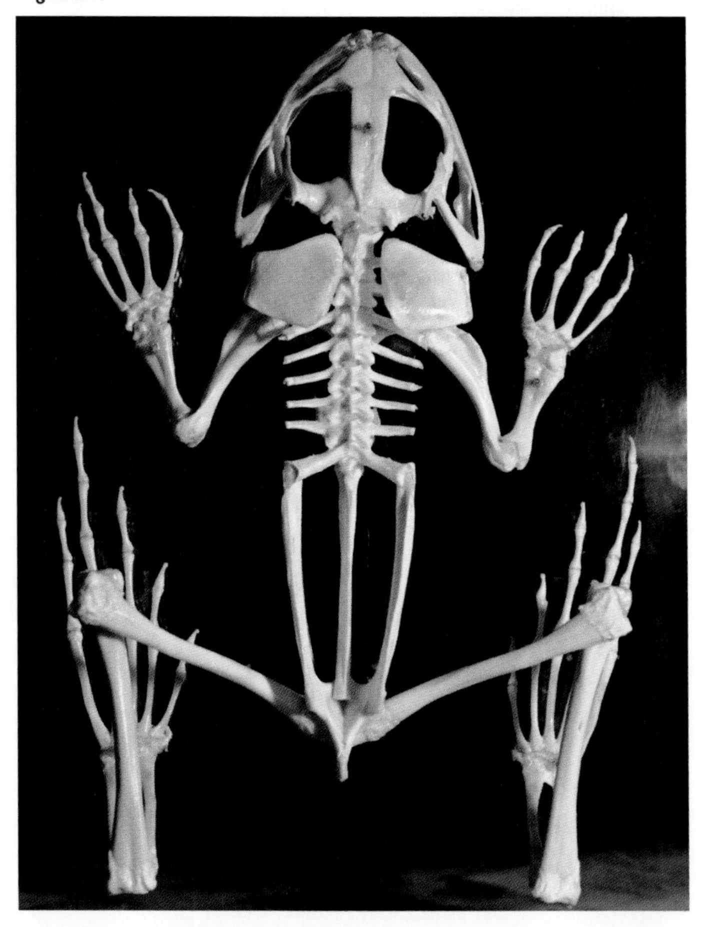

Willard Libby

dead remains with the amount in living organisms, the age of the remains could be determined. He designed equipment that he successfully tested on tree samples, since the age of these samples could be proven by counting their rings.

FAMOUS FIRST

While Libby was a graduate student at the University of California at Berkeley in the early 1930s, he built the United States' first **Geiger**-Müller counter for detecting radioactivity.

As Libby refined his technique he was able to date ever-older fossils, objects, and events. In one case, by dating tree remains once buried under glaciers, he showed that the most recent **ice age** ended about 11,000 years ago.

RESOURCES

- MORE ABOUT WILLARD LIBBY.

  http://www.nobel.se/chemistry/laureates/1960/libby-bio.html

  http://www.nobel.se/chemistry/laureates/1960/press.html

- HOW CARBON-14 DATING WORKS.

  http://www.howstuffworks.com/carbon-14.htm

Light

Plato (light begins at eye) ➤ **GREECE** (properties of light) ➤ **al Haytham** [Alhazen] (eye receives light) ➤ **KEPLER** (how lenses and eyes work) ➤ **Snell/Descartes** (laws of refraction) ➤ **NEWTON** (white light is mixture of colors) ➤ **Römer** (calculated light's speed) ➤ **HUYGENS** (light as waves) ➤ **YOUNG** (confirmed wave theory) ➤ **MAXWELL** (light a form of electromagnetic wave) ➤ **HERTZ** (discovery of radio waves) ➤ **EINSTEIN** (light as particles) ➤ **DE BROGLIE** (particles act like waves) ➤ Current theory that light is both particles and wave

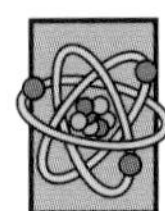

The early Greek philosophers disagreed about whether we see visible objects because light proceeds from the object to the eye or because the eye emits rays that "feel" the object. The influential Plato [Greek: c. 420–340 B.C.E.] favored rays from eye to object, but about 1000 C.E., Ibn al Haytham [Egyptian: c. 965–1038], known in the West as Alhazen, established that light is produced by some objects, such as the Sun or a fire, and reflected from others. He showed that the eye receives rays instead of producing them.

Although scientists knew by the 17th century how light behaves, it wasn't until the 20th century that they understood what light is.

Ancient Greeks discovered many properties of light, such as that light travels in straight lines and that the angle of reflection matches the angle at which light strikes a mirror. The advances of al Haytham, including laws of reflection in curved mirrors, became known after a 1572 Latin translation of his work. **Johannes Kepler** began with al Haytham's ideas and, in books published in 1604 and 1611, showed how lenses and eyes work.

In 1621, Willebrord Snell [Dutch: 1580–1626] discovered experimentally the laws of refraction—how light bends when passing through transparent materials. These were independently discovered and reformulated mathematically by René Descartes [French: 1596–1650] in 1637. About 1665, **Isaac Newton** discovered that refraction can spread white light into the colors of the rainbow (published in 1672). In 1676, Ole Römer [Danish: 1644–1710] calculated light's speed, using eclipses of the satellites of Jupiter.

Although scientists knew by 1676 how light behaves, it was unclear what light is. Newton argued that light consists of tiny particles, while **Christiaan Huygens** in 1678 explained light as waves. Throughout the 1700s, most scientists followed Newton, but in 1800, **Thomas Young** observed several phenomena that could only be explained in terms of light waves. Experiments throughout the 1800s confirmed the wave theory and in 1873, **James Clerk Maxwell** published a complete mathematical explanation based on waves of electricity and magnetism, or electromagnetic waves. Maxwell's theory soon led, in 1888, to **Heinrich Hertz's** discovery of radio waves, electromagnetic waves longer than those of light.

In 1887, Hertz discovered that light influences how an electric charge leaves a metal surface. This photoelectric effect does not obey Maxwell's theory. In 1905, **Albert Einstein** showed that the photoelectric effect can be explained only if light acts as a particle. Following an idea from 1922 of **Louis-Victor De Broglie**, physicists showed that all small particles also act as waves, which led to the current theory of light, which says that it is both a particle, called the photon, and an electromagnetic wave. Whether a particle or a wave is observed depends on the experiment performed.

RESOURCES

- Ardley, Neil. *Science Book of Light*. San Diego: Harcourt Brace, 1991. (JUV/YA)
- Fiarotta, Phyllis and Noel Fiarotta. *Great Experiments with Light*. New York: Sterling, 1999. (JUV/YA)
- MORE ABOUT LIGHT.

  http://www.phys.virginia.edu/classes/109N/lectures/spedlite.html

  http://library.thinkquest.org/C005705/English/Light/history.htm

  http://www.learner.org/channel/workshops/sheddinglight/lighthistory.html

Lighting

Learned to make fire ➤ Lamps that burned animal and plant fats ➤ **China** (burned natural gas) ➤ Development of wick and candles ➤ Development of coal burning ➤ **Argand** (brighter oil lamp) ➤ **Murdock** (purify and transport coal gas) ➤ **FRANKLIN** (lightning is electricity) ➤ **Auer** (mantle) ➤ **DAVY** (arc light) ➤ Development of electric current ➤ **EDISON/Swan** (incandescent light) ➤ **BECQUEREL** (fluorescent lamps) ➤ Development of LED

The first lighting humans learned to make was **fire**, perhaps a million years ago. Originally, open fires burned on the ground, but by 40,000 years ago, humans made lamps—shallow stone bowls in which animal fats burned. Lamps based on liquid fat (oil made by cooking animal fats or by squeezing it from oil-rich plants, such as olives or nuts) were introduced before 1000 B.C.E. People discovered that a sliver of wood or, better yet, a thin rope called a wick, burns brightly when dipped in oil. Putting one end of the wick in oil and lighting the other creates a lamp that burns for hours.

Until the 1800s, the history of lighting consisted of improvements in ways to use fire. New oils were found that burned brighter or with less smoke, such as whale oil and oils from petroleum. Candles—one-piece, self-contained lamps with fat called tallow or wax, such as beeswax, wrapped around the wick—were in use by at least 250 B.C.E. In 1784, Aimé Argand [Swiss: 1755–1803] invented a much brighter oil lamp that fed air to the flame and exposed more of the burning wick.

As early as 400 B.C.E., the Chinese learned to burn the natural gas found when drilling deep wells. Bamboo tubes carried gas from wells to light buildings. In the West, heating coal for use in iron manufacture released coal gas. In the late 1700s, several inventors experimented with using coal gas for lighting. The first major success came when William Murdock [Scottish: 1754–1839], in a series of experiments that began in 1792, developed methods to purify and transport coal gas for lighting. In 1803, he lit a factory with coal gas. Starting in 1812, London—and soon all major cities—adopted coal-gas lamps. After 1887, such lamps could produce a bright white light, using a kind of wick invented by Karl Auer [Austrian: 1858–1929] called a mantle.

Artificial light from sources other than fire came later. People had observed sparks from **static electricity** and, in 1752, **Benjamin Franklin** showed that the bright lightning bolt is also electricity. When current electricity became available after 1800, inventors began to develop lighting based on electricity. As early as 1809,

Different types of lighting

Humphry Davy produced a bright light from a continuous spark, called an arc light. Practical arc lamps were used for lighthouses in the 1870s, but they were too bright and too expensive for most other purposes. By 1820, inventors were enclosing thin wires in glass bulbs and using electric currents to heat the wires to glowing. By 1879 this idea led to the incandescent light of **Thomas Alva Edison** and, independently, Joseph Swan [English: 1828–1914], the ancestor of most common lights of today.

How It Works

A modern incandescent lamp uses a coil of tungsten as the lighting element, which is surrounded by a nonreactive gas such as argon. Tungsten, which has a high melting point, is coiled to provide more light-emitting surface. As a current passes through the metal, it interacts with the tungsten atoms, making them move faster, so the metal becomes very hot—perhaps 4550° F (2500° C)—and the moving charges on the atoms produce electromagnetic waves, or light. The gas helps keep the tungsten atoms at the surface from flying off and sticking to the inside of the bulb. Some fly off anyway, and after many hours some part of the coil becomes so thin that it breaks. The bulb has burned out.

Development of other forms° of electric light also required much experimentation. An electric current makes thin gases glow, which led to commercial mercury-vapor lamps in 1903, after 50 years of experimentation. The two-step process used in fluorescent lamps, commercially introduced in 1938, was first tried by Alexandre Becquerel [French: 1820–1891] in 1857.

In 1970, the light-emitting diode (LED), which directly converts electricity to light, was invented, but commercial use of the LED for lighting is still experimental.

RESOURCES

- Bowers, Brian. *Lengthening the Day: A History of Lighting Technology*. New York: Oxford University, 1998.
- Wallace, Joseph. *The Lightbulb* (Turning Point Inventions). New York: Atheneum, 1999. (JUV/YA)
- MORE ABOUT LIGHTING. **http://www.americanhistory.si.edu/lighting/**
- A LIGHTING PROJECT. **http://www.americanhistory.si.edu/csr/lightproject/**

Lind, James

Naval surgeon: found cure for scurvy
Born: 1716, Edinburgh, Scotland
Died: July 13, 1794, Gosport, England

"On the 20th May, 1747, I took twelve patients in the scurvy on board the Salisbury at sea," wrote Lind. Scurvy is a disease characterized by bleeding gums, poor healing of wounds, joint and muscle pain, weakness, and sometimes death. In those days, it was common among sailors, who often were away from land for many months at a time.

Citrus fruit contains vitamin C, which prevents scurvy.

Lind suspected that scurvy was caused by a diet deficiency. He divided his twelve patients into six groups and gave each group different foods. At the end of six days, two sailors were so improved that they were able to leave the sickroom and report for duty. Unlike the other patients, these two men had been given two oranges and a lemon to eat each day.

Repeated tests by Lind confirmed the value of oranges and lemons in preventing and curing scurvy. He published the results of his studies in 1753, with recommendations that sailors on long voyages be given fresh citrus fruits. But his work was largely ignored. It wasn't until 1795 that the English navy adopted this dietary practice, giving sailors lime juice every day—the origin of their nickname, "limeys." It wasn't until the 1900s that scientists discovered **vitamins** and learned that lack of vitamin C is responsible for scurvy.

RESOURCES

- Lind, James, "Of the Prevention of the Scurvy." **http://www.people.virginia.edu/rjh9u/scurvy.html**

Linnaeus, Carolus

Botanist: developed system of classifying organisms
Born: May 23, 1707, Råshult, Sweden
Died: January 10, 1778, Uppsala, Sweden

Linnaeus invented the system for **classification of life** that we use today. It is a hierarchical system, consisting of groups within groups and based on similarities and differences among organisms. The smallest group is the species—a specific kind of organism.

Carolus Linnaeus

Similar species are grouped together in a genus (sing.), similar genera (pl.) in a family, and so on.

Linnaeus also established the use of binomial, or two-word, Latin names for species. For example, he named white pine *Pinus alba*, with *Pinus* ("pine") the genus and *alba* ("white") the species. Today, every species identified by biologists is given a binomial name.

YEARBOOK: 1735

- Linnaeus publishes *Systema naturae*, which introduces his system of classification.
- **John Harrison** makes his first chronometer.
- Johann Gmelin [German: 1709–1755] discovers permafrost (permanently frozen soil in arctic regions).

By establishing a consistent classification scheme and system for naming species, Linnaeus motivated biologists to collect and study organisms, both during his lifetime and ever since. As his fame spread, students, explorers, and others sent him specimens from around the world. In his publications, he named and classified all the plant and animal species then known—some 7,700 plants and 4,400 animals.

In 1761, Linnaeus was granted nobility and became known as Carl von Linné.

RESOURCES

- Anderson, Margaret J. *Carl Linnaeus: Father of Classification*. Berkeley Heights, NJ: Enslow, 2001.(JUV/YA)
- CARL LINNAEUS. **http://www.ucmp.berkeley.edu/history/linnaeus.html**

Lister, Joseph

Surgeon: introduced antiseptic surgery
Born: April 5, 1827, Upton, England
Died: February 10, 1912, Walmer, England

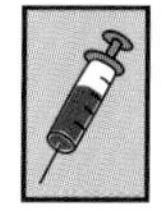

Until the mid-1800s, surgery was extremely risky. Death was common as wounds became infected with gangrene and other diseases. It was widely believed that these infections were caused by "bad air," though Lister suspected airborne dust particles. Lister tried to keep his operating room clean by spraying the air with a solution of carbolic acid. This helped somewhat, but Lister considered the 49 percent death rate still much too high.

In 1865, Lister read about **Louis Pasteur**'s experiments proving that microorganisms cause decay and fermentation. Lister hypothesized that microorganisms also are responsible for postsurgical infections. He began cleaning his hands, patients' skin, and surgical instruments with carbolic acid, and sprayed carbolic acid on wounds and bandages. Before using equipment he heated it to a high temperature, copying Pasteur's method of inhibiting the growth of microorganisms in wine and milk. These tactics reduced mortality in Lister's surgery to about 15 percent by 1869.

Lister also found that silk—the material then most widely used to stitch together wounds—did not absorb carbolic acid. He advocated that absorbable catgut be used instead—and that surgical personnel should stop holding sutures in their mouths!

Lister's introduction of **antiseptics** radically changed surgical practices, and made it possible to perform operations that had previously been considered too risky.

Joseph Lister

• More about Joseph Lister.
http://www.fordham.edu/halsall/mod/1867lister.html

Locks and Keys

The oldest known lock-and-key arrangement is called the Egyptian lock, although the earliest examples come from Nineveh in Mesopotamia and date from about 2000 B.C.E. These were carved from wood. The keys look rather like toothbrushes with pegs instead of bristles. Inserted in the lock and depressed (not turned), they lift corresponding pegs to free a bolt that can then be pulled aside.

The Greeks used a lock-and-key that lifted a bolt when the key was turned, but any key that would fit through the keyhole would work. Roman inventors improved this idea by putting circular impediments called wards below the bolt. Slots in the blade of the key had to match the position of the wards before it could turn and lift the bolt. Warded locks are still in use in older homes.

Door lock

In a Yale lock, notches in the key raise a series of catches called pin tumblers (much as pegs in Egyptian locks lift corresponding pegs) so a cylinder can be turned, which then pulls back a bolt. Furthermore, slots in the key must fit the keyhole, as in a Roman lock, or the key cannot be inserted.

Improved locks based on these ideas were introduced in the 1700s, but most U.S. locks today are descendants of a type invented in 1861 by Linus Yale [American: 1821–1868]. Yale locks are still common in homes and automobiles. Electronic locks that use keys with magnetic patterns have become popular in hotels.

Locks on Waterways

A lock is a large walled basin between two different heights of a waterway. Admitting water from the upper level into the lock raises water in the basin, while draining lowers it. A vessel in the lock is also raised or lowered, enabling it to travel between levels of the waterway.

Before locks, ships were carried around falls and rapids or dragged up and down chutes in canals. The first lock was built in China in 983 C.E. primarily to stop thieves from looting vessels that broke up while being dragged on chutes. **Canal** building increased greatly after locks were invented. The Chinese Grand Canal, completed in 1327, used locks to raise parts of the thousand-mile-long canal 138 feet (42 m)

Canal locks

above its sea-level origin. Lock building also spread to Europe about this time, where locks enabled canal construction in previously unusable paths. In 1395, a lock was installed on the Po River in Italy so ships could transport marble to Milan. In 1497, **Leonardo da Vinci** designed and built an improved lock with gates that folded into the walls and better placement of pipes to carry water. Leonardo's design is the basis of most canal locks used today.

RESOURCES

- More about Locks.

http://www.pigpen.demon.co.uk/locks.htm

http://ds.dial.pipex.com/town/square/gd86/locks.htm

Lorenz, Konrad

Zoologist: described imprinting
Born: November 7, 1903, Vienna, Austria
Died: February 27, 1989, Altenburg, Austria

Even in childhood, Lorenz enjoyed observing animals. While studying medicine, he kept a diary detailing his pet bird's activities. The diary's publication by a scientific journal in 1927 helped turn Lorenz's interests away from medicine and toward a career in **animal behavior**.

During the summers of 1935 to 1938, Lorenz studied greylag geese—for "many reasons, but the most important is that greylag geese exhibit a family existence that is analogous in many significant ways to human family life," he later wrote. During this period Lorenz developed the concept of imprinting, a phenomenon named by Oskar Heinroth [German: 1871–1945] in 1911. Imprinting is a form of learning that takes place early in the life of certain animals, causing a fixed behavior in response to specific stimuli.

Notable Quotable

Truth in science can be defined as the working hypothesis best suited to open the way to the next better one.

—Konrad Lorenz

Lorenz showed that within the first few hours after birth, a greylag gosling imprints to the first moving object it sees. Typically, it imprints on its mother, whom it closely follows. This is a valuable protective mechanism until the gosling is old enough to be independent. But when goslings were exposed only to Lorenz during the critical

Newborn ducklings typically imprint on their mother.

imprinting period after birth, they instead followed him around.

Lorenz also studied aggression, arguing that aggression in animals is solely a survival mechanism. His analogies between human and animal behavior, particularly in his book *On Aggression*, remain controversial.

RESOURCES

- Lorenz, Konrad Z. *King Solomon's Ring*. New York: Plume, 1997. Reprint.
- Lorenz, Konrad. *On Aggression*. New York: Harcourt Brace & World, 1966.
- Autobiography of Konrad Lorenz. **http://www.nobel.se/medicine/laureates/1973/lorenz-autobio.html**

Lovelace, Ada

Mathematician: first computer programmer
Born: December 10, 1815, London, England
Died: November 27, 1852, London, England

While still a teenager, Augusta Ada Byron met **Charles Babbage** and was fascinated by his idea for a new mechanical calculating machine, the Difference Engine. (Daughter of the poet Lord Byron, she later married, becoming Countess of Lovelace.) Babbage soon designed a more advanced calculating machine, the Analytical Engine. In 1842, Luigi F. Menabrea [Italian: 1809–1896] published an article summarizing the concept behind the Analytical Engine. Lovelace translated Menabrea's article into English and added her own notes as well as diagrams and other information supplied by Babbage. She explained how the machine might be instructed to perform a series of calculations—a description that foreshadowed today's **computer** programs. "The Analytical Engine weaves algebraic patterns, just as the **Jacquard** loom weaves flowers and leaves," she wrote. She also saw that such a machine, which Babbage never built, would have many applications beyond arithmetic calculations, from scientific research to composing music and producing graphics.

FAMOUS FIRST

Lovelace socialized with some of the most brilliant people of her time, including author Charles Dickens, physicist **Michael Faraday**, and inventor Sir David Brewster [Scottish: 1781–1868], who in 1816 made the first kaleidoscope.

Modern computer

RESOURCES

- Toole, Better A. *Ada, the Enchantress of Numbers: A Selection from the Letters of Lord Byron's Daughter and Her Description of the First Computer.* Mill Valley, CA: Strawberry, 1998.
- Wade, Mary D. *Ada Byron Lovelace: The Lady and the Computer.* Parsippany, NJ: Silver Burdett, 1994. (JUV/YA)
- MORE ABOUT ADA LOVELACE.

  http://www.sdsc.edu/ScienceWomen/lovelace.html

  http://cc.kzoo.edu/k97pe01/ada.html

Lumbering

Development of axes ➤ Development of wood-cutting axes ➤ Development of stone axes, stone adzes ➤ Development of stone or bone saws ➤ First metal tools ➤ Development of iron and steel ➤ **North America** (ax handle in middle of blade) ➤ Development of steam, power tools ➤ **Stihl** (chain saw)

Lumbering is cutting down trees to provide wood for lumber (wood sawed into planks). Although tools called hand "axes" were made over a million years ago, they probably were weapons, not lumbering tools. Axes

Lumbering became more efficient with the introduction of iron and steel saws, power tools, and heavy equipment.

used for cutting wood first appeared in Europe at the end of the last **ice age**, almost 12,000 years ago. A thousand years later, as farming began, humans began to grind and polish stone axes, making stronger tools that can be sharpened. Beside axes, tools called adzes were made from ground stone. An adze has its sharp edge perpendicular to its handle and shapes wood into flat-sided beams and planks. Another tool, the saw, was made from flaked stone or chipped bone.

In the Copper and Bronze Ages, people fashioned lumbering tools from metal. Bronze was no better than stone for axes but made excellent saws.

Iron and steel tools were great advances. Iron or steel axes and saws were used for lumbering well into the 20th century. Improvements were made along the way. Different saws were developed for cutting down (felling) trees, for cutting logs from trees, and for cutting boards. In the 1700s, North American loggers created an ax blade with the handle inserted in the middle instead of at one end, a small change that was a great improvement.

Power tools began with steam engines. But small, lightweight **internal combustion engines** enabled lumber workers to replace axes and saws in some uses with a power tool. The chain saw was invented in 1926 by Andreas Stihl [German: 1896–1973] and is now the main tool for felling trees.

RESOURCES

- Andrews, Ralph W. *Glory Days of Logging/Action in the Big Woods, British Columbia to California.* Atglen, PA: Schiffler, 1994.
- Pike, Robert E. *Tall Trees, Tough Men*. New York: W.W. Norton, 1999.

Lumière Brothers

Inventors and filmmakers: developed the cinematograph

Auguste-Marie **Born:** October 19, 1862, Besançon, France
Died: April 10, 1954, Lyon, France

Louis-Jean **Born:** October 5, 1864, Besançon, France
Died: June 6, 1948, Bandol, France

In the early 1890s, when Auguste and Louis were running the **photography** business founded by their father, the concept of moving pictures was new and intriguing. After learning of **Thomas Alva Edison**'s kinetoscope in 1894, which allowed peephole viewing of seemingly moving images, the young men decided to develop a machine that combined animation with projection on a large screen. They patented their cinematograph in 1895. This machine had a camera that could be used for both photographing and projecting images. A system of claws moved 35-millimeter film at a speed of 16 frames per second—fast enough to give viewers a sense of motion.

FAMOUS FIRST

On December 28, 1895, the Lumière brothers showed ten short films to an audience at a café in Paris. It was the world's first public demonstration of motion pictures. Despite public enthusiasm, Louis didn't think much of their achievement. "The cinema is an invention without a future," he said.

Also in 1895, the Lumière brothers made their first films. Their two-minute film, "Workers Leaving the Lumière Factory," is considered the world's first

motion picture. During the following years they made hundreds of short films, documentaries, and newsreels.

The Lumière brothers also developed Autochrome, the first practical color photography process, introduced commercially in 1907.

RESOURCES

- Lumière, Auguste, and Lumière, Louis. *Letters: Inventing the Cinema.* New York: Faber & Faber, 1997.
- MORE ABOUT THE LUMIÈRE BROTHERS.

  http://www.lyon-city.org/en/specif_lumiere.html

MacArthur, Robert

Ecologist: discovered warbler feeding zones
Born: April 7, 1930, Toronto, Canada
Died: November 1, 1972, Princeton, New Jersey

Five species of insect-eating wood warblers lived in a spruce forest on the Maine coast. Did they occupy the same niche, or position in the community? Some scientists believed they did, though this contradicted a basic rule of **ecology**: in any community no two species can share exactly the same environment and way of life. If they do, the species that is the better competitor eventually causes the elimination of the other species.

MacArthur showed that different species of warblers have different feeding habits.

MacArthur observed the warblers beginning in 1958. He divided individual trees into zones—new growth at the top of the tree, branches with dead needles near the top, the middle interior, branches near the ground, and so on. The data he collected showed that the five species had different niches. For example, Cape May warblers hunted for insects mostly in the top outside portion of trees but yellow-rumped warblers fed mostly on trees' lowest branches. By concentrating on different parts of trees, competition for food was limited, enabling the species to co-exist.

MacArthur discovered additional differences in the species' feeding habits. Cape May warblers, for instance, were more likely than the other species to hunt in flight. Also, the species nested at slightly different times, thus limiting competition during periods when food was needed for babies.

- AVIAN ECOLOGY.
  http://www.ornithology.com/lectures/Avian%20Ecology.html
- MACARTHUR'S WARBLERS.
  http://www.stanfordalumni.org/birdsite/text/essays/MacArthur's_Warblers.html

Maglev Trains

Imagine flying at hundreds of miles per hour only a few inches above the ground. That vision has propelled researchers into using magnets to suspend trains above tracks. These vehicles are called magnetically levitated transport, or maglev for short. Research and development on maglev started in the United States in 1968. This effort ran out of support in 1975, but Japan, using **superconductivity**, and Germany, employing ordinary electromagnets, continued maglev research. Late in the 1990s, the United States decided to re-enter the field, and, in 1999, funded projects at sites from Baltimore to Los Angeles. Plans are for trains to be operational by 2010.

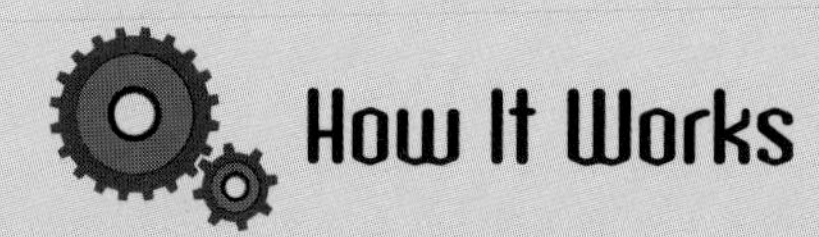

There are two kinds of maglev, suspending and repelling. Suspension systems use ordinary electromagnets to lift the train by means of a part that travels below electromagnets housed in the top of a T-shaped rail. This part is attracted and pulled upward by the rail magnets, and in the process the whole train is pushed upward. Repelling systems use superconductivity. The magnetic field produced by an ordinary magnet cannot enter a superconducting material, so a magnet is repelled by superconducting material and can be suspended above it.

The Japanese intend to connect Tokyo and Aichi with a superconducting maglev traveling 300 miles (500 km) per hour. German plans for a train levitated by conventional magnets that would travel from Berlin to Hamburg—a distance of 185 miles (292 km)—have been delayed by concerns that powerful magnetic fields might be environmental hazards. China, however, plans to install a German system. The only commercial operating maglev system, a 0.4-mile (0.6-km) low-speed carrier at the Birmingham, England, airport, ran for 11 years before being replaced by a conventional bus in 1995.

RESOURCES

- Vranich, Joseph. *Supertrains: Solutions to America's Transportation Gridlock*. New York: St. Martin's, 1993.
- MORE ABOUT MAGLEV TRAINS AND TECHNOLOGY.

  http://www.bwmaglev.com/what_maglev/whatmaglevfrmset.html

  http://www.wpi.edu/kmfdm/ph1121.html

  http://www.calpoly.edu/cm/studpage/clottich/fund.html

  http://www.fra.dot.gov/o/hsgt/maglev.htm

  http://www.howstuffworks.com/maglev-train1.htm

Magnetism

Gilbert (first investigation of magnets, Earth as giant magnet, pole theory) ➤ **OERSTED** (current attracts one pole of magnet) ➤ **FARADAY** (interaction of electricity and magnetism)

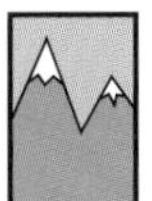

Natural magnets, called lodestones, were discussed by scientists of ancient Greece. They also learned how to make iron magnetic by stroking it with a lodestone, but most early ideas about magnets were mystical or speculative.

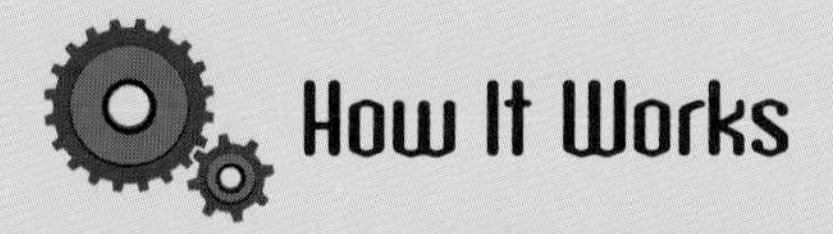

How It Works

Moving electrons in atoms produce electric and magnetic fields, but in most substances random orientation of atoms cancels out any force. Materials called ferromagnetic, which include iron, nickel, and cobalt, include small regions, called domains, where magnetic fields align. Stroking iron with another magnet makes the domains themselves align, resulting in a "permanent" magnet (magnetism can be removed by heating or by a sharp blow). An electric current also makes domains align, forming an electromagnet.

A magnet has two poles.

In 1600, William Gilbert [English: 1544–1603] published the first scientific investigation of magnets. It was also the first book of science completely based on experiments. He recognized that Earth is a giant magnet whose north pole attracts the south pole of a compass.

Gilbert was also the first scientist to identify **static electricity** as different from magnetism. Gilbert demonstrated that any two magnets attract each other when one pair of ends are close and repel each other when one magnetic pole is reversed. The regions of attraction and repulsion define the poles—like poles repel, while opposite poles attract. But either pole of a magnet attracts iron.

In 1820, **Hans Oersted** observed that electric current attracts one pole of a magnet. **Michael Faraday** studied the interaction of magnetism and electricity, concluding by 1846 that magnets and currents each produce a change in space called a field. Each point of the field embodies a particular force—a push or a pull—and direction. Lines of force of a magnetic field can be observed by sprinkling iron powder on a surface that has a magnet below it. A moving magnetic field creates an electric field, while a moving electric field, such as a current, creates a magnetic field.

RESOURCES

- DiSpezio, Michael Anthony. *Awesome Experiments in Electricity & Magnetism*. New York: Sterling, 2000. (JUV/YA)
- Livingston, James. D. *Driving Force: The Natural Magic of Magnets*. Cambridge, MA: Harvard University, 1977.
- MORE ABOUT MAGNETISM.

  http://www-spof.gsfc.nasa.gov/Education/Imagnet.html

  http://library.thinkquest.org/16600/intermediate/magnetism.shtml

  http://www.wondermagnet.com/dev/magfaq.html

Maiman, Theodore Harold

Physicist: made the first laser
Born: July 11, 1927, Los Angeles, California

The concept of **lasers** was first described in 1958, setting off a race to build such devices. The winner was Maiman, who built the first working laser in 1960. It was a solid-state laser based on a rod of pink ruby coated with silver at both ends. An electric flash lamp was coiled around the rod. When light from the lamp shined on the rod, the rod was stimulated to produce a narrow beam of highly concentrated monochromatic

Since Maiman built the first laser in 1960, these devices have evolved and found numerous applications.

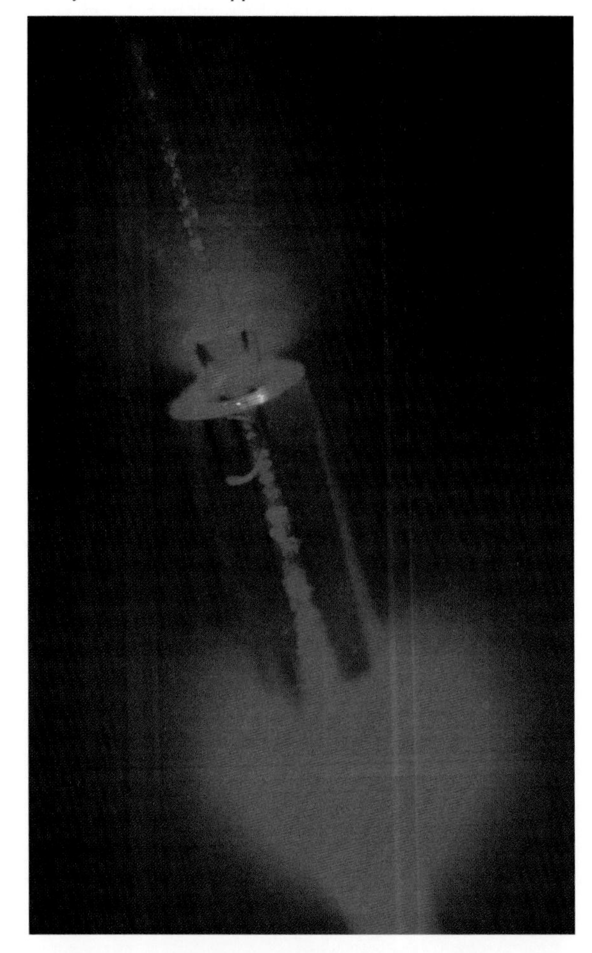

YEARBOOK: 1960

- Maiman creates the first laser.
- **Jane Goodall** observes tool-making by a chimpanzee.
- The United States launches *Tiros 1,* the first weather satellite.
- Digital Equipment Corporation introduces the PDP-1, the first commercial **computer** with a keyboard and monitor.

light (light of a single wavelength).

At a press conference announcing his invention, Maiman envisioned many possible applications for lasers. He noted, for example, that the high temperatures produced at the point where the beam of light touches a material would make lasers useful for cutting and welding. But journalists focused on lasers' potential use in weapons, even writing that Maiman had invented the "death ray."

Maiman continued to research, develop, and manufacture lasers. In 1983, he became involved with medical lasers, which have become important **surgical instruments**.

RESOURCES

- MORE ABOUT THEODORE HAROLD MAIMAN AND LASERS.

  http://www.spie.org/web/oer/august/augoo/maiman.html

  http://www.laserfaq.com/laserfaq.htm

Malpighi, Marcello

Anatomist, physiologist: discovered capillaries
Born: March 10, 1628, Crevalcore, Italy
Died: November 30, 1694, Rome, Italy

Armed with a new invention, the compound **microscope**, Malpighi made numerous discoveries that greatly expanded knowledge of the structure

Marcello Malpighi

of living things. He is best known for describing capillaries, the tiny vessels that carry blood from arteries to veins. This discovery, made while studying frog lungs, confirmed **William Harvey**'s explanation of how blood circulates.

Malpighi was the first person to study fingerprints scientifically. He was the

YEARBOOK: 1672

- Malpighi publishes a pioneering work on the formation of a chick in an egg.
- Regnier de Graaf [Dutch: 1641–1673] discovers structures in a female animal's ovary where, it later is learned, eggs mature.
- **Francis Glisson** explains that living tissues react to their environment.

first to describe papillae, the small projections on the upper surface of the tongue, and nephrons, the microscopic structures in the kidney where urine is formed. He showed that bile is secreted by the liver, not by the bile duct, as had been believed.

In botany, Malpighi found the annular rings produced in stems of oaks and other trees. He recognized that sap flows through vessels from one part of a plant to another, and discovered openings (stomata) in the surface layer of leaves.

RESOURCES

- DISCOVERY OF THE CIRCULATION OF THE BLOOD.
  http://www.usyd.edu.au/su/hps/tutes/lecture18.html
- THE KIDNEY THROUGH THE AGES.
  http://www.nnsg.com/kidneystoria.htm

Maps

First map engraved on ivory ➤ Map on silver ➤ **Mesopotamia** (land maps, first scale) ➤ Egypt (papyrus) ➤ **Anaximander** (first attempt to show whole world) ➤ **Pythagoras** (Earth as sphere) ➤ **ERATOSTHENES** (size of Earth) ➤ **HIPPARCHUS** (idea of longitude and latitude) ➤ **PTOLEMY** (projections) ➤ **MERCATOR** (straight line projection)

A map uses symbols to show how objects are related in physical space. Most maps today are drawn or printed on flat sheets of paper and show the locations of buildings, natural features, settlements, and boundaries, but the earliest known map was engraved on ivory about 15,000 years ago. It appears to show huts and a stream in the settlement Mezhirich in Ukraine. A later map on silver from Maikop in Ukraine, dating from about 3000 B.C.E., shows rivers and mountains.

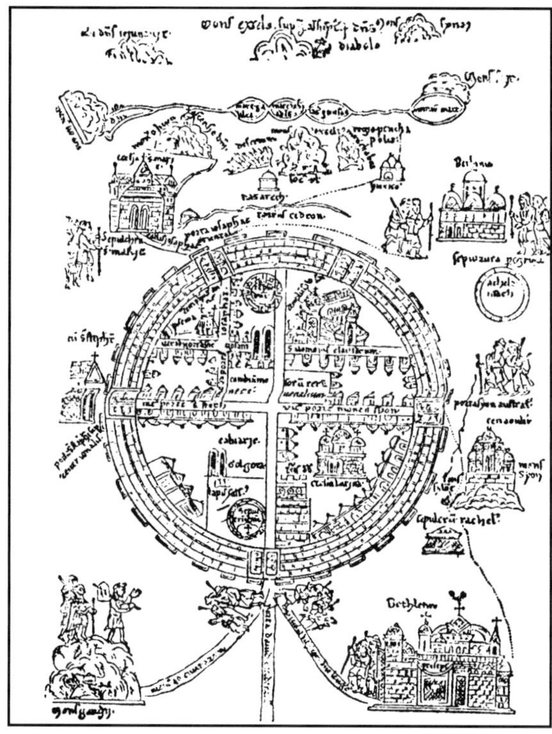

A 12th-century map of pilgrim routes to Jerusalem.

The next known maps are from Mesopotamia starting about 2300 B.C.E. Land maps used for taxation and marked with north, south, east, and west were drawn on clay tablets, and a map of the city of Lagash was carved in stone. The map of Lagash includes the first scale, an indication of how the size of symbols on the map relates to the actual size of the objects being mapped. The ancient map most like one of today is an Egyptian map on papyrus from about 1150 B.C.E. that shows a mountain region near the Red Sea. Color indicates mountains that contain gold. Ancient sailors are reported to have mapped coasts and islands, but none of these maps has survived.

Anaximander [Greek: 610 B.C.E. – c. 546 B.C.E.] reportedly drew the first map intended to show the whole world. People had observed that stars appear higher and lower

A map from the 1600s and a modern satellite map.

in the sky as one travels north and south, which Anaximander recognized as indicating that Earth's surface is curved—so he drew his map on the curved surface of a cylinder. A few years later, Pythagoras [Greek: c. 560 B.C.E. – c. 480 B.C.E.] correctly recognized that Earth is a sphere (ball). **Eratosthenes** about 240 B.C.E. determined the size of the sphere and made the best map of Earth to that date. Greek maps of this period showed southern Europe and the British Isles, western Asia, and northern Africa.

Sailors' maps were based on the Mediterranean Sea, which they divided by length (longitude) and width (latitude). About 130 B.C.E., **Hipparchus** extended the idea of longitude and latitude over all Earth and into space to locate stars.

Another astronomer, **Claudius Ptolemy**, created the best map of ancient times about 150 C.E. Ptolemy developed good mathematical techniques for mapping the curved surface of Earth onto a flat sheet of paper. Such techniques are called projections and are an important aspect of mapmaking. Some projections distort sizes, others shapes. The correct projection for a map depends on how it will be used.

When America was explored, there was a great need for new maps. The best cartographer, or mapmaker, of the 1500s was Gerardus Mercator [Flemish: 1512–1594; born Gerhard Kremer]. He developed a projection in 1569 that is especially good for navigation because a straight line on a Mercator projection represents constant direction. No map can represent a spherical surface exactly on a flat plane. Mercator's maps have correct angles, but areas near the poles are shown much larger and those near the equator much smaller than they are in reality. Other projections, developed since Mercator's work, have correct areas at the expense of incorrect shapes.

Modern maps still use the system of longitude and latitude to locate places. Latitude extends from 0° at Earth's equator to 90° north and south at the poles, which are the ends of the axis on which Earth rotates. But there is no natural line for 0° longitude corresponding to that for latitude. In 1884, an international conference of geographers accepted an arbitrary line through Greenwich Observatory in England as 0°—longitude.

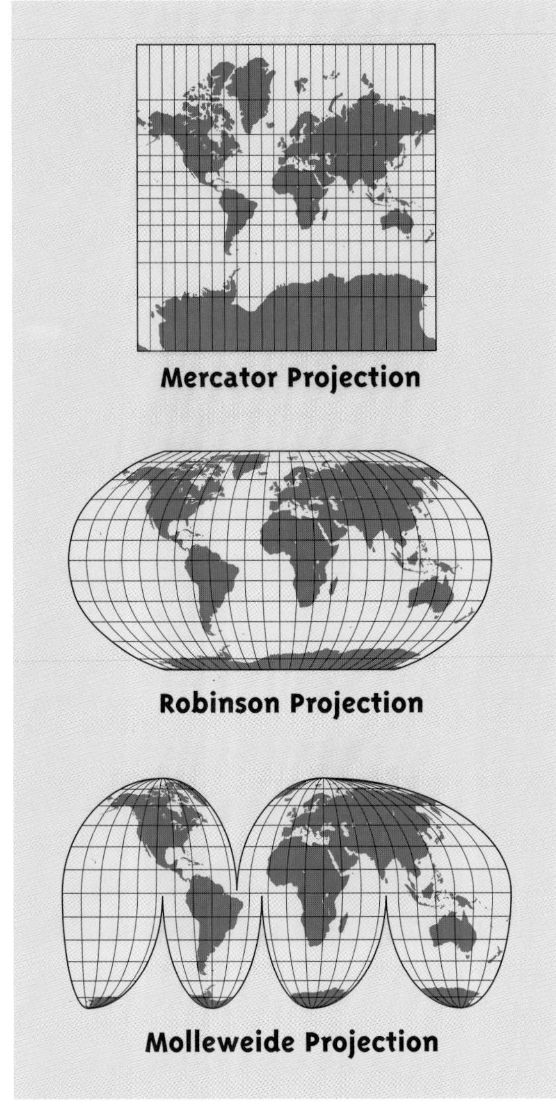

Mapmakers have developed various techniques, called projections, to map Earth's curved surface.

RESOURCES

- Brown, Lloyd Arnold. *The Story of Maps.* Mineola, NY: Dover, 1979.
- Wilford, John Noble. *The Mapmakers*. Rev. ed. New York: Alfred Knopf, 2000.
- NASA's Athena Project's Cartography Page. **http://www.athena.ivv.nasa.gov/curric/land/geograph/carto/**

Marconi, Guglielmo

Inventor: invented radio
Born: April 25, 1874, Bologna, Italy
Died: July 20, 1937, Rome, Italy

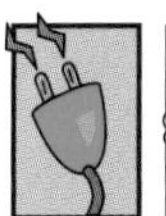

Fascinated by electricity from childhood, Marconi was inspired to create an entirely new communication device, which he called the wireless and which we know as the **radio**.

In 1894, Marconi read that **Heinrich Hertz**, by inducing an electric spark to jump across a gap, had produced invisible waves that travel through space. Marconi realized that the waves might be used to send wireless messages similar to the dot-and-dash messages sent by **telegraphs**. He began experimenting and within a year was sending messages over distances of more than a mile (1.6 km).

Marconi continually improved his device, and interest in the invention grew. Widespread use of radio was assured on December 12, 1901, when assistants in England sent the first transatlantic signals to Marconi in Newfoundland, a distance of some 3,000 miles (4,800 km).

Guglielmo Marconi

Nobel Prize 1909

Marconi was awarded the Nobel Prize in physics for his invention. He shared the prize with Karl Ferdinand Braun [German: 1850–1918], who invented the crystal rectifier, which improved radio transmission.

RESOURCES

- Garratt, G.R. *The Early History of Radio, from Faraday to Marconi*. Edison, NJ: INSPEC, Inc./Institution of Electrical Engineers, 1994.
- Godfrey, Donald G. and Frederic A. Leigh, eds. *Historical Dictionary of American Radio*. Westport, CT: Greenwood, 1998.
- Biography of Guglielmo Marconi. **http://www.nobel.se/physics/laureates/1909/marconi-bio.html**

Mass Extinctions

Extinction is the death of a single species of organism. Mass extinction is the death of many different kinds of species all around the world in a relatively short period of geological time—a million years, perhaps. Based on the study of **fossils**, most scientists agree that there have been five big mass extinctions.

Luis W. Alvarez and his son Walter [American: 1940–] inspired interest in the causes of these events. In 1980, he suggested that the mass extinction some 65 million years ago—which wiped out the dinosaurs—was due to a giant asteroid smashing into

Some scientists believe that destruction of habitats by humans will result in extinction of some animal and plant species.

Earth. This hypothesis received important support in 1990, when an impact crater some 125 miles (200 km) in diameter was discovered on Mexico's Yucatan Peninsula. Scientists theorize that the impact vaporized huge amounts of rock in the area, throwing a huge cloud of debris into the atmosphere. The cloud circled Earth, blocking sunlight, causing acid rain, and dropping temperatures to below freezing for months. In 1998, a fragment thought to be from the large object that smashed into Yucatan was reported; chemical analysis suggested it had been part of an asteroid.

There is no indication that all mass extinctions had the same cause. Other proposed causes include comet showers, widespread volcano eruptions, and changes in sea level. Recently, a new cause has been added: human activities. Many scientists believe we are in the midst of a sixth big mass extinction. They predict that humanity's impact on Earth, including destruction of natural habitats, will result in the extinction of one- to two-thirds of all current plant and animal species during the 21st century.

RESOURCES

- Hallman, A. and P.B. Wignall. *Mass Extinctions and Their Aftermath*. New York: Oxford University, 1997.
- MORE ABOUT MASS EXTINCTIONS.

  http://www.bbc.co.uk/education/darwin/exfiles/massintro.htm

  http://advlearn.lrdc.pitt.edu/belvedere/materials/Mass Extinctions/Massext.htm

Matches

Brand (isolated phosphorus) ➤ **Walker** (first match lit by striking) ➤ France/U.S. (white phosphorus added to friction matches) ➤ **Pasch** (first safety match)

Although the 19th century saw the birth of many inventions that changed lives, a popular choice in 1900 for the greatest invention of the previous century was the match. Before matches, starting a **fire** was a tedious, chancy procedure involving lengthy friction or tiny sparks struck from flint.

FAMOUS FIRST

The first match was invented in 577 C.E., when a group of Chinese women in a besieged town put sulfur tips on splinters of wood. These were easily lit from a struck spark.

Modern matches are based on a discovery of Hennig Brand [German: born c. 1630]. In 1669 he isolated phosphorus, a white nonmetal that catches fire spontaneously in air. It can be converted to a more stable red form.

The first match that could be lit by striking did not use phosphorus. In 1827,

Almost all modern matches are safety matches.

John Walker [English: 1771–1859] used heat from friction to light flammable chemicals. These friction matches were struck on sandpaper. In 1830, chemists in France and the United States added white phosphorus to friction matches. These matches often lit by themselves, setting many accidental fires. Gustaf Erik Pasch [Swedish: 1788–1862] in 1844 made the first safety matches. Red phosphorus coats a side of the matchbox rather than the match itself so the match lights only when struck on the box. Nearly all matches today are safety matches.

RESOURCES

- History of Swedish Match Manufacture. **http://enterprise.shv.hb.se/match/history.html**

Maury, Antonia

Astronomer: classified stars
Born: March 21,1866, Cold Spring, New York
Died: January 8, 1952, Dobbs Ferry, New York

A project to classify the brightest 250,000 **stars** in the sky was underway at Harvard College Observatory in Boston when Maury joined the team in 1888. Project director Edward C. Pickering [American: 1867–1919], a pioneer in using **spectroscopes** to obtain the spectra of light emitted by stars, put Maury to work classifying northern stars

Maury classified stars using lines in their spectra.

according to lines in their spectra. Maury soon found the existing classification scheme inadequate and set about revising it, using the intensity, width, and spacing of lines in a star's spectrum as her basis. Early in the 1900s her system was adopted by Ejnar Hertzsprung [Danish: 1873–1967], who laid the foundations for the modern study of how stars form and evolve. It became clear that Maury's series begins with the hottest stars, consisting mainly of helium, oxygen, and nitrogen; at the other end are the coolest stars, with significant amounts of heavier elements.

RESOURCES

- Reaching for the Stars.
  http://www.hno.harvard.edu/gazette/1998/03.19/ReachingfortheS.html

Maxwell, James Clerk

Physicist: formulated electromagnetic theory
Born: June 13, 1831, Edinburgh, Scotland
Died: November 5, 1879, Cambridge, England

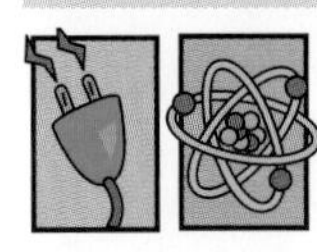

Maxwell's fascination with how and why things work was evident from early childhood. He constantly experimented, observed, and asked his parents, "What's the go of that?" and "Show me how it does." This curiosity remained strong throughout Maxwell's life, as he pursued investigations in many fields.

His major contribution was the electromagnetic theory, which provided a unified explanation of electricity and magnetism. In a series of papers published in the 1860s and 1870s, Maxwell presented a set of mathematical equations describing the behavior of electric and magnetic fields. He theorized that light is a combination of electric and magnetic waves, and predicted longer and shorter electromagnetic waves far beyond visible light. The theory was confirmed in the late 1880s when **Heinrich Hertz** discovered radio waves.

Maxwell also studied optics, primarily how humans perceive color, made one of the earlier color photographs, and was the first scientist to use statistical methods to describe movement of gas molecules.

FAMOUS FIRST

Maxwell wrote his first scientific paper, describing a method for making oval curves, at age 14. An adult read the paper to the Royal Society of Edinburgh, "for it was not thought proper for a boy in a round jacket to mount the rostrum there."

RESOURCES

- Tolstoy, Ivan. *James Clerk Maxwell, A Biography*. Chicago: University of Chicago, 1983.
- More about James Clerk Maxwell.
  http://physics.uwstout.edu/sotw/maxwell.htm

McClintock, Barbara

Geneticist: discovered transposons
Born: June 16, 1902, Hartford, Connecticut
Died: September 2, 1992, Huntington, New York

McClintock spent her long career working with corn, or maize. Her most important discovery came in the 1940s, when she realized that some sections of **DNA** can change their positions on chromosomes. Some of these "jumping genes," called transposons, are responsible for the colors of maize kernels. Depending on where transposons move,

Nobel Prize 1983

For her discovery of transposons, McClintock received the Nobel Prize for physiology or medicine. "It might seem unfair," she once said, "to reward a person for having so much pleasure over the years, asking the maize plant to solve specific problems and then watching its responses."

kernels will be dark, pale, or speckled.

McClintock published her discovery in 1950. Because it contradicted the widely held belief that genes have fixed positions on chromosomes, the discovery was ridiculed and ignored for almost twenty years. It wasn't until the 1970s, after transposons were discovered in bacteria and other organisms, that McClintock's work received general acceptance. Today it is believed that transposons play important roles in **evolution** and **disease**.

Barbara McClintock

Changes in DNA create different-colored corn kernels.

RESOURCES

- Fine, Edith H. *Barbara McClintock, Nobel Prize Geneticist.* Springfield, NJ: Enslow, 1998. (JUV/YA)
- Kent, Charlotte. *Barbara McClintock, Biologist.* Broomall, PA: Chelsea House, 1991. (JUV/YA)
- More about Barbara McClintock.
  http://clio1.cshl.org/public/mcclintock.html
  http://www.nobel.se/medicine/articles/green/

McCormick, Cyrus

Inventor: developed first mechanical reaper
Born: February 15, 1809, Rockbridge County, Virginia
Died: May 13, 1884, Chicago, Illinois

"Fifteen acres a day!" promised McCormick. On the family farm in Virginia in 1831, McCormick designed, built, and demonstrated the world's first mechanical reaper, a machine for harvesting grain. It took a while for the reaper to catch on. It was much more efficient than reaping by hand but farmers were reluctant to try it, in part because early models were unreliable and tired the horses that pulled them.

McCormick continued to work on and improve his reaper. In 1847, thanks to growing demand for the machine and realizing that it worked better on flat grain fields, such as those of the American Midwest, he left hilly Virginia and opened a factory in Chicago.

Cyrus McCormick

FAMOUS FIRST

Although McCormick was the first to demonstrate a mechanical reaper, he did not patent his machine until 1834, one year after Obed Hussey [American: 1792–1860] received the first patent for a reaper. The two machines were competitive in field tests but McCormick was the better businessman and marketer.

Because the reaper revolutionized **farming,** allowing farmers to produce much more grain, McCormick has been called the "founder of modern agriculture."

RESOURCES

- More about Cyrus McCormick. **http://web.mit.edu/invent/www/inventorsI-Q/mccormick.html**

Mead, Margaret

Anthropologist: studied human cultures
Born: December 16, 1901, Philadelphia, Pennsylvania
Died: November 15, 1978, New York, New York

Mead was a psychology student at Barnard College in New York City when she met **Ruth Benedict,** who inspired her to study anthropology with Franz Boas [German-American: 1858–1942] at neighboring Columbia University. Mead became particularly interested in cultures that were rapidly changing and dying out as a result of modern influences. In 1925 she began field work in the Samoan Islands, focusing on attitudes and behavior of teenage girls. She

Margaret Mead (above left) compared the roles of males and females in various South Pacific cultures.

described her findings in *Coming of Age in Samoa*, published in 1928. This best-selling book showed that much of "human nature" actually is learned behavior shaped by cultural expectations.

Mead also studied other South Pacific cultures as well as American Indians. She compared cultures, showing for example that the roles of males and females are not based solely on biology but differ from one society to another. She demonstrated the interrelationships among various aspects of a culture—such as politics, environmental attitudes, warfare, and child-rearing—and showed the influence of culture on personality. She also stressed the possibility and value of learning from other cultures.

RESOURCES

- Burby, Liza N. *Margaret Mead*. New York: Rosen, 1997. (JUV/YA)
- Mark, Joan. *Margaret Mead: Coming of Age in America*. New York: Oxford University, 1999. (JUV/YA)
- Pollard, Michael. *Margaret Mead: Bringing World Cultures Together*. Woodbridge, CT: Blackbirch, 1999. (JUV/YA)

Measurement

Sumeria (standard weight and length measures) ➤ **Egypt** (time measure) ➤ **Mesopotamia** (60-minute/second measure) ➤ **France** (metric system) ➤ Development of International System

The earliest signs of measurement are fired clay tokens from about 8000 B.C.E. These were used in Mesopotamia to represent, among other things, jars of oil or other goods used in trade. This idea is useful only if the jars are all about the same size, so that five jars of wheat is a specific amount. A specifically sized measure is called a standard. Measurements of ancient structures from 3000 B.C.E. onward indicate that an early standard length was used in construction, but the first known standard measures are weights in Sumeria from about 2500 B.C.E. By 2000 B.C.E. the Sumerians also had standard lengths. A whole number of smaller standard measures defines a larger measure; for example, 60 shekels is 1 mina (weight). Time was originally measured in Egypt in hours,

Standard measures eliminate confusion in science and other fields.

with 12 equal hours to the day and 12 to the night, so the hour varied with the length of daylight. The division into 60 minutes and 60 seconds, however, reflects the numeration system of Mesopotamia.

Despite the advantages of universal standard measures, nations and even towns often established their own standards, especially after the fall of the Roman Empire. In 1795, the French Republic eliminated all older standard measures and started with a new set based on the size of the Earth (the meter, the fundamental unit, was one ten-millionth of the distance from the north pole to the equator on a line through Paris).

The French metric system spread through much of Europe and became popular with scientists around the world.

The balance scale is a popular measuring device.

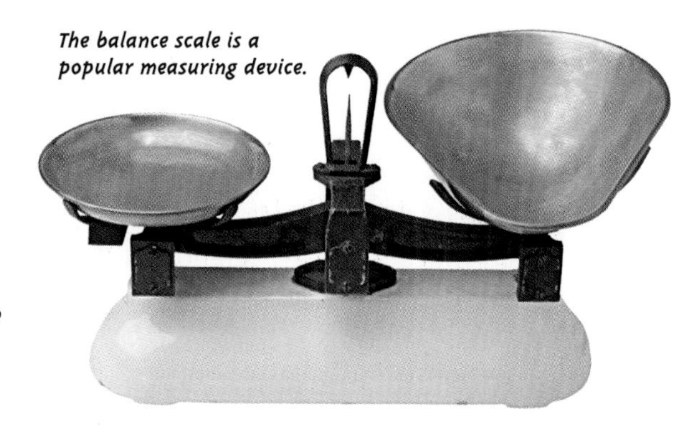

Variations from standard rules within the metric system persisted, however. In 1960, a revised standard, called the International System (or SI from the French name, *Systèm International*), was created. Today the meter is based on the speed of light in a vacuum and the SI second is defined in terms of vibrations of an atom, but the kilogram, the standard unit of mass, is based on a specific metal object kept in a special measurement center near Paris. Nearly every nation uses the SI system or slight variations of it. An exception is the United States, where most measurement is based on a customary system originally adapted from the British system, but since 1893, has been legally established in terms of metric measure—for example, today the inch is defined as 0.0254 meter.

RESOURCES

- Glover, Thomas J. and Richard Alan Young. *Measure for Measure*. Littleton, CO: Sequoia, 1996.
- Johnstone, William D. *For Good Measure*. New York: Holt, Rinehart and Winston, 1975.
- DICTIONARIES OF MEASUREMENT UNITS. **http://www.ex.ac.uk/cimt/dictunit/dictunit.htm** **http://www.unc.edu/rowlett/units/**

Medical Imaging

RÖNTGEN (discovered X rays) ➤ Development of chest X ray ➤ Development of mammogram ➤ Development of artery imaging ➤ Development of radioactive isotope imaging ➤ Development of CT scans ➤ Development of PET scans ➤ Development of MRI ➤ Development of ultrasound

Medical imaging allows organs and tissues inside the body to be shown without cutting through skin. It began in 1895, when **Wilhelm Konrad Röntgen** discovered **X rays**. One account has Röntgen using a fluorescent screen to observe bones in his own hand. Within months, physicians were using X rays to help set broken bones. With longer exposures on film, the difference between normal tissue and scars caused by diseases such as tuberculosis or tumors could be observed. The chest X ray for tuberculosis was in use by 1900 and by 1913 the first mammograms, X-ray images for detection of breast cancer, were performed.

As early as 1897, scientists began to fill soft organs with liquids that block X rays, imaging the stomach, kidneys, and intestines. Making blood visible on X rays is difficult, but by 1927, physicians could image arteries in the brain. Since 1945, imaging arteries in the heart has been an important diagnostic technique.

Starting in the early 1950s, a technique has been used to produce X rays from inside the body. A radioactive **isotope** that produces **subatomic particles** called positrons is included in a compound that the body uses, such as glucose. Positron production concentrates where the compound does, such as at active regions of the brain or in tumors. As positrons encounter the electrons normally present in atoms, they combine to produce

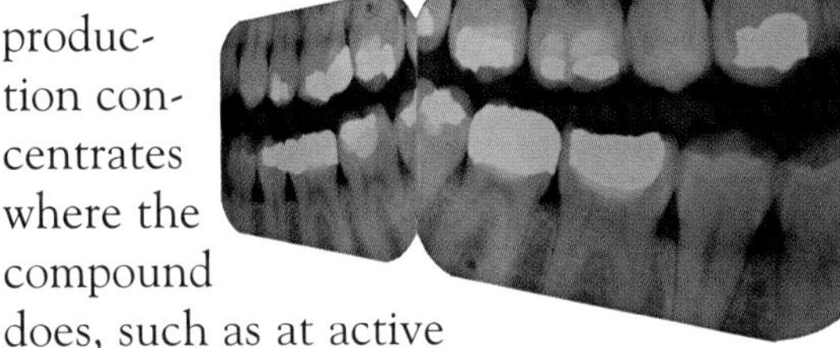

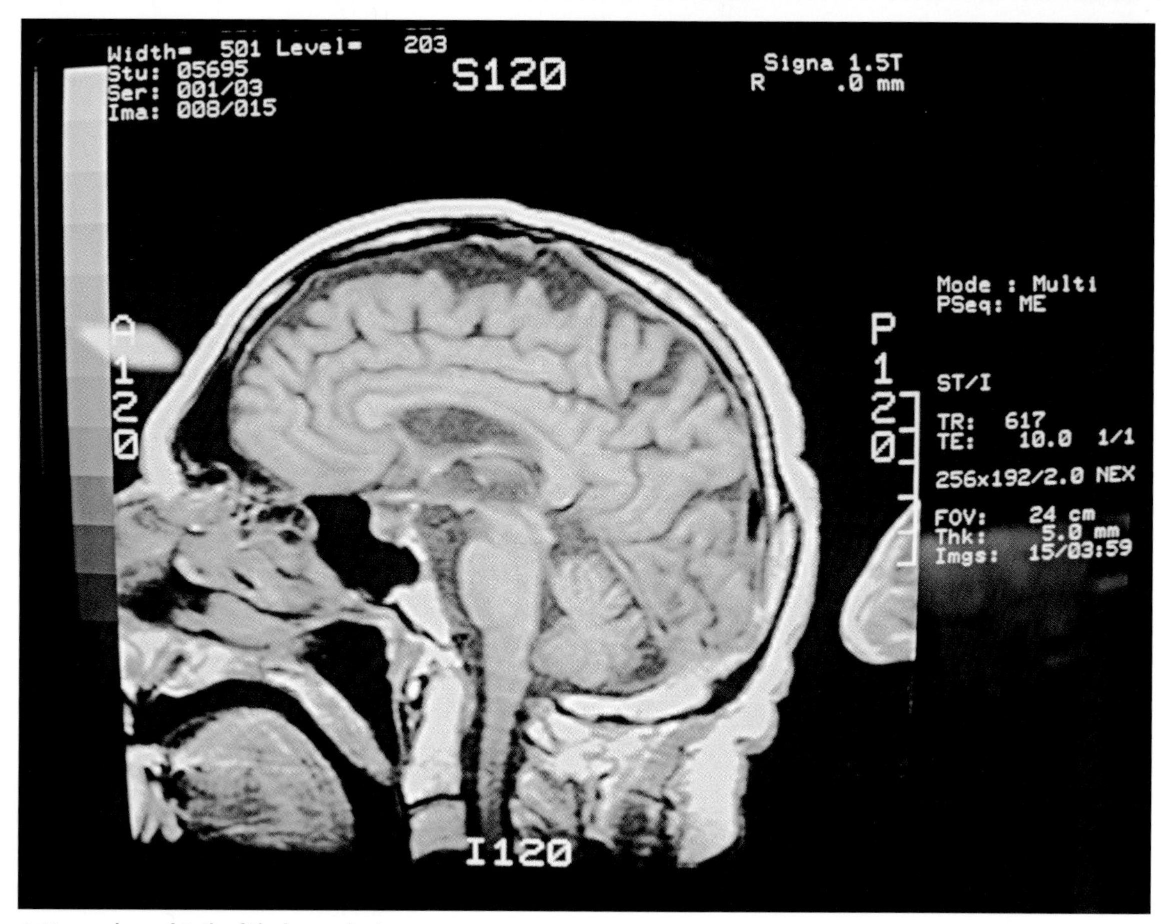

A CT scan shows details of the human brain.

a high-energy X ray, which can be detected outside the body.

A different use of X rays was first tested on living subjects in England in 1972: computerized tomography, or the CT scan. Tomography is the mathematical combining of multiple images to produce three dimensions. The positron method is also combined with tomography to create a three-dimensional image known as a PET (positron-emission tomography) scan.

X rays can damage cells, but other methods of imaging are safer. Magnetic resonance imaging (MRI), first used in Scotland in 1973, is the medical version of a technique that uses a strong magnetic field and radio waves to image groups of specific atoms. MRI does not damage cells, and images appear that would not be revealed by X rays.

Ultrasound uses high-frequency sound waves—higher frequencies correspond to shorter wavelengths that can picture more detail. These waves move at different speeds through different tissues. Ian Donald [Scottish: 1910–1987] noted in 1959 that ultrasound can be used to obtain clear images of a fetus, and the technology has developed into an important tool for examining unborn children.

RESOURCES

- More about Medical Imaging.
  http://imasun.lbl.gov/budinger/medhome.html

Medical Technology

China (acupuncture) ➤ **Egypt** (leg and arm operations) ➤ Development of human anatomy understanding ➤ Development of compound microscope ➤ **LAËNNEC** (invented stethoscope) ➤ **HELMHOLTZ** (invented ophthalmoscope) ➤ **Garcia** (invented laryngoscope) ➤ **Allbutt** (invented clinical thermometer ➤ Development of anesthetics and antiseptics ➤ **RÖNTGEN** (discovered X rays) ➤ Development of electronics, computers, fiber optics, lasers, ultrasound ➤ **Einthoven** (invented electrocardiograph) ➤ **Berger** (first electroencephalograms) ➤ **Kolff** (invented kidney dialysis) ➤ **Greatbatch** (invented implantable pacemaker) ➤ Development of genetic engineering

Medicine has been practiced since prehistoric times, as evidenced by drawings and tools uncovered at archeological sites. Drugs, mainly plant extracts, were used to treat various ills. Splints supported broken limbs. Wounds were cauterized with hot irons. **Surgical instruments** included drills to bore holes in the skulls of people afflicted with headaches or those considered insane.

By 2700 B.C.E., Chinese physicians practiced acupuncture and by 2500 B.C.E. Egyptians were operating on arms and legs, though many patients died from bleeding or infection.

Over the next 4,000 years, few significant advances occurred. Only in the 16th century C.E. did scientists begin to understand human **anatomy**. Modern **physiology** began in the 17th century, and discovery of the germ theory of **disease** came late in the 19th century. These were essential steps toward developing effective medical technologies.

One of the most important diagnostic tools in medicine, helping physicians recognize signs of disease, is the compound **microscope**, invented at the end of the 16th century. Many tools commonly used by modern physicians were invented in the 1800s. **René Laënnec** invented the stethoscope, for listening to chest sounds, in 1816. **Hermann von Helmholtz** invented the ophthalmoscope, for examining eyes, in 1851. Manuel Garcia [Spanish: 1805–1906] invented the modern laryngoscope, for examining the throat, in 1855; and Thomas Allbutt [English: 1836–1925] the clinical thermometer in 1866. The 19th century also saw the introduction of **anesthetics** and **antiseptics**.

A major medical advance began with the discovery of **X rays** in 1895. Within

FAMOUS FIRST

The hypodermic syringe was invented independently in the 1850s by Alexander Wood [Scottish: 1817-1884] and Charles Gabriel Pravaz [French: 1791–1853]. It was first used to inject morphine as an anesthetic.

YEARBOOK: 1929

- Hans Berger [German: 1873–1941] publishes the first human electroencephalograms (tracings of brain waves).
- FM **radio** is introduced.
- **Robert Goddard** launches the first instrument-carrying rocket.
- **Edwin Hubble** shows that the **universe** is expanding.

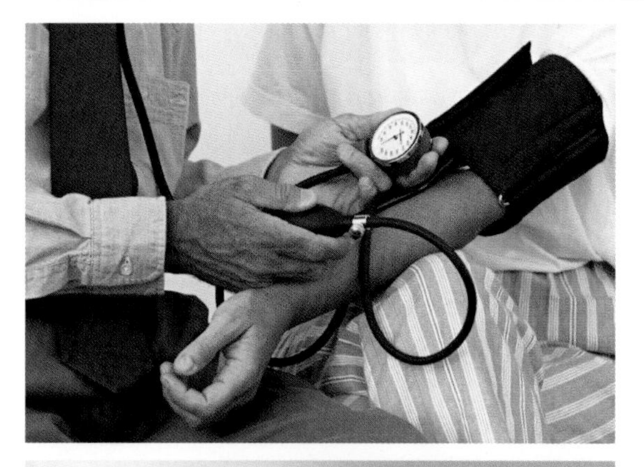

A great variety of tools are used to diagnose and treat patients.

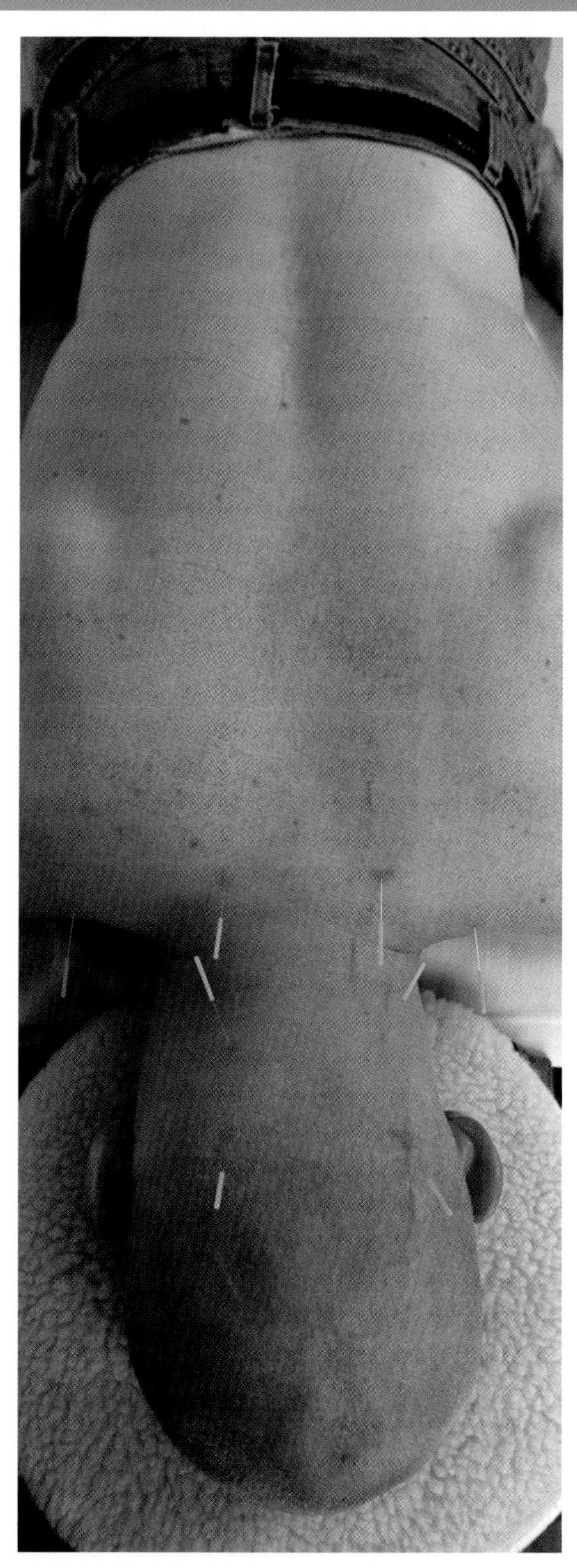

months, physicians were using X rays to help set broken bones. Additional applications of X rays plus new **medical imaging** techniques were developed throughout the 20th century. The 20th century also saw the introduction of technologies such as **computers**, **electronics**, **fiber optics**,

lasers, and **ultrasound**, all of which have found their way into medicine. **Willem Einthoven** designed a reliable electrocardiograph, for diagnosing heart abnormalities, around 1901. Hans Berger [German: 1873–1941] published the first human electroencephalograms (tracings of brain waves) in 1929. Willem Kolff [Dutch-American: 1911–] developed the first kidney dialysis machine, to remove wastes from the blood, in 1944. Wilson Greatbatch [American 1919–] invented the implantable pacemaker, for regulating heartbeat, in 1958.

Genetic engineering is a recent technology that shows promise for curing and treating illness. Development of durable **plastics** is leading to improved **artificial limbs and organs**, including artificial hearts. Advances in **vaccines**, **antibiotics**, and other medicines continue to help physicians conquer disease.

• DICTIONARY OF MEDICAL EQUIPMENT. **http://www.themedweb.co.uk/Dictionary.htm**

Meitner, Lise

Physicist: co-discovered nuclear fission
Born: November 7, 1878, Vienna, Austria
Died: October 27, 1968, Cambridge, England

"I am not important; why is everyone making a fuss over me?" questioned Meitner late in her career. Perhaps the fuss was an attempt to make up for the many years during which the scientific establishment ignored Meitner and her work. Even the Nobel Foundation, which awards Nobel Prizes, overlooked Meitner's many significant contributions.

Lise Meitner

Inspired by her childhood heroine **Marie Curie**, Meitner received a Ph.D. in physics—the first such doctorate awarded to a woman by the University of Vienna since its founding in 1365. In 1907, she joined the laboratory of chemist Otto Hahn [German: 1879–1968] in Berlin, beginning a long collaboration.

Meitner and Hahn were interested in **radioactivity** and in 1917 discovered the radioactive element protactinium. In the 1930s, Meitner suggested to Hahn that he and Fritz Strassmann [German: 1902–1980] try to discover what happens when uranium atoms are bombarded with neutrons.

In 1938, Meitner fled from Nazi Germany to Sweden, but kept contact with Hahn via mail and telephone. When Hahn reported

NOBEL PRIZE 1944

Hahn received the Nobel Prize in chemistry for the discovery of nuclear fission.

FAMOUS FIRST

In 1982, a team of German scientists reported the existence of a previously unknown element. In 1997, this radioactive element was given the name meitnerium.

that bombardments of uranium produced barium, Meitner realized that the uranium atoms must capture neutrons, causing the atoms to become unstable and split in two. She called the process fission, and correctly proposed that splitting uranium produces barium, krypton, and energy. Hahn and Strassmann confirmed this, as did Meitner's nephew Otto R. Frisch [Austrian-English: 1904–1979], working in Denmark.

See also nuclear reactors, nuclear weapons.

RESOURCES

- Barron, Rachel. *Lise Meitner, Discoverer of Nuclear Fission*. Greensboro, NC: Morgan Reynolds, 1999. (JUV/YA)
- Sime, Ruth Lewin. *Lise Meitner: A Life in Physics*. Berkeley, CA: University of California, 1997.
- More about Lise Meitner. **http://www.energy.ca/gov/education/scientists/meitner.html**

Mendel, Gregor

Monk: discovered basic laws of heredity
Born: July 22, 1822, Heinzendorf, Austria (now Hynčice, Czech Republic)
Died: January 6, 1884, Brünn, Austria-Hungary (now Brno, Czech Republic)

Mendel spent most of his adult life in the monastery at Brünn. His interest in the way characteristics are passed from one generation to the next led him to experiment with pea plants in the monastery garden. Between 1856 and 1863 he grew at least 28,000 pea plants and analyzed characteristics such as height, flower color, and pod shape. He carefully cross-pollinated plants, then noted what sort of plants developed from the seeds.

Mendel concluded that a plant has two "factors" for each characteristic, one inherited from each parent. Today these factors are called **genes**. For example, a pea plant has two genes for seed color. A gene may be for green (y) or yellow (Y) seeds. According to Mendel's principle of

Gregor Mendel

dominance, in some cases one gene is dominant and the other is less powerful, or recessive. In pea plants, the gene for yellow seeds is dominant while that for green seeds is recessive. In a plant with one yellow gene and one green gene (Yy), the recessive green gene is masked; the plant has yellow seeds.

Mendel's principle of incomplete dominance says that for some characteristics neither gene is dominant. Cross-breeding two pure organisms results in a hybrid intermediate in appearance. For example, when a four-o'clock plant with red flowers (RR) is crossed with one having white flowers (WW), the offspring have pink flowers (RW).

Mendel published his findings in 1866 but they were overlooked until 1900, when three botanists independently rediscovered them.

RESOURCES

- Edelson, Edward. *Gregor Mendel*. New York: Oxford University, 1999. (JUV/YA)
- Henig, Robin Marantz. *The Monk in the Garden: How Gregor Mendel and His Pea Plants Solved the Mystery of Inheritance.* Boston: Houghton Mifflin, 2000.
- MORE ABOUT GREGOR MENDEL.
  http://www.netspace.org/MendelWeb/MWtime1.html

Mendeleyev, Dmitri Ivanovich

Chemist: formulated periodic table
Born: February 8, 1834, Tobolsk, Russia
Died: February 2, 1907, St. Petersburg, Russia

"If all the elements be arranged in order of their atomic weights a periodic repetition of properties is obtained," announced Mendeleyev. His periodic table had its beginnings in 1860,

Dmitri Ivanovich Mendeleyev

when Mendeleyev learned about **Amedeo Avogadro**'s hypothesis for determining atomic weights. Then in 1868, Mendeleyev sat down to write a chemistry textbook and looked for a way to classify all sixty of the known elements.

His original classification scheme listed elements in order of their atomic weights. He lined up elements with similar properties in rows, or periods. One row, for example, contained lithium, sodium, potassium, rubidium, cesium, and (incorrectly) tellurium, elements that react strongly with water. As he finished one row, he found that the next row also contained a group, or family, of elements with similar properties.

Mendeleyev left blank spaces in the table for elements he thought existed but had not yet been identified. When other scientists discovered three of the predicted elements—gallium, scandium, and germanium—Mendeleyev's table gained acceptance. Since he published the first version in 1869, this periodic table has expanded well beyond 100 elements, now listed in columns of elements with similar properties instead of rows. Also, scientists have explained that members of each family have similar properties because they have the same valence, or number of electrons available for chemical reactions.

RESOURCES

- Atkins, P.W. *The Periodic Kingdom, a Journey into the Land of the Chemical Elements.* Upland, PA: Diane, 1998.
- Strathern, Paul. *Mendeleyev's Dream: The Quest for the Elements.* New York: St. Martin's, 2001.
- MORE ABOUT DMITRI IVANOVICH MENDELEYEV.
  http://www.chem.mtu.edu/pcharles/SCIHISTORY/Mendeleyev.html

Metabolism

Von Liebig (first metabolic studies) ➤ **Berzelius** (enzymes are catalysts) ➤ **Mayer** (first law of thermodynamics) ➤ **Rubner** (metabolic rate proportional to surface area) ➤ **KREBS** (discovered citric acid cycle)

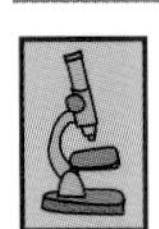

Metabolism is the sum of all of the chemical reactions that occur within a living cell. Metabolic studies began in the 1830s with the work of Justus von Liebig [German: 1802–1873], who believed that all **physiology** (life activity) could be explained in chemical and physical terms. Liebig developed a reliable technique to determine the proportions of elements in a compound, and used this technique to analyze hundreds of organic compounds.

Around the same time, the first **enzymes** were discovered, and Jöns Berzelius [Swedish: 1779–1848] correctly hypothesized that enzymes are catalysts that speed up reactions without themselves being changed. Today, it is known that enzymes enable many metabolic reactions to take place.

Metabolism includes the digestion of food.

Metabolism has two major phases: anabolism and catabolism. During anabolism, energy is stored in complex carbohydrates,

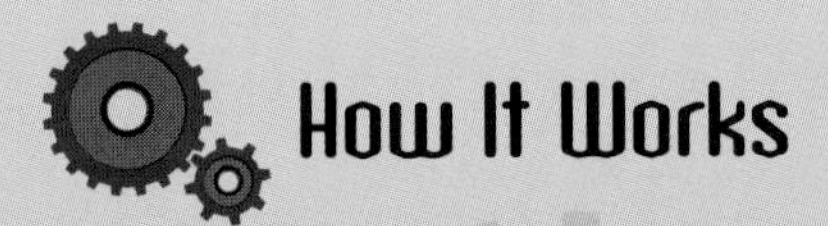

When a cell needs energy, molecules of carbohydrates and fats are broken down and their chemical energy is captured by the compound adenosine triphosphate (ATP). ATP then carries the energy to parts of the cell where it is needed to drive energy-consuming reactions. ATP was discovered in 1929. Its role as the carrier of energy in living cells was determined by Fritz Albert Lipmann [German-American: 1899–1986] in 1941.

proteins, and fats, which are synthesized from simple substances such as carbon dioxide and water. During catabolism, energy is released as the complex substances are broken down into simple substances.

In 1842, Julius Robert Mayer [German: 1814–1878] enunciated the first law of thermodynamics—energy can be neither created nor destroyed—and said the law applied to living organisms. But energy can be converted from one form to another, and discovering the metabolic pathways in which this occurs continues to occupy chemists. The most important pathway, the citric acid cycle, was discovered in the 1930s by **Hans Adolf Krebs**.

Also of interest is the metabolic rate—the total metabolism of an organism at a given time. In 1883, Max Rubner [German: 1854–1932] discovered that the metabolic rate is proportional to the surface area of the body. Thus mice and other small mammals must metabolize more rapidly than larger mammals in order to maintain the same body temperature.

- Cell Metabolism.
  http://www.mindquest.net/biology/anatomy/guides/outline_cell_metabolism.html
- The 1997 Nobel Prize in Chemistry.
  http://www.nobel.se/chemistry/laureates/1997/press.html

Meteor Expedition

Began: 1925
Ended: 1927

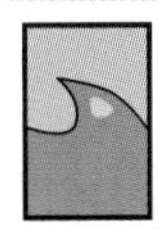

Until the 1920s, the ocean floor was thought to be a flat, almost featureless plain. An expedition by the German research vessel *Meteor* painted a startlingly different picture. The ship was the first to use a newly developed device, the echo sounder, to measure the depth of an ocean basin. It crossed the southern Atlantic Ocean, taking 67,400 echo soundings and creating thirteen east-west bottom profiles. It discovered that the Atlantic basin is divided by a great submarine mountain range, the Mid-Atlantic Ridge. A long valley, or rift, runs through the center of the ridge.

The expedition also provided new insights into other ocean features. For example, using temperature and salinity (saltiness) data it collected, George Wüst [German: 1890–1977] and Albert Defant [German: 1884–1974] showed that the deep ocean has strong currents, disproving the belief that it is a quiet, calm environment.

By the early 1960s expeditions by other

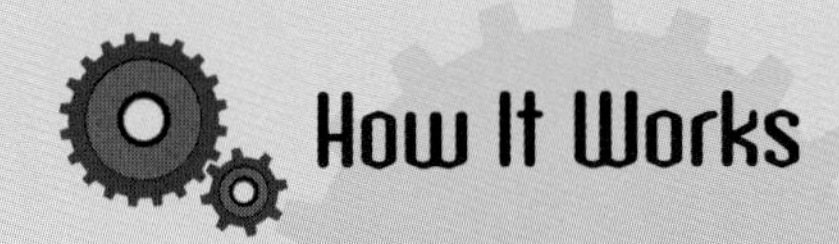

Echo-sounding equipment sends sound waves from a ship to the ocean bottom. A detector aboard the ship picks up sound waves reflected from the bottom. The deeper the water, the greater the time required for a wave to be reflected back to the ship.

FAMOUS FIRST

The rift valley in the Mid-Atlantic Ridge was first visited in 1973 by the French submersible *Archimede*, helping confirm **Alfred Lothar Wegener**'s theory of continental drift.

countries showed that the Mid-Atlantic Ridge is part of a continuous feature, the Mid-Oceanic Ridge, that extends for almost 40,000 miles (65,000 km) throughout all the major oceans.

RESOURCES

- A CHRONOLOGY OF UNDERSEA EXPLORATION. **http://www.pbs.org/wgbh/nova/abyss/frontier/discoveries.html**

Meteoroids

Chladni (fireballs are stones from space) ➤ **Biot** (confirmed stones fall from sky) ➤ **Newton** (explained meteor shower is comet debris)

In ancient times, people believed that streaks of light and balls of fire in the sky were effects of the weather and called them meteors (from the Greek for "high in the air"). Sometimes stones fell from the sky, but most scientists rejected stories of falling stones. In 1794, however,

Large meteor or fireball

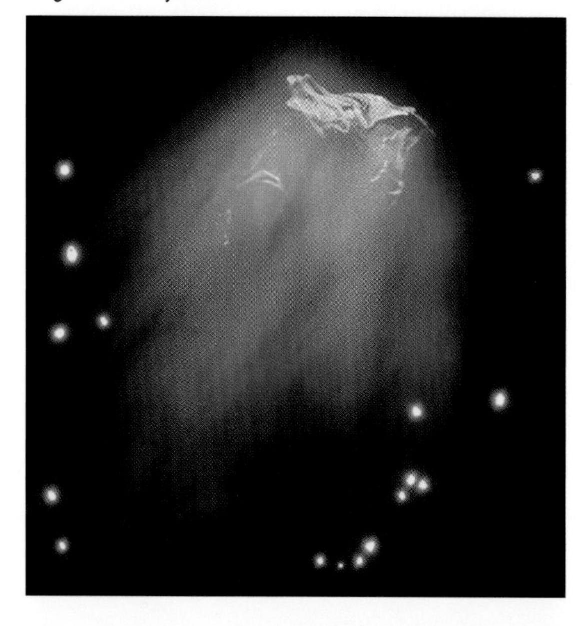

FAMOUS FIRST

Anaxagoras [Greek: c. 500–c. 428 b.c.E.] concluded that a large rock that fell from the sky in 467 B.C.E. did not originate on Earth.

Ernst Chladni [German: 1756–1827] proposed that fireballs are caused by stones falling from space. A report on an 1803 fall at L'Aigle, France, by Jean-Baptiste Biot [French: 1774–1862] finally convinced scientists that stones do sometimes fall from the sky.

In 1863, Hubert Newton [American: 1830–1896] correctly explained that a shower of many meteors occurring at the same time every 33 years was debris from a comet. Nearly all other meteor showers originate in comets also. The tiny particles burn completely in the sky. Stones or pieces of iron that reach the ground are called meteorites. Objects in space that will become meteors or meteorites are meteoroids.

Meteorites can be rock or iron or a mixture. Most are fragments of broken asteroids. A meteoroid found in Antarctica in 1982 was once part of the Moon. It had been blasted into space by a different meteoroid that struck the Moon. Since then, several unusual meteorites blasted from Mars have been found and identified on Earth.

RESOURCES

- Simon, Seymour. *Comets, Meteors, and Asteroids*. New York: Mulberry, 1998. (JUV/YA)
- Olson, Roberta J.M., Jay M. Pasachoff, and Colin T. Pillinger. *Fire in the Sky: Comets and Meteors, the Decisive Centuries, in British Art and*

Meteor crater, Arizona

Science. New York: Cambridge University, 1998.

- Littmann, Mark. *The Heavens on Fire: The Great Leonid Meteor Storms*. New York: Cambridge University, 1998.
- Atkinson, Austen. *Impact Earth: Asteroids, Comets and Meteors: The Growing Threat.* London: Virgin, 1999.
- More about Meteors, Meteoroids, and Meteorites.

http://www.seds.org/nineplanets/nineplanets/meteorites.html

http://liftoff.msfc.nasa.gov/academy/space/solarsystem/meteors/meteors.html

http://starchild.gsfc.nasa.gov/docs/StarChild/solar_system_level2/meteoroids.html

http://www.morehead.unc.edu/Astronomy/meteor/

http://www.planetscapes.com/solar/eng/meteor.htm

Microprocessors

Kilby (integrated circuit) ➤ **Noyce/Hoerni** (planar process) ➤ Development of computer chips ➤ **Hoff** (first microprocessor)

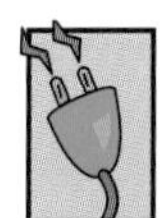

Inside every personal **computer** is a microprocessor, a complete central processing unit assembled on a wafer of silicon. It interprets software instructions, executes arithmetic and logical operations, and maintains control over the system's hardware.

The first important step toward development of microprocessors was the integrated circuit, with two or more electronic components on a single silicon wafer, or chip. The first integrated circuit was created in

YEARBOOK: 1971

- Intel officially introduces the first microprocessor.
- Texas Instruments introduces the first pocket **calculator**.
- The U.S. spacecraft Mariner 9 enters orbit around Mars—the first **artificial satellite** to orbit another planet.

1958 by Jack St. Clair Kilby [American: 1923–]. The following year, Robert Noyce [American: 1927–1990] and Jean Hoerni [Swiss-American: 1924–1997] developed the planar process, which uses photoengraving to connect components of an integrated circuit. This meant that components no longer had to be manufactured separately and linked together by soldered wire connectors. Chips greatly reduced the size and increased the speed of computers.

Early integrated circuits had a few **transistors** and other components. As silicon chip technology improved, so did the number of components that could be put on a single chip. By the 1970s, chips held circuits with thousands of components. Today they hold millions of components.

Marcian ("Ted") Hoff [American: 1937–] began developing the first micro-

Microprocessors have numerous applications in computers and other electronic equipment.

processor in 1969. It evolved into the Intel 4004, which Intel introduced in 1971 as a "microprogrammable computer on a chip." It had 2,300 transistors and could process four bits of data at a cycle rate of 60,000 per second. By 2001, microprocessors with 42 million transistors that processed 32 bits of data at a speed of 1.5 gigahertz—1.5 billion cycles per second—were being sold.

RESOURCES

- Jackson, Tim. *Inside Intel; Andrew Grove and the Rise of the World's Most Powerful Chip Company*. New York: Dutton, 1997.
- MORE ABOUT MICROPROCESSORS.

  http://www.intel.com/intel/museum/25anniv/index.htm

  http://www.softwarecat.com/microprocessor.htm
- MORE ABOUT TED HOFF.

  http://www.digitalcentury.com/encyclo/update/hoff.html

Microscopes

Nero (used emerald for magnification) ➤ Development of single-glass lens ➤ **Janssen** (first compound microscope) ➤ **VAN LEEUWENHOEK** (single-lens microscopes) ➤ Development of three-lens microscope ➤ Development of binocular microscope ➤ **Nicol** (polarizing microscope) ➤ **Zernike** (phase-contrast microscope) ➤ **RUSKA/Knoll** (electron microscope) ➤ **Knoll** (scanning electron microscope) ➤ Development of X-ray microscope ➤ **Binnig/Rohrer** (scanning tunneling microscope) ➤ Development of acoustic microscope

People in ancient times discovered that there were ways to magnify objects. For instance, Nero, emperor of Rome from 54 to 68 C.E., is believed to have compensated for nearsightedness by watching fighting gladiators through an emerald.

By the late 1200s, single glass lenses were being used to magnify objects. Then in 1590, Zacharias Janssen [Dutch: 1580–c. 1638] took two lenses, aligned them in a tube, and created the first compound microscope. News of this invention traveled rapidly throughout Europe. The name "microscope" was given to it by an Italian scientific society whose members included **Galileo.** Not everyone, however, immediately switched to compound microscopes. Some of the most incredible microscopic discoveries of the 17th century were made around 1670 by **Antoni van Leeuwenhoek**, with single-lens microscopes he made himself.

Many improvements have been made to compound microscopes since Janssen's time. Among the most important, early in the 17th century, was the addition of a third lens to better concentrate light on specimens. In 1860, the binocular microscope, with two eyepieces so a person could view specimens using both eyes, was invented. The three-lens, binocular compound microscope is used today in almost every field of science.

Through experimentation, scientists invented special light microscopes. William Nicol [Scottish: 1768–1851] invented the polarizing microscope, which uses a prism to polarize light, allowing people to better study colorless specimens such as quartz crystals. Frits Zernike [Dutch: 1888–1966] invented the phase-contrast microscope, which

Nobel Prize 1953

Zernike received the Nobel Prize in physics for inventing the phase-contrast microscope.

changes light waves so that parts of a specimen can be distinguished more easily.

Even the best light microscopes cannot magnify objects more than about 2,000 times. The study of extremely tiny objects was expanded enormously in 1931 when **Ernst Ruska** and Max Knoll [German: 1897–1969] invented the transmission electron microscope. This device uses beams of electrons instead of light waves to produce images on a screen. Their model enlarged objects 17 times, but improvements since then have resulted in transmission electron microscopes that can magnify 2 million times. In 1935, Knoll created the scanning electron microscope, which moves a beam of electrons back and forth over a specimen, producing an image that appears to be three-dimensional.

In 1948, the first practical X-ray microscope was invented, and in 1981, Gerd Binnig [German: 1947–] and Heinrich Rohrer [Swiss: 1933–] introduced the scanning tunneling microscope, which produces images by recording electrical currents and is routinely used to image atoms.

Scientists also learned from animals such as bats, which use sound to "see."

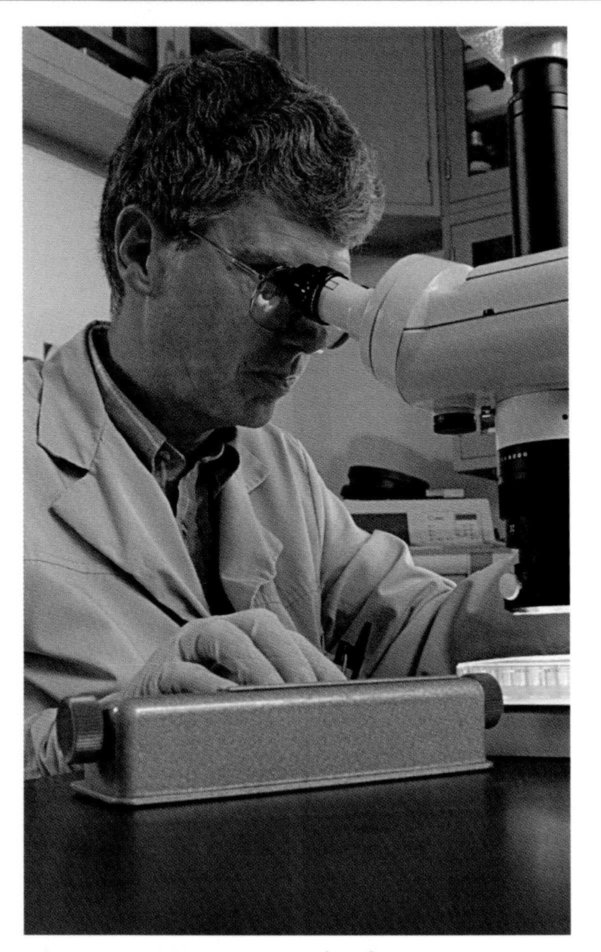

Microscopes are important research tools.

Timeline of Microscopes

1590	Compound microscope
c. 1850	Polarizing microscope
1931	Electron microscope
1932	Phase-contrast microscope
1935	Scanning electron microscope
1948	X-ray microscope
1950s	Field ion emission microscope
1970s	Acoustic microscope
1981	Scanning tunneling microscope

NOBEL PRIZE 1986

Ruska, Binnig, and Rohrer shared the Nobel Prize in physics for their microscope inventions.

Acoustic microscopes were developed in the 1970s. They send high-frequency sound waves through solid objects; the waves are detected by lasers and made visible on a monitor. Acoustic microscopes are useful in studying the interiors of specimens that cannot be destroyed, such as parts of a person's body or the girders that hold up a bridge.

RESOURCES

- Croft, William J. *Under the Microscope: A Brief History of Microscopy*. River Edge, NJ: World Scientific, 1999.
- Ruestow, E.G. *The Microscope in the Dutch Republic: The Shaping of Discovery*. New York: Cambridge University, 1996.
- MORE ABOUT MICROSCOPES.
  http://www.utmem.edu/personal/thjones/hist/hist_mic.htm
  http://library.utmb.edu/scopes/welcome.htm

Microwaves

HERTZ (discovery made existence of microwaves apparent) ➤ Discovery that electromagnetic wave echoes can detect objects ➤ **England** (magnetron) ➤ **England/U.S.** (radar) ➤ **Spencer** (first microwave oven)

The existence of microwaves was apparent after 1888. That year **Heinrich Hertz** discovered **radio** waves, extending knowledge of the electromagnetic spectrum far past **infrared radiation**. Microwaves are just the electromagnetic waves between infrared and radio, with lengths from about 1/25 inch (1 mm) to 1 foot (30 cm).

As early as 1900, some scientists recognized that echoes from electromagnetic waves could detect objects, but radio waves are so long that they pass completely around most objects instead of bouncing back. As World War II approached, scientists in England began to create a special electronic tube, called a magnetron because it combines magnetism with

Cooking food is a popular application of microwaves.

electronics, that would generate powerful microwaves. The first truly successful magnetron was built in 1939, and English and American scientists used it to build **radar**.

Microwaves have other uses as well. Today's **television** and FM radio both use microwaves, as do cellular **telephones**. But the word "microwave" is most closely associated with cooking. In 1946, Percy L. Spencer [American: 1894–1970], one of the contributors to radar, noticed that a candy bar in his pocket melted while he was testing a new magnetron. Spencer cooked other foods with the magnetron and, with other engineers, designed the first microwave oven, introduced commercially in 1947. Microwaves are also familiar from **cosmic background radiation**, discovered in 1964, which is microwave radiation with a wavelength of 2.9 inches (7.3 cm).

RESOURCES

- Scott, Allan W. *Understanding Microwaves*. New York: John Wiley & Sons, 1993.
- MORE ABOUT MICROWAVES.
  http://www.colorado.edu/physics/2000/microwaves/
  http://www.gallawa.com/microtech/history.html

Midgley, Thomas

Engineer: created leaded gas and chlorofluorocarbons (CFCs)
Born: May 18, 1889, Beaver Falls, Pennsylvania
Died: November 2, 1944, Worthington, Ohio

Although educated as an engineer, Midgley's major contributions came in chemistry. Chemicals that he discovered quickly found widespread use, but eventually had to be banned.

Thomas Midgley

In 1916, Midgley joined the lab of **Charles Kettering**, where his first assignment was to find a solution for the knocking in **internal combustion engines**. In 1921, after experimenting with many different gasoline additives, he found that tetraethyl lead completely suppressed the knocking. Leaded gasoline became popular even though there were concerns about the serious health problems caused by lead pollution. It wasn't until 1984 that the U.S. government took steps to ban leaded gasoline. Today, less toxic anti-knock additives are used.

In 1928, Kettering asked Midgley to find a safer, cheaper refrigerant (cooling agent). Midgley synthesized a chlorine-fluorine-carbon compound called dichlorodifluoromethane, sold under the name Freon. It was the first chlorofluorocarbon (CFC), and worked extremely well not only as a refrigerant but in other applications as well. Then in 1974, **F. Sherwood Rowland** and an associate announced that CFCs were destroying the atmosphere's ozone layer. This led to a worldwide ban on the use of CFCs in 1990 and to their replacement with chlorine-free chemicals.

RESOURCES

- MORE ABOUT THOMAS MIDGLEY. **http://www.uh.edu/engines/epi684.htm**

Migration

Migration is the regular movement of animals from one place to another. It allows animals to avoid competition and take advantage of seasonal resources such as food and breeding sites.

People have been aware of migration since ancient times. For example, **Aristotle** noted that cranes, geese, and swans move to warmer places for the winter. But people often had odd explanations for the disappearance of certain animals at the end of a season. As late as the 1500s some naturalists believed that swallows hibernated underwater through the cold months. A 1703 essay hypothesized that migratory birds wintered on the Moon.

It wasn't until the 20th century that scientists began to track animals carefully, using increasingly sophisticated equipment that today includes radio transmitters and artificial satellites. Also during the 20th century, scientists began to understand the **physiology** of migration. In 1925 came the first evidence that the photoperiod (seasonal

Sandhill cranes are among many bird species that migrate with the seasons.

increases and decreases in daylight) triggers migration. Subsequent studies showed that the photoperiod affects feeding behavior, fat deposition, and changes in reproductive organs.

FAMOUS FIRST

Although scientists suspected since at least the 1850s that monarch butterflies migrate, this wasn't confirmed until 1930. But where monarchs spend the winter remained unknown. Then on January 2, 1975, American businessman Kenneth Brugger discovered their winter home high in the mountains west of Mexico City. Hundreds of millions of monarchs congregate in the fir forests there each year from November to March.

Since the 1950s, it has been learned that some migrating birds determine direction according to the position of the Sun, some use specific star constellations to navigate, some orient themselves according to Earth's magnetic field—and some use combinations of these and perhaps other methods. Fish may depend on Earth's magnetic field or chemical odors from their home rivers. Sea turtles may follow bands of warm water.

RESOURCES

- Simon, Seymour. *They Swim the Seas: The Mystery of Animal Migration*. Orlando, FL: Harcourt, 1998. (JUV/YA)
- Bird Navigation and Migration.

  http://www.earthfoot.org/backyard/birdnavi.html

  http://www.manzanodragon.com/manzanovalley/cyberlibraryIII/hist.htm

Milstein, César

Immunologist: produced monoclonal antibodies
Born: October 8, 1927, Bahía Bianca, Argentina

Blood contains many different kinds of antibodies—proteins that attack bacteria and other materials that invade the body. Early research on **immunity** showed that antibodies are specific—a given antibody attacks a specific foreign chemical. However, the amount of any one type of antibody in the blood is too little for research or for many medical applications.

Working in Cambridge, England in the 1970s, Milstein and Georges J.F. Köhler [German: 1946–1995] found a way to produce large amounts of a specific antibody. They injected mice with a desired foreign chemical, causing the mice to produce antibodies to the chemical. Then they removed the antibody-producing cells from the mice and fused them with mice cancer cells. The fused cells, called hybridomas, can survive indefinitely and thus are "factories" able to make a limitless supply of the antibody.

Identical antibodies produced in this manner are called monoclonal antibodies. They have proven very useful in medical diagnosis, including identifying patients at risk for heart disease and stroke.

NOBEL PRIZE 1984

The Nobel Prize in physiology or medicine was given to Milstein, Köhler, and Niels K. Jerne [Danish: 1911–1994] for their work on immunity.

Monoclonal antibodies also have been attached to drugs, to target diseased cells while leaving healthy cells alone.

RESOURCES

- Autobiography of César Milstein. **http://www.nobel.se/medicine/laureates/1984/milstein-autobio.html**

Mining

Early humans (flint pits) ➤ Development of mining for copper, silver, gold, gemstones ➤ Development of mining for copper, tin, iron ➤ **Serbia** (shafts dug with deer antlers) ➤ **Negev Desert** (vertical shafts and galleries) ➤ **China** (coal mining) ➤ Development of iron tools, pumps ➤ Introduction of carts on rails ➤ **Germany** (blasting with gunpowder) ➤ Development of steam engines, compressed air tools ➤ Development of open pit mining

Mining was invented by early humans, who dug pits to obtain flint, a stone useful for sharp tools. Australian flint mines 20,000 years old have been discovered. Later, native metals such as copper, silver, and gold and gemstones were mined, followed by ores for copper, tin, and iron.

One early mining tool was the antler of a deer. A Serbian copper mine from 4500 B.C.E. with shafts 60 feet (20 m) deep was dug with antler picks. Baskets of ore were lifted up the shafts with ropes. **Fire** was often used to heat rocks, which shattered when cold water was poured on them. By 2800 B.C.E., copper mines in the Negev Desert on the Sinai Peninsula combined vertical shafts with large underground rooms called galleries. These were probably lit with bronze mirrors that cast sunlight into the depths.

Coal was later mined in China by the same shaft-and-gallery system perhaps as early as 100 B.C.E. Antler picks by then had long been replaced with iron tools—not only picks, but also hammers, wedges, and saws. Aside from introducing **pumps** to remove water from mines, known from Roman mines in Spain, mining did not change for thousands of years. Improvements began again in Europe about 1450 C.E. Carts on rails were used to

After substances such as coal are mined, they are processed.

Above: *Hydraulic mining dominated the California gold mining industry in the 1800s.* Below: *Strip mining removes deposits that lie close to the surface.*

remove ore, the first step toward development of the railroad. Blasting with gunpowder began in Germany about 1625. In 1698, the very first workable **steam engine** was designed for use in pumping out mines. As improved steam engines were developed, they powered new hammers and drills that revolutionized mining, using tools based on **compressed air**, a system developed as early as 1843 for tunnel building. In the 20th century, internal combustion engines, including diesels, replaced steam and new **explosives** replaced gunpowder.

With the advent of heavy steam shovels and powerful bulldozers, it became economically possible to remove overlying rock completely from ores or coal. This method is called open pit mining or strip mining. Such mines produce large holes, sometimes refilled with rock and soil after mining operations cease.

RESOURCES

- Francaviglia, Richard V. *Hard Places: Reading the Landscape of American's Historic Mining Districts* (American Land and Life Series). Iowa City, IA: University of Iowa, 1997.

Missiles, Guided and Ballistic

Germany (early missiles) ➤ **Germany** (V-1s, V-2s) ➤ Development of ICBMs ➤ Development of MIRVs

Today's military missiles are pilotless, self-propelled weapons, usually rocket-based. Germany experimented with missiles as early as 1934. During World War II, Germany attacked England with jet-propelled missiles called V-1s and rocket-powered ones called V-2s. V-1s steered themselves toward the target, so they were guided missiles. V-2s were guided ballistic missiles; that is, power shut off after launch started them on the right path, and they then free-fell to their destination. The first V-2 missiles began to land in London in September 1944.

After World War II, German rocket engineers aided both the United States and the Soviet Union in developing missiles and space vehicles based on missile technology. The range of weapons similar to the V-2 was extended so much that rockets launched in the United States could transport nuclear weapons to targets in the then-Soviet Union. The Soviet Union also had such weapons, called intercontinental ballistic missiles, or ICBMs.

Missiles like V-2s launched from permanent installations and aimed at cities or military bases are called surface-to-surface, while those launched by airplanes are labeled air-to-surface, air-to-air, or air-to-sea missiles; similar categories are used for missiles launched from ships and submarines. Torpedoes directed at other submarines are underwater-to-underwater guided missiles.

A missile silo

Surface-to-air missiles had a noteworthy success in 1960 when a Soviet rocket downed a high-flying U-2 airplane that flew above other ground-based weaponry and even out of the range of other airplanes.

In 1968, the United States added several warheads (explosive parts) to each ICBM, each warhead aimed at a different target. These MIRVs, or multiple independently targeted re-entry vehicles, made missiles into more potent weapons. In recent years, international treaties have reduced the number of guided missiles, especially such dangerous weapons as MIRVed ICBMs.

• MacKenzie, Donald. *Inventing Accuracy: A Historical Sociology of Nuclear Missile Guidance* (Inside Technology). Cambridge, MA: MIT, 1993.

Moissan, Henri

Chemist: isolated fluorine
Born: September 28, 1852, Paris, France
Died: February 20, 1907, Paris, France

By the 1880s many scientists had tried unsuccessfully to isolate fluorine—an extremely poisonous element that is highly reactive, combining quickly with other elements. Moissan attacked the problem beginning in 1884. In 1886 he succeeded in producing gaseous fluorine at -76° F (–50° C). During the next several years he studied the properties of fluorine and its compounds. Later, working with **James Dewar**, he produced fluorine in its liquid and solid forms.

Moissan also was interested in the possibility of transforming graphite into diamonds—that is, changing an ordinary form of carbon into a very dense form of the same element. Hypothesizing that this could be accomplished under great heat and pressure, in 1892 he developed an electric furnace capable of producing temperatures up to 6300° F (3500° C).

Henri Moissan

Later scientists showed that Moissan's equipment did not produce sufficient pressure to create diamonds. However, the furnace inaugurated the field of high-temperature chemistry. Moissan used it to prepare pure samples of chromium, manganese,

Nobel Prize 1906

Moissan received the Nobel Prize in chemistry for isolating fluorine and developing his electric furnace.

uranium, and other elements, plus many new compounds.

RESOURCES

- Biography of Henri Moissan.
  http://www.nobel.se/chemistry/laureates/1906/moissan-bio.html

Molecules

BOYLE (distinguished elements from compounds) ➤ **AVOGADRO** (molecule is smallest unit of a compound) ➤ **Lewis** (described ionic compounds) ➤ **KEKULÉ** (first explanation of organic molecules) ➤ **PAULING** (used quantum theory to analyze organic molecules)

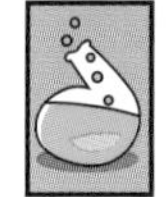

People long ago observed that one substance can change into another —fire changes wood to ash, heat changes water to steam or ore to copper, and dampness changes iron to rust. Greek philosophers theorized that such changes imply all matter is a combination of a few elements, such as earth, air, fire, and water, perhaps consisting of tiny particles called **atoms.** Atoms of different shapes, some suggested, link to create substances more complex than simple elements. These ideas were offered with little or no evidence but are not far from what we now believe.

Robert Boyle in 1661 was one of the first to separate elements, such as gold or carbon, that cannot be broken into other substances, from compounds, made from closely joined elements. In 1811, **Amedeo Avogadro** invented the word "molecule" to describe the tiniest particles of compounds. He was also first to recognize that many elements also occur normally as molecules with more than one atom—both hydrogen and

Scientists study the relationship between a molecule's structure and its chemical properties.

oxygen gases consist of two-atom, or diatomic, molecules. It took 50 years for Avogadro's ideas to be completely accepted, but soon after 1860, the molecule was recognized as the main building block of chemistry.

Avogadro's molecule theory was based largely on gases; when applied to solutions and solids, complications arose. Many compounds break into electrically charged parts (ions) when in solution or in crystals, so that the compound consists of ions floating in solution or bound into crystals by **static electricity** rather than molecules. Rocks, salts, ice, and bone are examples of ionic compounds. Ionic compounds were first correctly described in 1916, by Gilbert Lewis [American: 1875–1946] using current ideas of atomic structure.

Organic compounds such as hydrocarbons and carbohydrates consist of complex molecules based on carbon, whose atoms can form chains or other structures. The first explanation of organic molecules was provided by **Friedrich Kekulé** in 1858, with the modern theory, based in **quantum theory,** developed by Nobel Prize-winning American chemist **Linus Pauling** in 1933.

Long chains of molecular links are called polymers—**plastics** are polymers, as is a molecule of **DNA**. Unlike a simple molecule of carbon dioxide, which always has one carbon atom joined to two oxygen atoms, most polymers can be almost any size. **Proteins,** however, are polymers whose molecules have specific sizes—for example, the molecule of human insulin always has 777 atoms linked in the same way each time.

- Atkins, P.W. *Molecules*. New York: Scientific American Library (W.H. Freeman), 1987.

Montgolfier Brothers

Inventors: invented the hot-air balloon

Joseph-Michel	**Born:** August 26, 1740, Annonay, France **Died:** June 26, 1810, Balaruc-les-Bains, France
Jacques-Étienne	**Born:** January 6, 1745, Annonay, France **Died:** August 2, 1799, Serières, France

"With all haste, gather together provisions of fabric and ropes, and you will surely see the most astonishing things in the world," wrote Joseph Montgolfier to his brother Étienne in late 1782. Joseph had a brilliant idea while watching smoke rise from a **fire**: if hot air could be captured in a bag, the bag would float upward.

On June 5, 1783, after six months of experiments, Joseph and Étienne launched a huge bag filled with hot air. It rose 6,600 feet (2,000 m) into the sky and traveled about 1.5 miles (2.4 km) before it cooled, and gently returned to earth. This was the first flight of a hot-air **balloon**.

Could people survive such a flight? A basket was attached to a balloon and on September 19 the Montgolfiers launched a duck, a chicken, and a sheep. After an 8-minute flight, they were found safe. And so on November 21, Pilâtre de Rozier and the Marquis d'Arlandes ascended in a Montgolfier balloon. They were the first humans to fly.

The Montgolfiers continued to build

Hot air balloons

balloons, and their successes inspired many others around the world.

RESOURCES

- History of the Hot-Air Balloon. **http://messel.emse.fr/tdaurat/montgolf/haballoon.html**

Moons

Parmenides (moonlight is reflected sunlight, explained phases) ➤ **Empedocles** (explained eclipses) ➤ **Aristarchus** (estimated distance to Moon) ➤ **HIPPARCHUS** (correct distance and size) ➤ **GALILEO** (observed "seas," discovered moons of Jupiter) ➤ **HUYGENS** (observed a Saturn moon) ➤ **Cassini** (found additional Saturn moons) ➤ **HERSCHEL** (discovered Uranus, two moons) ➤ **Lassell** (found moons of Neptune and Uranus) ➤ **Hall** (discovered moons of Mars) ➤ **WEGENER** (impact crater theory) ➤ Apollo astronauts (collect rocks, confirm impact theory) ➤ **Christy** (found Pluto moon)

Earth's Moon is visible on clear nights and often during the day. Early humans have left drawings of the Moon's phases, or regular changes in shape, from as early as 30,000 years ago. Parmenides [Greek: c. 515–c. 450 B.C.E] recognized that moonlight is reflected sunlight, also explaining the phases. Empedocles [Greek: c. 492–c. 432 B.C.E] agreed and noted that eclipses of the Sun are caused by the Moon blocking light from the Sun. Aristarchus [Greek: c. 310–c. 230 B.C.E] used the shadow of Earth on the Moon in a lunar eclipse to estimate, rather inaccurately, the distance to the Moon and its size. About a hundred years later, **Hipparchus** determined the correct distance and size, which today we describe as 238,856 miles (384,401 km) for the average distance and 2,160 miles (3,476 km) for the diameter.

No one correctly explained the Moon's blotchy appearance ("the man in the Moon") until **Galileo** in 1609 pointed his newly made telescope at the Moon. He saw that the bright and dark regions are mountains and level plains, which he called "maria" (Latin for "seas"). It seemed at first that there could be air, water, and even life on the Moon, but better telescopes eventually revealed that the Moon lacks an atmosphere and the "seas" are frozen lava. Until the 20th century, astronomers argued over whether the giant craters observed on the Moon had been produced by volcanoes or by impacts of large meteoroids. In 1921, **Alfred Wegener** put forth a convincing argument based on experiments that favored impact craters. Rocks collected by *Apollo* astronauts in 1969–1972 confirmed the impact theory and contributed to establishing that the Moon originated as debris from a giant impact on the early Earth.

Galileo's telescope also found that

At least 30 moons orbit the ringed planet Saturn, most too small to be seen here.

Jupiter has its own moons, observing in 1610 four bodies orbiting that planet. The concept of "moon" was extended from Earth's Moon in orbit about Earth to any large natural body in orbit about a planet. In 1655, **Christiaan Huygens** observed that Saturn has a moon (Titan). Giovanni Cassini [Italian-French: 1625–1712] found a second moon of Saturn in 1671 and two more in 1684. Now, after visits to the planets by space probes and some additional discoveries from Earth, we count 28 moons at Jupiter and 30 orbiting Saturn. **William Herschel**, who discovered Uranus, also located two of its 21 moons in 1787. In 1846, William Lassell [English: 1799–1880] observed Triton, the largest of Neptune's eight moons, and later found another moon at Neptune and two of those orbiting Uranus. In 1877, Asaph Hall [American: 1829–1907] found both of the small moons of Mars during the same week. Finally, in 1978, James W. Christy [American: 1938–] recognized that a series of photographs showed a single moon for Pluto, which was named Charon. Mercury and Venus are the only planets in the solar system without moons.

The 91 moons in our solar system range in size from Jupiter's Ganymede at 5,276 miles (8,484 km) in diameter to tiny, unnamed moons of Saturn less than 6 miles (10 km) across. Unlike Earth's Moon, some of the larger moons of the planets have atmospheres, active volcanoes, and water, making it possible that they might even harbor life.

RESOURCES

- Burnham, Robert. *The Reader's Digest Children's Atlas of the Universe*. Pleasantville, NY: Reader's Digest Children's Books, 2000. (JUV/YA)
- MORE ABOUT MOONS.

  http://www.seasky.org/cosmic/sky7a03.html

  http://www.windows.ucar.edu/cgi-bin/tour_def/our_solar_system/moons_table.html

Earth's Moon is the only moon that has been visited by humans, beginning in 1969.

Morgan, Garrett

Inventor: developed automatic traffic signals
Born: March 4, 1877, Paris, Kentucky
Died: August 27, 1963, Cleveland, Ohio

The son of former slaves, Morgan's formal education ended with elementary school. Nonetheless, he built a notable career doing what he enjoyed most: inventing new and improved gadgets.

Morgan's first major invention was the Breathing Device, a forerunner of modern gas masks. On July 25, 1916, he used it to rescue men trapped by an explosion in a tunnel beneath Lake Erie. News of the rescue spurred fire departments to buy the masks to protect firefighters in smoke-filled buildings. Morgan's equipment also was used by the U.S. Army during World War I to protect soldiers against poison gases.

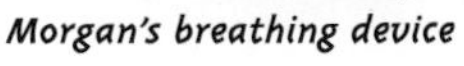

Morgan's breathing device

Morgan's second major invention was the electric traffic signal. At the time, police officers manually operated a stop-go mechanism at intersections. Morgan's device had green GO signs and red STOP signs that were systematically raised and lowered. In addition, there was an all-direction stop signal that allowed pedestrians to cross the street safely. This traffic control system was installed in cities across North America and led to today's red-amber-green traffic lights.

YEARBOOK: 1914

- Morgan's Breathing Device is patented.
- The first **telephone** link between the U.S. East and West coasts is completed.
- The Panama **Canal** opens.
- Edwin C. Kendall [American: 1886–1972] identifies the **hormone** thyroxin.
- Henry Hallet Dale [English: 1875–1968] proposes that acetylcholine is a **neurotransmitter**.

RESOURCES

- More about Garrett Morgan.

http://education.dot.gov/aboutmorgan.html

http://www.princeton.edu/mcbrown/display/morgan.html

http://www.sciencemuseum.org.uk/collections/exhiblets/morgan/gallery.htm

Modern traffic signal

Morgan, Thomas Hunt

Geneticist: proved chromosome theory
Born: September 25, 1866, Lexington, Kentucky
Died: December 4, 1945, Pasadena, California

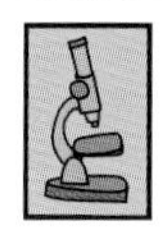

Morgan was skeptical about **Gregor Mendel**'s laws of inheritance. In 1908 he and his colleagues began a series of experiments using the *Drosophila* fruit fly to study how characteristics are passed from generation to generation. Morgan soon confirmed Mendel's laws. He also proved the hypothesis by Walter Sutton [American: 1877–1916] that **genes** are carried on chromosomes and that an organism inherits pairs of **chromosomes**—one chromosome of each pair from each parent.

Drosophila typically have red eyes. One day, a white-eyed fly appeared in one of Morgan's bottles of fruit flies. Breeding experiments showed that this **mutation** occurred only in male flies. Morgan called *Drosophila*'s eye color a sex-linked characteristic, hypothesizing that the gene for this trait is on the X chromosome. Females have two X chromosomes while males have one X and one Y. For a female to have white eyes, she has to inherit white-eye genes from both parents, but a male need only inherit the white-eye gene from his mother. (The red-eye gene is dominant, so a female with one red-eye gene and one white-eye gene has red eyes.) Many sex-linked characteristics have been identified since, including in humans.

Thomas Hunt Morgan

Nobel Prize 1933

Morgan received the Nobel Prize in physiology or medicine for "his discoveries concerning the function of the chromosome in the transmission of heredity."

Morgan's team, particularly **Hermann Joseph Muller**, also advanced understanding of the phenomenon called "crossing over." During cell division, when the two chromosomes of a pair lie next to one another, they can become tangled, break, and exchange segments. In this manner a Drosophila chromosome carrying genes for ebony body and curly wings may end up with genes for ebony body and straight wings.

Morgan reasoned that the farther apart two genes are on a chromosome, the more likely they are to be separated by crossing over. His student Alfred H. Sturtevant [American: 1891–1970] used this concept to make the first chromosome map, which showed the relative position of five genes on *Drosophila*'s X chromosome. By 1922, Morgan and his associates had mapped more than 2,000 *Drosophila* genes.

RESOURCES

• More about Thomas Hunt Morgan.

http://www.nobel.se/medicine/laureates/1933/morgan-bio.html

http://www.nobel.se/medicine/articles/lewis/

Morse, Samuel F. B.

Artist and inventor: developed telegraph
Born: April 27, 1791, Charlestown, Massachusetts
Died: April 2, 1872, New York, New York

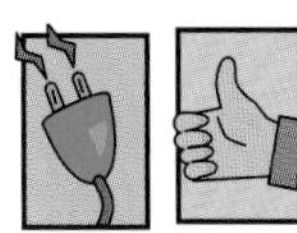

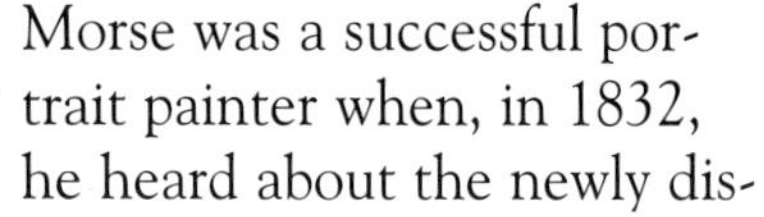

Morse was a successful portrait painter when, in 1832, he heard about the newly discovered phenomenon of electromagnetism. He quickly recognized that a combination of electric pulses could be used as a **code** to send messages over a wire—the basic concept of the **telegraph**. By 1837, with assistance from **Joseph Henry** and Leonard Gale [American: 1800– 1883], Morse sent a message over 1,700 feet (500 m) of wire. He then developed a dot-dash code for letters and numbers, which came to be known as Morse code.

There was little interest in Morse's device, because few people believed it could send messages over great distances. Finally, Morse received money from Congress to build a telegraph line between Baltimore and Washington, D.C. On May 24, 1844, he sent a historic message from the Capitol to his assistant in Baltimore: "What hath God wrought?"

Samuel F.B. Morse

RESOURCES

• More about Samuel F.B. Morse.

http://web.mit.edu/invent/www/inventorsI-Q/morse.html

http://www.morsehistoricsite.org/

http://lcweb2.loc.gov/ammem/atthtml/mrshome.html

Motion

Zeno (argued that motion could not exist) ➤ **ARISTOTLE** (measured motion as speed and acceleration) ➤ **GALILEO** (predicted speed of falling bodies in a vacuum) ➤ **NEWTON** (laws of motion)

If you push something hard enough, it moves. Sometimes it keeps moving after you stop pushing. Drop it, and it moves without a push. Such experiences lead to our ideas about motion. Nevertheless, early scientists found motion hard to understand. Some early philosophers, such as Zeno [Greek: c. 490–c. 425 B.C.], argued that logically motion could not exist. **Aristotle** developed ideas about motion some 200 years after Zeno. He measured motion as speed (change of distance with time) and acceleration (change of speed). He correctly observed that objects accelerate—gain speed—as they fall, but he also made errors. For example, since he observed feathers falling more slowly than rocks, Aristotle concluded that falling heavy objects accelerate faster than light ones.

In 1590, **Galileo** showed that eliminating friction or air resistance produces different conclusions from Aristotle's. His experiments correctly predicted that all falling bodies accelerate at the same rate in a vacuum. Also, without friction, a body moving along a flat surface keeps moving at the same speed. In the 1660s, **Isaac Newton** went beyond Galileo in establishing the laws of motion, including motion in

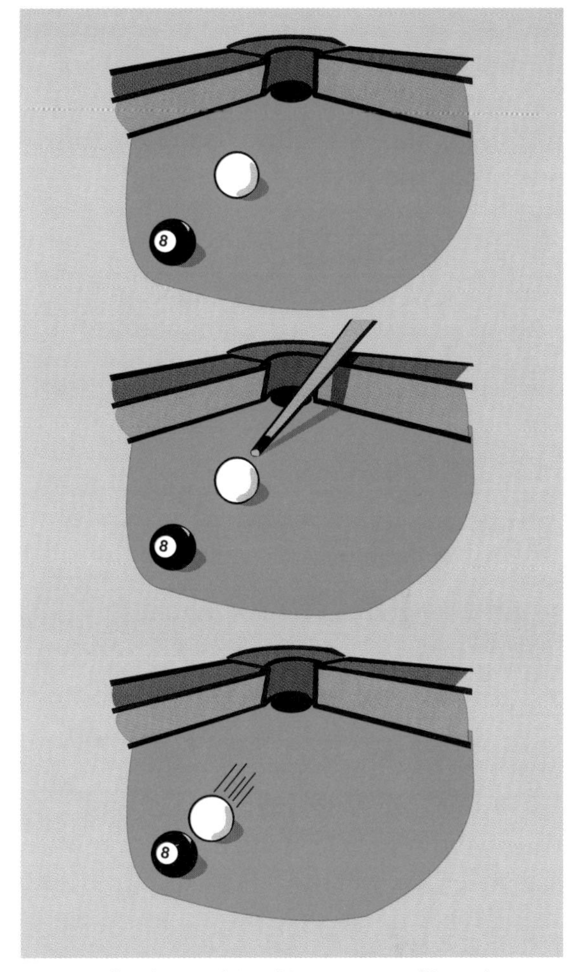

Newton's first law explains objects at rest and in motion.

FAMOUS FIRST

Simon Stevinus [Dutch: 1548–1620] in 1586 dropped a heavy and a light object from a tall building and observed them fall at the same rate, an experiment that may have been repeated later from the Leaning Tower of Pisa by Galileo.

circles. Newton developed the mathematical theory of force, acceleration, and **gravity**. He showed that a few simple laws provide a basis for understanding motion on Earth and in the heavens.

RESOURCES

- NEWTON'S LAWS AND SIMPLE MOTION EXPERIMENTS. **http://www.rose-hulman.edu/bartonrj/project.htm**

Motion Pictures

Roget (established that images persist in mind) ➤ **MUYBRIDGE** (motion as a series of stills) ➤ **EDISON** (first camera to simulate motion) ➤ **LUMIÈRE BROTHERS** (invented projection) ➤ **DE FOREST** (recording sound on film) ➤ Development of color film ➤ Development of 3-dimensional effects

In 1824, Peter Mark Roget [English: 1779–1869] established that an image persists briefly in the mind of a viewer after the image has vanished. As a result, a rapidly shown series of still pictures with small changes in parts of an image from picture to picture can make the image appear to move. In the 19th century some books and toys used this concept to produce pictures showing such scenes as a man tipping his hat.

In 1879, **Eadweard James Muybridge** used multiple cameras to capture motion as a series of stills. When **Thomas Alva Edison** visited Muybridge in 1888, he was inspired to develop a camera whose images could be used to simulate motion, patenting some ideas that year. By 1891, Edison had a prototype that took photographs in quick succession with a single camera and a device to view the apparently moving pictures while looking through a peephole. A finished version was publicly demonstrated in 1893 and quickly put on the market.

In 1894, the **Lumière brothers** studied one of Edison's viewers and adopted it for projection on a large screen, instead of peephole viewing. Others also developed projectors, including one manufactured by Edison's plant along with his peephole viewers. Edison's own projector was introduced in 1896.

Early in the 20th century, motion pictures began to tell whole stories, including fairy tales, science fiction (*A Voyage to the Moon* in 1902), and westerns (*The Great Train Robbery* in 1903). By the 1920s, story films with no soundtrack were popular entertainment. Then, in 1927, audiences streamed to see the first full-length picture that included sound. Nearly every motion picture since pairs sound with images, most using a system of recording sound on the film devised in 1931 by **Lee De Forest**.

How It Works

A motion-picture film camera takes a succession of still photographs, using a rotating shutter with a cutout portion to prevent any photo being taken while the film advances. The projector has the same kind of arrangement, so each photo is shown briefly as a still (typically for 1/24th of a second) and then the film is advanced to the next photo. Each image persists during the time it takes the film to advance, so the viewer interprets the series of still images as continuous motion.

Color images instead of black and white were included in some early films, often by hand tinting. From 1922, Technicolor,

Movies are a popular form of entertainment.

which combined two or three different films to make color images, was often used for special effects and in animation. Technicolor was the basis of the first all-color feature, *Becky Sharp* in 1935. Other innovations, such as 3-dimensional effects based on stereovision (introduced in 1953), have been less effective. Larger screen images, also introduced in 1953, produce some illusion of three dimensions and remain popular.

RESOURCES

- Parkinson, David. *The Young Oxford Book of the Movies*. New York: Oxford University, 1998. (JUV/YA)
- MORE ABOUT MOTION PICTURES.
  http://memory.loc.gov/ammem/edhtml/edmvhist.html
  http://www.cinemedia.net/SFCV-RMIT-Annex/rnaughton/ENC_CINEMA.html

Mountains

A mountain is distinguished from a hill by greater size and steeper inclines, but there is no hard-and-fast distinction. Most mountains occur in long chains called ranges, although some mountains rise in more compact groups. **Volcanoes**, which usually are mountains, exist both in ranges and individually.

Throughout history, humans have discovered **fossils** of ocean creatures on top of high mountains. As recently as the 18th century, most scientists believed that these fossils were deposited at a time when the sea rose over permanent mountains. But in the 19th century, geologists such as Charles Lyell [Scottish: 1797–1875] recognized that erosion removes mountains over the eons of geological time. Scientists looked for a mechanism that would grow new mountains. One popular idea for about a hundred years, starting in 1866, was that Earth is cooling and shrinking, wrinkling Earth's crust into mountain chains. Another idea was that since mountain rock is lighter (less dense) than other rock, mountains float in Earth's crust like icebergs in the sea. But these ideas were flawed in various ways. By 1960, geologists recognized that they did not know what causes mountains to rise.

In the 1960s, **plate tectonics** provided an explanation. When two slabs of the

Many mountains form in chains called ranges.

Earth's crust, called plates, move toward each other, their combined motion lifts the crust, creating mountain regions such as the Himalayas. Similarly, the Hawaiian Islands, which rise as mountains from the sea's floor, or the Black Hills of the Dakotas, have appeared where plumes of rising rock push up the crust. Ranges also occur where giant faults drop part of the crust and lift the adjacent portion, producing mountains such as the Grand Tetons.

RESOURCES

- Bevan, Finn. *Mighty Mountains: The Facts and the Fables*. Danbury, CT: Children's, 1998. (JUV/YA)
- Tesar, Jenny E. *America's Top 10 Mountains*. Woodbridge, CT: Blackbirch, 1998. (JUV/YA)
- More about Mountains.

  http://www.platetectonics.com/book/page_11.htm

  http://www.peakware.com/encyclopedia/pwindex_ranges.htm

Muller, Hermann Joseph

Geneticist: demonstrated danger of X rays
Born: December 21, 1890, New York, New York
Died: April 5, 1967, Indianapolis, Indiana

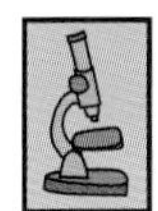

The rate at which **mutations**, or changes in **genes**, occur in nature is very low. In the 1920s, Muller, who became interested in mutations while working with **Thomas Hunt Morgan**, wondered if it was possible to increase the mutation rate. He exposed *Drosophila* fruit flies to heat, which increased the rate somewhat. Then he switched to **X rays** and discovered that exposure to X rays increases the mutation rate in *Drosophila* up to 150 times. This led him to warn of the potential danger of such radiation to humans. Muller also concluded that most mutations are harmful, generally causing an organism's death, often before it can reproduce and pass on the mutations to future generations.

Hermann Joseph Muller

Nobel Prize 1946

Herman Muller received the Nobel Prize in physiology or medicine for his discovery that X rays cause mutations.

- Biography of Hermann Joseph Muller.

  http://www.nobel.se/medicine/laureates/1946/muller-bio.html

Müller, Paul

Chemist: discovered DDT's insect-killing properties
Born: January 12, 1899, Olten, Switzerland
Died: October 12, 1965, Basel, Switzerland

The few insecticides—**pesticides** that kill insects—available in 1935 were expensive or poisonous to humans and other vertebrates. Müller observed that chemicals are absorbed and metabolized (processed) differently in insects than in vertebrates. For this reason, he thought there might be chemicals that are poisonous only to insects.

After four years of intensive research, Müller synthesized and tested DDT (dichlorodiphenyltrichloroethane). This chemical was first synthesized in 1874 by German chemist Othmar Zeidler, who failed to recognize its properties. To Müller, DDT appeared to be an ideal insecticide. It was highly toxic to insects but did not seem to harm other animals. It was inexpensive to manufacture and easy to apply in a spray or dust.

DDT became extremely useful in combating disease and agricultural pests. But discovery of DDT's negative effects on valued organisms led to bans of its use in the United States and elsewhere in the 1970s.

Paul Müller

Nobel Prize 1948

Paul Müller received the Nobel Prize in physiology or medicine "for his discovery of the high efficiency of DDT as a contact poison against several arthropods."

RESOURCES

- Biography of Paul Hermann Müller.
  http://www.nobel.se/medicine/laureates/1948/muller-bio.html
- More about Insecticides and DDT.
  http://ipmworld.umn.edu/chapters/ware.htm
  http://chppm-www.apgea.army.mil/ento/timefram/DDT.htm

Mullis, Kary B.

Biochemist: invented PCR
Born: December 28, 1944, Lenoir, North Carolina

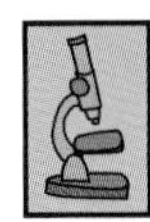

"I do my best thinking while driving," Mullis once explained. One night in 1983, he was driving north from San Francisco when he devised a simple technique that would revolutionize many areas of biology and medicine. Called polymerase chain reaction (PCR), the technique allows scientists to take a microscopic segment of the genetic material **DNA** and rapidly reproduce the segment to make millions or even billions of copies. It can be done in a test tube, but today automated equipment is generally used.

Before PCR, copies of DNA were made one at a time; it was almost impossible to make quantities large enough for further study. PCR has been extremely valuable to the **Human Genome Project** and other research efforts. It has been used to diagnose genetic diseases, develop tests for detecting acquired immunodeficiency syndrome (AIDS), examine remains of ancient humans, and perform DNA fingerprinting in criminal cases.

Kary B. Mullis

Nobel Prize 1993

Mullis received the Nobel Prize in chemistry for his invention of PCR. He shared the prize with Michael Smith [British-Canadian: 1932–], who developed site-directed mutagenesis, another technique for manipulating DNA.

RESOURCES

- More about Kary B. Mullis.
  http://www.nobel.se/chemistry/laureates/1993/mullis-autobio.html
  http://www.invent.org/98mullis.html
- Polymerase Chain Reaction—Xeroxing DNA.
  http://esg-www.mit.edu:8001/esgbio/rdna/pcr.html

Musical Instruments

Neandertal (bone whistles, flutes) ➤ **Greece** (panpipes) ➤ **Near East** (harp, lyre) ➤ Development of lute, guitar, violin, horns ➤ **Crete** (pottery bells) ➤ **China** (brass bells) ➤ **Ancient Greece, Rome** (aulos, organ, early keyboard instruments,sackbut, zink) ➤ Development of modern orchestra instruments ➤ Development of first piano ➤ Development of electronic keyboards, electrified instruments

Hitting an object to make a rhythmic sound may be the oldest form of music. An ice-age site in Ukraine has yielded red-painted mammoth bones that

may have been struck to make rhythms and simple tunes. But the earliest definite musical instruments are whistles or flutes made from bone. Some are from Neandertal times, over 40,000 years ago. Bone flutes, similar to modern instruments called recorders, were common around 28,000 years ago. Blowing into the flute makes a sound, and opening and closing holes changes the pitch. Another way to obtain different pitches is to use several different-sized whistles, as in the panpipes of ancient Greece.

The earliest stringed instruments were the harp or lyre, invented at least 5,000 years ago in the Near East. Notes are created by plucking on the instrument's strings. Around 4,000 years ago, the lute could produce different notes by changing the length of a single string. Guitars are modified lutes, and members of the violin family are essentially lutes played by pulling a bow across the strings. Other types of early instruments developed from blowing into an animal horn or seashell, which created the first kinds of horns. A metal horn makes louder and brighter sounds than one made of a horn or shell. Instruments such as the bassoon and oboe family vibrate a small piece of hollow

Today's electronic instruments produce high-quality sound.

reed pressed between the lips. About 3,000 years ago bells were used in Crete (made from pottery) and China (made from brass). Chinese bell sets were tuned so that each bell played a different note.

During Greek and Roman times, about 2,500 to 1,500 years ago, the ancestor of the clarinet and saxophone was very popular. Called the aulos, it used a pair of single-reed instruments, each played with one hand. Another Greek invention was the organ, a large set of pipes with airflow controlled by a keyboard. Another early keyboard instrument, used about 1100 C.E., was the mechanically plucked harp.

By the 1700s, modern orchestra instruments began to take shape. In 1709, when the first piano was made, the keys caused small hammers to strike the strings. The first horns could only play a few notes; to change keys the player inserted or removed extra tubing. The sackbut solved this problem with a piece of tube that slides back and forth to change the length, becoming today's slide trombone. The zink was a wooden trumpet with holes to change the tones, like a flute. In 1813, the modern system of valves was introduced to change the pitch of trumpets.

The modern keyboard, available commercially since 1983, controls electrically generated sounds, which can imitate traditional instruments. Other instruments, such as the guitar or even wind instruments, are often electrically amplified, changing the way they are played and often how they sound.

RESOURCES

- Ardley, Neil. *Eyewitness: Music.* New York: Dorling Kindersley, 2000.
- Baines, Anthony. *The Oxford Companion to Musical Instruments.* New York: Oxford University, 1992.
- Dearing, Robert. *Keyboard Instruments & Ensembles* (The Encyclopedia of Musical Instruments). Broomall, PA: Cheslea House, 2000. (JUV/YA)
- More about Musical Instruments.
  http://sports.onysd.wednet.edu/academics/science/chemistry/biochem/sound/history.html
  http://www.si.umich.edu/CHICO/MHN/enclpdia.html
  http://www.eyeneer.com/World/Instruments/

Mutations

DE VRIES (discovered mutations) ➤ **MULLER** (X-ray effect) ➤ Mutations are changes in DNA ➤ **Luria/Hershey** (mutations in bacteriophages)

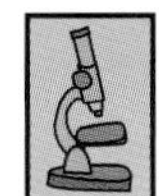

Abrupt hereditary changes in organisms were discovered at the beginning of the 20th century by **Hugo Marie de Vries**. He called the changes mutations, and correctly theorized that they are changes in **genes**.

Naturally occurring mutations are rare events, but in the 1920s, **Hermann Joseph Muller** demonstrated that the mutation rate can be increased by exposure to X rays. His work inspired other scientists to try to artificially induce mutations; today many mutagens (mutation-causing factors) are known, including ultraviolet rays, radioactive materials, and numerous chemicals.

In the 1940s, scientists demonstrated that genes are composed of **DNA**. In the 1950s, DNA's structure was clarified. These discoveries led to the understanding that a mutation is a change in the sequence or number of building blocks in a DNA molecule. Sometimes cells can correct the damage. However, if it is not repaired or is repaired incorrectly, the mutated gene is passed on to the next generation when the cell divides.

By the 1940s, it had been established that mutations occur in all organisms. But, researchers asked, what about **viruses**, which are not considered to be organisms because they do not carry out **metabolism** and multiply only within living cells? In 1945, Salvador Luria [American: 1912–1991] and Alfred Hershey [American: 1908–1997] demonstrated that bacteriophages (viruses that infect bacteria) can mutate. This suggested the possibility, which has since been proven, that mutations also occur in other viruses.

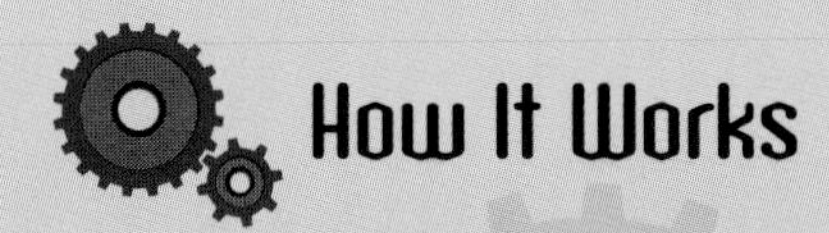

How It Works

In the late 1960s, Bruce Ames [American: 1928–] developed a simple method for determining the mutagen-causing potential of chemicals. The test chemical is added to a culture of a particular strain of the bacterium *Salmonella typhimurium*. Then the rate at which the bacteria mutate is measured. Mutations play a significant role in the development of cancer, and the Ames test can help identify cancer-causing chemicals.

Researchers proved that mutations are common in viruses, including the AIDS virus shown here.

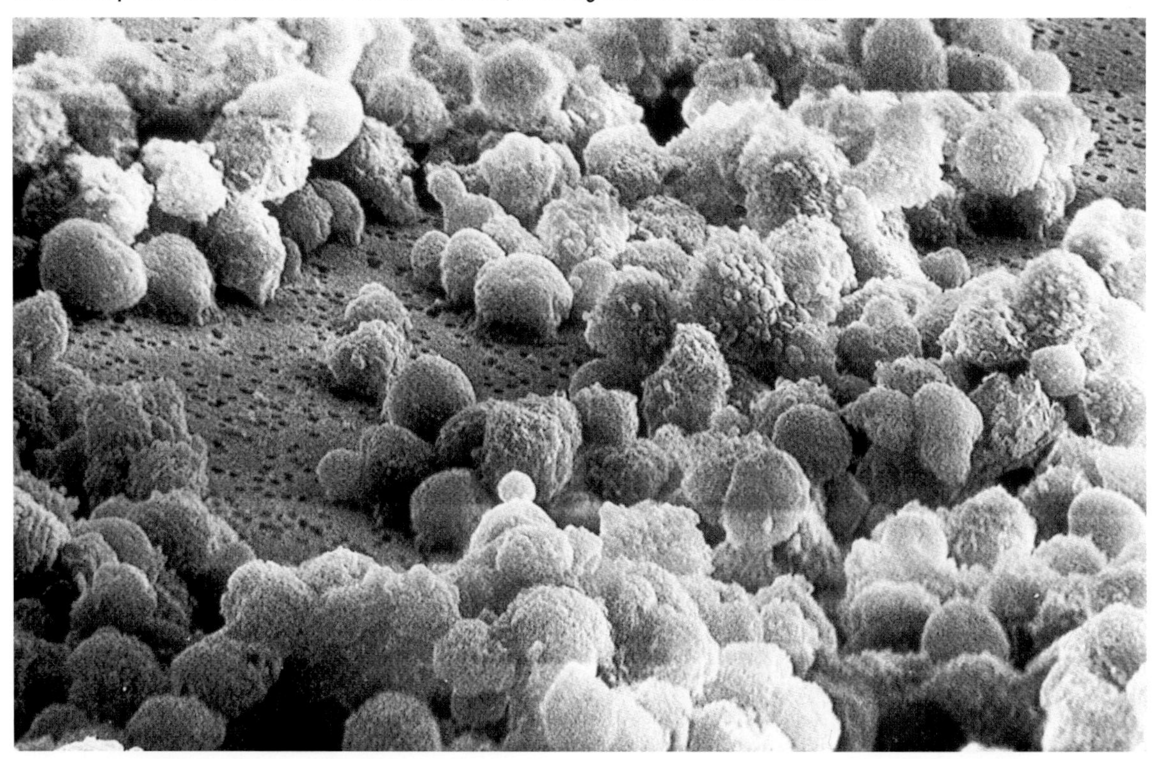

Such mutations make it difficult to develop cures for influenza, colds, AIDS, and other viral diseases.

RESOURCES

- More about Mutations.
  http://www.brooklyn.cuny.edu/bc/ahp/BioInfo/SD.Mut.HP.html

Muybridge, Eadweard James

Inventor: pioneered photography of motion
Born: April 9, 1830, Kingston upon Thames, England
Died: May 8, 1904, Kingston upon Thames, England

Before **motion pictures**, there was Muybridge's motion **photography**. While living in California during the 1860s, Muybridge became famous for his photographs of Yosemite Valley. In 1872, a wealthy horse breeder asked Muybridge if he could take photographs to settle an age-old question: are all four feet of a racing horse off the ground simultaneously? Muybridge used a series of cameras triggered by strings stretched across a racetrack. The resulting photo sequence showed that at times a horse does have all its feet in the air.

During the following years, Muybridge improved his technique for photographing motion and studied animal and human locomotion. In 1880 he invented the zoopraxiscope, which projected images in rapid succession onto a screen, creating the illusion of movement.

RESOURCES

- Muybridge, Eadweard. *Horses & Other Animals in Motion, Forty-Five Classic Photographic Sequences*. Mineola, NY: Dover, 1985.
- More about Eadweard James Muybridge.
  http://www.kingston.ac.uk/muytexto.htm

Nanotechnology

Feynman (idea of nanotechnology) ➤ Advances based on scanning tunneling microscope ➤ Use of paired lasers ➤ Development of electric micrometer ➤ Development of artificial molecules, self-replicating ➤ **Adleman** (molecular computer memory) ➤ Applications such as nanowires

The prefix nano- (Greek for "dwarf") means billionth—a billionth of a meter is a nanometer—but is also applied to small devices whose size might conveniently be measured in nanometers. Creation of such devices, usually those less than 100 nanometers in any dimension, is called nanotechnology.

The idea of nanotechnology was introduced in1959 by Richard Feynman [American: 1918–1988]. He envisioned making devices by joining as few as 7 atoms—about 2 nanometers. Feynman was inspired by the miniaturization introduced in the U.S. space program in 1958, and by **microprocessors** (computer chips), also invented in 1958. Soon, tiny motors and other devices—still hundreds or thousands of nanometers in size—were built. Some became commercially useful, embedded in such devices as automobile airbags or switching networks for telephones.

The word *nanotechnology* was coined in 1974, but the first real advances near atomic levels came in the 1980s. The scanning tunneling **microscope** (STM), invented in 1981, provided the breakthrough. The STM can image individual atoms. A modification called the atomic force microscope (AFM) can also move them—demonstrated in 1989 when researchers spelled "IBM" with 35 xenon atoms. In 1985, physicists also began to

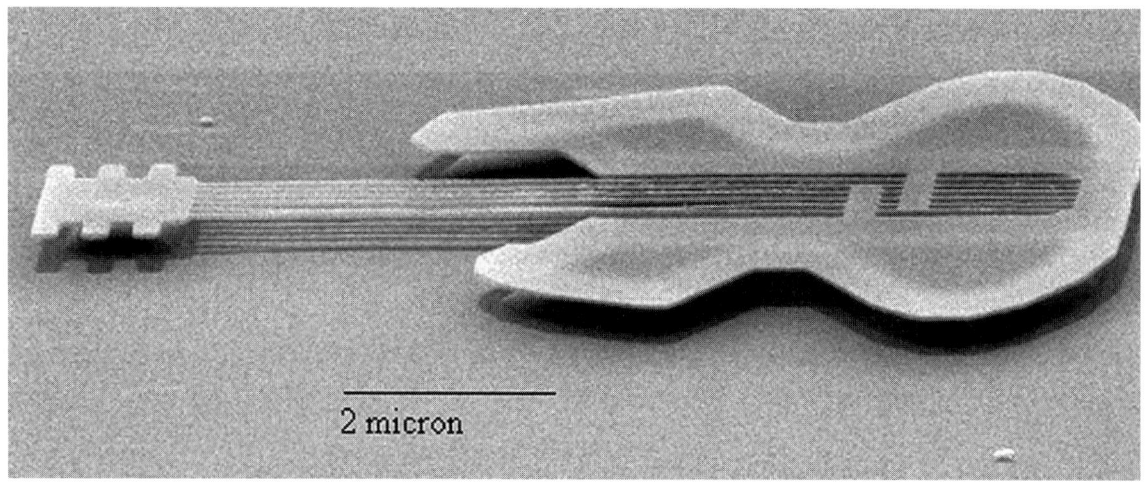

A nanoguitar only 10 microns (100 nanometers) long.

use paired lasers as pincers to handle individual atoms. Using technology developed for etching transistors into silicon chips, scientists at the University of California at Berkeley created the first electric micromotor in 1988, not from single atoms, but at a nanometer scale.

In the 1990s, chemists began to fabricate complex molecules that self-assemble from simpler molecules. Also in 1990, several groups of chemists announced successful creation of molecules that replicate themselves. In 1994, Leonard Adleman [American: 1945–] created a computer equipped with a memory and stored program consisting of single molecules, albeit giant molecules, of DNA. Another giant molecule, the carbon molecule called a nanotube—essentially an elongated **buckyball**—showed that it had many properties that could be exploited in nanotechnology.

Nanotechnology grew rapidly at the start of the 21st century. A modified AFM became an inkjet printer that sprays individual molecules into nanoscale designs. Workers used silicon-chip technology to fabricate "nanowires" a few hundred atoms in diameter that they then combined to make transistors only 20 nanometers across. Biochemists crafted a form of DNA with a metal conductor running along the middle of the molecule, creating a nanoscale combination that could be called "intelligent electronics." In 2000, the University of Michigan started a center to apply nanotechnology to medicine, aimed at cell manipulation with tools smaller than the cells themselves.

RESOURCES

- Gross, Michael. *Travels to the Nanoworld: Miniature Machinery in Nature and Technology*. New York: Perseus, 1999.
- Scientific American. *Key Technologies for the 21st Century*. New York: W.H. Freeman, 1996.
- More about Nanotechnology.

  http://nanozine.com/WHATNANO.HTM

  http://www.rand.org/publications/MR/MR615/mr615.html

  http://www.kheper.auz.com/future/nanotech/nanotech-history.htm

  http://nanotech.about.com/science/nanotech/library/blinhistory.htm

Navigation

Stars, Sun used for navigation ➤ Development of astrolabe) ➤ **China** (magnetic needles, compass) ➤ Development of cross-staff, back-staff ➤ Development of octant ➤ **Campbell** (invented sextant) ➤ **HARRISON** (chronometer) ➤ Development of radio beacon navigation ➤ Development of satellite-based navigation, GPS

Early people navigated—found locations and followed routes to specific destinations—using landmarks and **time** measured in days.

Around 3000 B.C.E., traders knew that different stars appear as one travels north or south. Measuring the height above the horizon of a familiar star or the position of the Sun became a navigation tool, especially for sailors out of sight of land. By 500 B.C.E., philosophers recognized that apparent changes in position of stars occur because Earth is a sphere. Astronomers developed instruments to measure star positions. The earliest was the astrolabe of 200 B.C.E., a disk marked in degrees combined with a movable pointer to aim at the Sun or a star.

Sailors often used a cross-staff, a simplified astrolabe for sighting along a movable pointer while a plumb line kept the device perpendicular. In 1590, the backstaff was introduced; sailors measured the staff's shadow instead of sighting into the Sun. In the 18th century, another modified astrolabe called the octant replaced the backstaff. Later, a more precise tool, the sextant, became standard in a version developed in 1757 by John Campbell [Scottish: 1720–1790].

When the Sun and other stars were hidden by clouds, mariners navigated by dead reckoning, combining direction of travel with speed to establish an approximate location. Dead reckoning was greatly improved by the Chinese discovery that a magnetized body free to spin orients itself in an approximately north-south direction. By 270 C.E. Chinese sailors had begun to use a magnetic needle, or compass, for direction. The compass reached Europe by at least 1080, and soon was used by sailors. Speed aboard ship was found by timing how long it took to pass a float, called a log, tossed from the ship.

Local time compared to time at a known location established a position east or west of the known location. Local noon occurs when the Sun reaches its highest point of the day, easily measured

An astrolabe

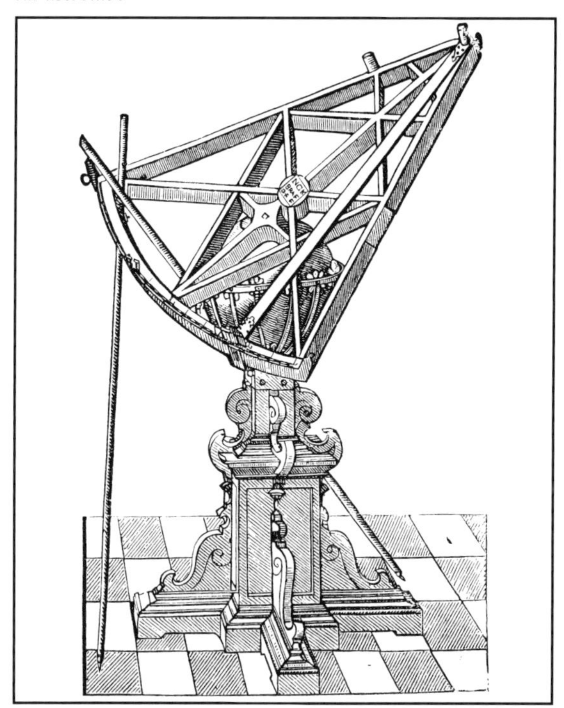

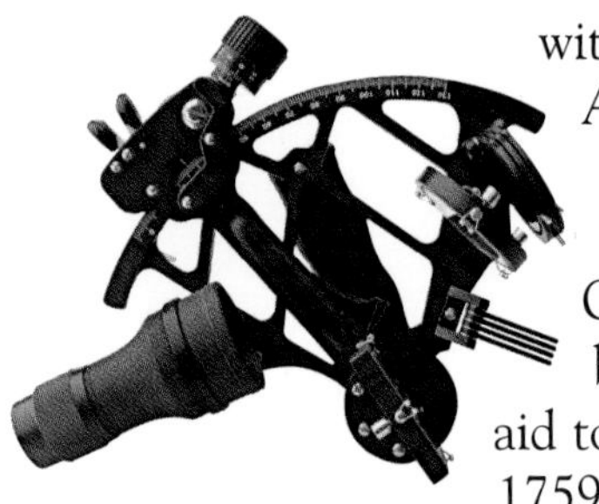

with a sextant. Although this concept was apparent to the ancient Greeks, it only became a practical aid to navigation after 1759, when **John Harrison** built the first accurate navigational clock, or chronometer.

When **radio** began regular broadcasts in the 1920s, sailors recognized that the direction of the broadcasting station could be determined by moving an antenna to find the strongest signal. In 1928, stations called radio beacons began broadcasting for navigational use. Such beacons could also be used by **airplanes**. Loran (from "long range navigation") was an improvement introduced in 1942; instead of depending on one beacon and radio waves, loran uses a pair of beacons and **microwaves** for more accuracy. In the 1970s, the U.S. military recognized that satellite-based navigation could be accurate enough to guide ships, planes, and **missiles**.

How It Works

The 24 GPS satellites each transmit digital radio signals that contain precise information on the time and the satellite's position. Four of the satellites are always visible from any point on Earth. A GPS receiver compares its clock with **atomic clocks** on the four satellites. Its computer calculates the distance to each based on the time. Each of the 4 distances is the radius of a sphere—all points equidistant from a center form a sphere in 3 dimensions. The 4 spheres intersect in only 1 point—the location of the receiver.

In 1993, the U.S. Air Force completed launch of the Global Positioning System (GPS) of satellites, which also became accessible for civilian navigation that year. Today, even automobiles and backpackers can use GPS for navigation.

RESOURCES

- Ganeri, Anita. *The Story of Maps and Navigation*. New York: Oxford University Children's Books, 1998. (JUV/YA)
- MORE ABOUT EARLY NAVIGATION. **http://www.yahooligans.com/Around_the_World/History/Maritime_History/Navigation/**

Nebulas

Messier (prepared list of fuzzy patches) ➤ **HERSCHEL** (cataloged thousands of nebulas) ➤ **Huggins** (some nebulas have glowing gases) ➤ Use of radiotelescopes to study nebulas

Some objects in the sky appear as fuzzy patches of light. Astronomers named these nebulas (Greek for "clouds"). Not all fuzzy patches are nebulas. Some become **comets** as they approach the Sun. Others reveal themselves as clusters of stars when seen through powerful telescopes.

Charles Messier (French: 1730–1817) became interested in comets in 1759 when he observed the reappearance of Comet Halley. His search for new comets was hindered by other fuzzy objects, so, from 1760 through 1784, Messier made a numbered list of more than 100 fuzzy patches that are not comets. The Messier list is still used to identify objects in the sky although not all on his list are nebulas—M1, the Crab nebula, is the remains of an exploded star; M31 is the Andromeda **galaxy**; M42, or Orion's Sword, is a shining cloud of dust and gas in which stars are born; and M45 is the Pleiades star cluster.

William Herschel received a version of Messier's list in 1781 and began to study nebulas himself in 1783, eventually listing thousands. Many nebulas cataloged by Herschel appeared as round disks, like planets, so he called them planetary nebulas, although they are actually spheres of expanding gases.

About 1865, William Huggins [English: 1824–1910] established that M31 consists of many stars, but both a planetary nebula called NGC 6543 and M42 (Orion's Sword) produce light of a type that comes from glowing gases. Late in the 1920s, astronomers established that some of the glow is **fluorescence** induced by nearby stars and some comes from high temperatures that cause atoms and molecules to crash into each other.

Since the 1940s, **radiotelescopes** have expanded what we know about nebulas. Dark patches of sky are cool nebulas. When stars begin to form, which takes place in nebulas, their energy heats and brightens their surroundings. A few nebulas are remains of supernova (huge star) explosions, but planetary nebulas are gases heated by a star that ejected the gas without exploding.

Many nebulas emit light. Others reflect light from nearby stars.

RESOURCES

- Malin, Stewart. *The Greenwich Guide to Stars, Galaxies and Nebulae*. New York: Cambridge University, 1990.
- Vogt, Gregory. *Nebulas*. Austin, TX: Raintree Steck-Vaughn, 2000. (JUV/YA)
- MORE ABOUT NEBULAS.

 http://fusedweb.pppl.gov/CPEP/Chart_Pages/5.Plasmas/Nebula.html

 http://www.seds.org/billa/twn/

 http://oposite.stsci.edu/pubinfo/nebulae.html

Neurotransmitters

RAMÓN Y CAJAL (nerve cell "buttons") ➤ **Sherrington** (synapse) ➤ **Dale** (acetylcholine a neurotransmitter) ➤ **Loewi** (chemical process at synapse) ➤ **von Euler** (noradrenaline as neurotransmitter) ➤ Discovery of dopamine, serotonin, enkephalins, endorphins

The nervous system rapidly transmits messages throughout the body. Until late in the 19th century, scientists assumed that messages pass directly from the end of one nerve cell to the beginning of the next. But, in 1889, **Santiago Ramón y Cajal** demonstrated that each nerve cell ends in a "button" that is close to, but never actually touches, neighboring nerve cells. In 1897, Charles Sherrington [English: 1857-1952] named this junction between two nerve cells a "synapse."

In 1914, Henry Hallet Dale [English: 1875–1968] published a study of the chemical acetylcholine and proposed that it might be a neurotransmitter: a chemical that carries impulses across synapses from nerve to nerve. In 1920, Otto Loewi [Austrian-American: 1873–1961] proved for the first time that a chemical is produced at the synapse. He called it **Vagustoff**, after the vagus nerve that he used in his experiments. He later identified this chemical as acetylcholine.

Acetylcholine was the first neurotransmitter to be identified. Today, over 100 substances are known to act as neurotransmitters. For instance, in 1949, Ulf von Euler [Swedish: 1905–1983] discovered that noradrenaline (also called norepinephrine) serves as a neurotransmitter at some synapses. He also showed how noradrenaline molecules are stored within Ramón y Cajal's "buttons." In the 1950s, dopamine was discovered and, in the 1970s serotonin, enkephalins, and endorphins—all involved with sensations of pleasure, among other functions.

Disturbances in levels of neurotransmitters in parts of the brain are implicated in several diseases, including Parkinson's disease (dopamine), Alzheimer's disease (acetylcholine), and clinical depression (serotonin).

RESOURCES

- MORE ABOUT NEUROTRANSMITTERS AND NEUROSCIENCE.

 http://faculty.washington.edu/chudler/hist.html

 http://faculty.washington.edu/chudler/chnt1.html

 http://neurolab.jsc.nasa.gov/timeline.htm

A molecule of the neurotransmitter dopamine

Newcomen, Thomas

Engineer: built first practical steam engine
Born: 1663, Dartmouth, England
Died: August 5, 1729, London, England

At the beginning of the 18th century, removing water from mines was costly. Animals powered pumps, but they tired and had to work in shifts. Newcomen, improving a device invented by Thomas Savery [English: c. 1650–1715], built a piston-operated **steam engine** to pump water from mines. The engine had a cylinder in which a piston moved. The piston was connected to a large rocking beam, which at its other end was connected to the pump rod that went down into the mine. When steam from a boiler entered the cylinder it pushed the piston upward. When the piston reached the top, water was sprayed into the cylinder, cooling the steam and creating a vacuum that let atmospheric pressure push the piston downward. The piston's up and down movement rocked the beam, thus creating a pumping action.

YEARBOOK: 1753

- The first Newcomen engine in the U.S. is installed at a copper mine in New Jersey.
- **James Lind** describes a preventive for scurvy.
- **Carolus Linnaeus** publishes *Species Plantarum*, classifying plants according to binomial names.

The first Newcomen engine was installed in 1712, pumping 120 gallons (454 L) of water a minute from a coal mine 150 feet (46 m) below the surface. In the decades that followed minor improvements were made to Newcomen's invention. In 1764, **James Watt** found a way to improve its efficiency significantly.

RESOURCES

- The World's First Steam Engine.
  http://www.historical.engines.btinternet.co.uk/newcomen.htm

Newton, Isaac

Mathematician and physicist: invented calculus, discovered laws of motion
Born: January 4, 1643, Woolsthorpe, England
Died: March 20, 1727, London, England

Newton's father, a farmer, died before his son was born and Newton was raised by his grandmother. An uncle recognized his talent for making mechanical devices and encouraged his schooling. Newton entered Cambridge University in 1661. In 1665, Cambridge closed because of a plague epidemic. Newton returned to the family farm for a year and a half, during which he worked on his own ideas.

He first developed new methods in mathematics, starting with the binomial theorem, which deals with fractional powers of an algebraic expression, and continuing with a useful method for approximating solutions as closely as one wishes. Newton was the first to show that processes with an infinite number of steps can give sensible and useful results. By the end of 1665, he had developed the methods for finding slopes of curves that we call differential calculus. In the following year, he completed his invention of calculus with the method of finding areas of curved regions, today known as the integral calculus.

During the same period, Newton experimented with **light** and found that white light is a mixture of colors. He also began to think about **gravity**—whether the same force that causes an apple to fall to Earth also affects the Moon.

When Cambridge reopened in 1666, Newton completed his studies and remained as a professor of mathematics. He continued to develop new ideas in mathematics. Instead of publishing his work, however, he circulated manuscripts to friends—a manuscript explaining calculus was circulated starting in 1669. In 1668, he built the first reflecting **telescope** and presented one to the Royal Society, a scientific organization that met in London in 1672. Newton became a member of the Royal Society and began to communicate some of his discoveries about optics to them.

In 1679, **Robert Hooke** of the Royal Society, who had been working on the problem of planetary orbits, wrote to Newton asking his views. Newton followed Hooke's line of thought and used calculus to produce a first version of the law of gravity. He did not tell Hooke, whom he viewed as a rival. Five years later, Hooke had still not solved the problem, so he asked **Edmond Halley**, who in turn asked Newton. Newton told Halley that he had already established the correct answer mathematically. Halley then prevailed on Newton to write an explanation of how the planets move, which became the two volumes called the *Principia*, published in 1687.

Isaac Newton

Newton's *Principia* contained his laws of **motion** and gravity as well as such topics as **artificial satellites**. Although the physics was entirely supported by traditional algebra and geometry, the *Principia* also explained calculus for the first time in print.

In 1696, Newton left Cambridge to run the British mint in London. In 1703 he became president of the Royal Society, keeping that post for the rest of his life. The following year he wrote a full account of his study of light, called *Opticks*. Although Newton devoted much time to alchemy, the predecessor of chemistry, he did not publish any results. Many of his notes on alchemy and other subjects are still being studied by science historians.

RESOURCES

- Berlinski, David. *Newton's Gift: How Sir Isaac Newton Unlocked the System of the World.* New York: Free Press, 2000.
- White, Michael. *Isaac Newton: Discovering Laws That Govern the Universe.* Woodbridge, CT: Blackbirch, 1999. (YA/JUV)
- MORE ABOUT ISAAC NEWTON.

  http://www-groups.dcs.st-and.ac.uk/history/Mathematicians/Newton.html

  http://www.newton.org.uk/

Nirenberg, Marshall

Biochemist: cracked the genetic code
Born: April 10, 1927, New York, New York

DNA consists of building blocks called nucleotides. There are only four DNA nucleotides, which differ in their nitrogen base: adenine (A), thymine (T), guanine (G), and cytosine (C). The nucleotides' bases determine the arrangement of 20 different amino acids in **proteins**. In the 1950s scientists were eager to discover how this genetic code works. George Gamow [Russian-American: 1904–1968] noted that if a sequence of DNA is considered three bases at a time—as triplets — there are 64 possible "messages" (AAA, AAT, AAG, etc.). This would be more than enough to code for the 20 amino acids.

Nirenberg and his colleagues carried out the experiments proving the triplets code for amino acids. Nirenberg announced in 1961 that they had discovered the three-letter code for the amino acid phenylalanine. They went on to study other triplets, creating a "dictionary" of the genetic code. In the process, they showed that more than one triplet can specify a particular amino acid. For example, both AAA and AAG code for lysine.

How It Works

GCT codes for the amino acid alanine, GGA codes for glycine, and AAG codes for lysine. Thus a DNA segment GCTGGAGGAAAG results in a protein sequence alanine-glycine-glycine-lysine. The code is transcribed from the DNA to a messenger molecule, which carries the code to the part of the cell where proteins are made.

Marshall Nirenberg

RESOURCES

- MORE ABOUT MARSHALL NIRENBERG.

  http://web.calstatela.edu/faculty/nthomas/nirenber.htm

  http://www.nobel.se/medicine/laureates/1968/index.html

Nobel, Alfred

Inventor: created dynamite
Born: October 21, 1833, Stockholm, Sweden
Died: December 10, 1896, San Remo, Italy

In the 1860s, Nobel revolutionized the field of explosives. He took nitroglycerin, an extremely sensitive liquid explosive discovered in 1846 by Ascanio Soberro [Italian: 1812–1888], and combined it with an absorbent material such as wood pulp to produce dynamite. Unlike pure

Alfred Nobel

nitroglycerin, dynamite can be safely packaged and transported, since it explodes only when triggered by a blasting cap, which Nobel also invented.

FAMOUS FIRST

The first Nobel Prizes were awarded on December 10, 1901. Each winner receives a gold medal, diploma, and large sum of money.

Nobel developed many other inventions and received more than 350 patents. In addition to his interest in science and technology, he loved literature and promoted peace among nations. He willed most of his money to establish the Nobel Prizes in physics, chemistry, physiology and medicine, literature, and peace. (A sixth prize, for economic sciences, was established in 1968 by the Bank of Sweden.)

YEARBOOK: 1867

- Nobel patents dynamite.
- Joseph Monier [French: 1823–1906] patents reinforced concrete.
- **George Westinghouse** invents the air brake.

RESOURCES

- Skagegard, Lars-Ake. *The Remarkable Story of Alfred Nobel and the Nobel Prize*. Philadelphia: Coronet, 1994.
- ALFRED NOBEL — MAN BEHIND THE PRIZE. **http://www.nobel.se/nobel/alfred-nobel/index.html**

Nuclear Reactors

Discovery of fission ➤ **FERMI** (designed first nuclear reactor) ➤ Development of nuclear reactors for electricity

In 1938, Otto Hahn [German: 1879–1968] and Fritz Strassmann [German: 1902–1980] established that some large atomic nuclei can break apart, or undergo fission, releasing energy. Soon after, the U.S. Government hired **Enrico Fermi** to develop a device to produce and control nuclear fission. Fermi succeeded on December 2, 1942. His "nuclear pile"—lumps of uranium and carbon interspersed with cadmium strips—was a step in producing materials for **nuclear weapons**, and it also released energy.

In the late 1940s, other nations also built nuclear piles, now called reactors. England's first reactor, Windscale, was finished in 1950. The **heat** from a chain reaction out of control, however, can cause the reactor to melt. Soon, acci-

A nuclear power plant

dents caused by too-rapid chain reactions occured, the first in Canada in 1952. A U.S. reactor underwent a meltdown in 1955. Windscale suffered a major meltdown in 1957, releasing radioactivity into the environment.

Reactors began to produce electric power starting in 1954. The Soviet Union led the way, but the first large-scale producer was an English power plant in 1956. In 1957, several reactors in the U.S. began producing electricity. A partial meltdown occurred at Three Mile Island in the U.S. in 1979, and a complete meltdown at Chernobyl in Ukraine in 1986 caused many lives to be lost. Although new reactor startups were drastically cut, nuclear energy production continued to rise, nearing 10 percent of all electric power in the U.S. by the late 1990s.

How It Works

Uranium atoms have large nuclei that tend to break in two from their own mass. The pieces—nuclei of smaller atoms and **subatomic particles**—fly apart, striking nearby atoms and setting them in faster motion. Some pieces are neutrons. These are slowed (moderated) by carbon or water molecules and captured by atoms, which then undergo fission. Since each fission produces more neutrons, a chain reaction starts. Collisions among fragments heat the reactor fuel and the moderators, which powers steam engines that generate electricity.

RESOURCES

- Cantelon, Philip L.; Robert C. Williams, and Richard G. Hewett (eds.). *The American Atom: A Documentary History of Nuclear Policies from the Discovery of Fission to the Present.* Philadelphia: University of Pennsylvania, 1994.
- Galperin, Anne L. *Nuclear Energy/Nuclear Waste.* Broomall, PA: Chelsea House, 1992. (JUV/ YA)
- Wilcox, Charlotte. *Powerhouse: Inside a Nuclear Power Plant.* Minneapolis: Carolrhoda, 1996. (JUV/YA)
- How a Nuclear Reactor Works. **http://www.sciencenet.org.uk/database/Physics/Atomic/p00417b.html**

Nuclear Weapons

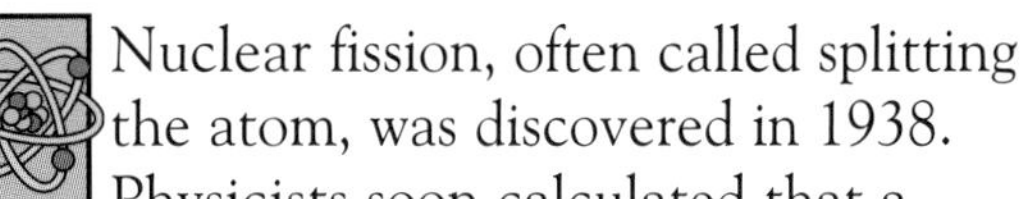

Eddington (energy of stars produced by fusion) ➤ Nuclear fission discovered ➤ **United States** (first fission, or atom, bombs) ➤ Atom bombs dropped on Japan ➤ Development of fusion (hydrogen) bombs

Nuclear fission, often called splitting the atom, was discovered in 1938. Physicists soon calculated that a large enough mass of the artificial element plutonium or of the rare **isotope** uranium-

Mushroom cloud from nuclear explosion.

235 would, if confined to a small enough space, undergo a spontaneous fission chain reaction, releasing vast amounts of **radioactivity** and **heat**. In 1939 the United States, with help from its allies, launched a project to build such weapons, known as atom bombs. The first device was exploded in a test on July 16, 1945. The following month, atomic bombs were dropped on the Japanese cities of Hiroshima and Nagasaki. Both cities were destroyed and much of the population killed, either outright from the blast and heat or later from radioactivity.

More energy than is produced from fission can be released when two atoms join into one, a process called fusion. As early as 1926, twelve years before the discovery of nuclear fission, Arthur Eddington [English: 1882–1944] concluded that the vast energy of stars is produced by fusion, induced by the great heat and pressure in the stars' centers. The invention of the atom bomb enabled humans to produce comparable heat and pressure. In 1952, the U.S. used an atom bomb to ignite the first fusion weapon, known as the hydrogen bomb; other nations followed in developing their own nuclear weapons.

No nuclear weapons have been used in war since 1945, but their existence has been a major factor in relations between nations.

RESOURCES

- More about Nuclear Weapons.
  http://www.fas.org/nuke/hew/
  http://www.mtholyoke.edu/acad/intrel/nukes.htm

Numeration

Scratches on bone ➤ **Middle East** (baked clay tokens) ➤ **Sumeria** (cuneiform) ➤ **Egypt** (system of tallies) ➤ **Mesopotamia, Central America, India, China** (place value) ➤ **India** (true zero) ➤ **Europe** (Roman numerals, use of subtraction) ➤ Adoption of Hindu-Arabic system

Writing numbers, called numeration, preceded writing words by thousands of years. Scratches on

A variety of numerals, or symbols for numbers.

bone artifacts 30,000 years old are thought to show numbers similar to today's tallies, such as marking 𝍸 // to mean seven.

In the Middle East, about 10,000 years ago, traders used small pieces of baked clay, called tokens, to record numbers. Specific shapes, such as animal heads or cones, indicated what each token meant, such as a sheep or jar of oil. A clay container would hold as many tokens as counted sheep or jars. Later, the individual pieces were pressed into soft clay to make images that were then baked hard. As this system was further simplified, some images came to mean numbers that could be applied to any item, while other symbols came to stand for words. This system of symbols pressed into clay is called cuneiform and is first associated with the Sumerians in about 3000 B.C.E.

At nearly the same time, Egyptians invented their own system of numeration. It started with single-unit scratch marks like tallies. Ten tallies were indicated by a wicket (see below), ten wickets by a scroll, and so forth. The Egyptian system was strictly additive—to show 36, the scribe wrote ∩∩∩ ||||||.

In Mesopotamia, Central America, China, and India, numeration systems began to use the place in which a symbol appears to mean multiples of that symbol—a system called place value. The oldest, the cuneiform system of Mesopotamia from about 2000 B.C.E., used an additive system of ones and tens like the Egyptian through 59, placing the symbol for the number one off to the left of a group of ones and tens to signify 60. In Central America, the Maya from about 300 B.C.E. developed a place-value system based on multiples of 20, while about that same time the Chinese system used multiples of ten. There were many different systems in use in India, but sometime between 600 C.E. and 900 C.E., Indians of the Hindu religion became the first to introduce a true zero into their system—the Maya had independently recognized zero some centuries earlier than this.

European writers at that time used Roman numerals for numeration, a system that had originally been additive like the Egyptian, but later also used a subtractive feature, replacing the numeral IIII for four (1 + 1 + 1 + 1) with IV (5 – 1) and VIIII for nine with IX (10 – 1). It is difficult to compute with Roman numerals and fractions must be treated separately. Arab mathematicians learned the Indian system of place value with zero, which is easy to use and allows decimal fractions. In the 13th century, European scholars such as Leonardo of Pisa, also known as Fibonacci [Italian: c. 1170–1250] campaigned successfully for changing to Hindu-Arabic numeration. Today every civilized country uses the Hindu-Arabic system.

RESOURCES

- Ganeri, Anita. *The Story of Numbers and Counting*. London: Evans Brothers, 1996. (JUV/YA)
- HISTORY OF NUMERATION. **http://www.cpsc.ucalgary.ca/williams/History_web_site/timeline3000BCE_1500CE/numeration.html**

Observatories

Early humans (observed Sun, stars) ➤ **Egypt** (pyramids) ➤ **Greeks** (measured angles to stars) ➤ **Beg** (giant observatory) ➤ **TYCHO** (best naked-eye observatory) ➤ **GALILEO** (telescope) ➤ **HERSCHEL** (first modern observatory) ➤ **Lowell** (mountaintop observatory) ➤ Development of large optical telescopes

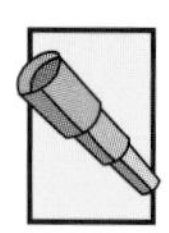

Early agricultural people observed the Sun, Moon, or specific stars from special places to determine dates of important days. The Hopi of North America appointed one Sun Watcher in each village, who observed the Sun from a designated place as it rose over the mountains. Its location was notched on a wooden stick and used to schedule festivals and determine planting dates.

Many ancient structures align with the Sun and stars. Openings in Egyptian temples and pyramids from as early as 2750 B.C.E were placed so that the Sun or a particular star shone through on special days. With this information, Egyptians determined that the year is 365 days long and learned to predict the annual Nile flood.

When agriculture began in Europe, people also built structures to align with particular stars or sunrise on significant days, such as the summer solstice when daylight is longest. The most famous such calendar structure is Stonehenge in England, built about the same time as early Egyptian pyramids. Like all structures created to observe stars or planets, these structures are called observatories.

About 300 B.C.E. Greeks at Alexandria, Egypt, built an observatory that used small instruments designed to measure angles to stars. Giant tools that measured angles more accurately were used in observatories erected by Arabian and Persian astronomers, starting in 829 C.E. In Samarkand, Uzbekistan, in 1420, Ulugh Beg [Timurid: 1394–1449] built a three-story observatory of this type inside a trench some 260 feet (80 m) across. From this stone observatory, Beg produced the best tables of planetary positions up to that time. **Tycho Brahe** built the best of all the naked-eye observatories in 1576. Tycho's measurements were vital in establishing the correct theory of the motions of the planets.

After **Galileo** introduced the astronomical **telescope** in 1609, there was no need at first for observatories—astronomers used portable telescopes. The Paris Observatory in France, which became important after 1669, when Giovanni Cassini [Italian-French: 1625–1712] began to work there, mingled old-fashioned—but precise—large naked-eye instruments with small telescopes. A similar observatory at Greenwich in England followed in 1676.

Modern observatories, like this one house giant optical telescopes.

William Herschel discovered the planet Uranus in 1781 with a backyard telescope but soon began to plan a large fixed instrument. His 1789 telescope was 40 feet (12 m) long and poked out of a small building. Its tube was held in place by a giant wooden scaffold. Herschel also used a 20-foot- (6-m-) long telescope and several smaller ones at the site, the first modern observatory.

Isaac Newton had suggested that high mountains make the best observatory sites. Lick Observatory on Mount Hamilton in California, which began observations in 1888, established that high elevations are practical. In 1893, Percival Lowell [American: 1855–1916] followed with a mountaintop observatory outside Flagstaff, Arizona. Nearly all major observatories since—such as the large **optical telescopes** installed at California's Mount Wilson in 1908 and Palomar Mountain in 1948—are similarly located. Among the greatest observatories of today are several on 13,825-foot (4,213-m) Mauna Kea in Hawaii and several high in the Andes Mountains.

RESOURCES

- Krisciunas, Kevin. *Astronomical Centers of the World*. New York: Cambridge University, 1988.
- Parker, Barry R. *Stairway to the Stars: The Story of the World's Largest Observatory*. New York: Perseus, 1994.
- MORE ABOUT OBSERVATORIES.

  http://tdc-www.harvard.edu/mthopkins/obstours.html

  http://www.asnsw.com/info/observatories.htm

  http://webhead.com/WWWVL/Astronomy/observatories-optical.html

Ocean Currents

Franklin (recognized ocean currents, plotted Gulf Stream) ➤ **Maury** (wind and current chart) ➤ **Challenger expedition** (mapped currents around the world) ➤ Development of modern current theory

Great rivers, called ocean currents, run through the seas. Among the first scientists to recognize this fact, long known to sailors, was **Benjamin Franklin**. In 1770, as deputy postmaster to the English colonies, Franklin learned that fishing boats crossed the Atlantic Ocean two weeks faster than mail ships. Franklin asked sailors why this occurred. He plotted sailors' reports on a map, revealing a large surface current, the Gulf Stream. Mail ships were slowed by sailing against this current, which fishers had learned to avoid.

FAMOUS FIRST

In 1513, Ponce de León [Spanish: 1460–1521] discovered the strong current along the east coast of Florida, becoming the first sailor to report the Gulf Stream.

In 1847, Matthew Maury [American: 1806–73] began to offer copies of his *Wind and Current Chart of the North Atlantic* to ship's captains who sent him their ship's logs (records). Maury also persuaded sailors to toss and recover bottles, noting dates and

Ocean currents have long been known to sailors.

locations. Maury, who summarized his data in 1855, is the "founder of oceanography."

In 1872–1876, the **Challenger expedition**, sent by the British navy to investigate oceans, mapped currents around the world. American, German, and French oceanographic expeditions also mapped currents in the late 1800s.

In the 1900s, oceanographers developed a theory of currents. Colder or saltier water is dense and flows along the bottom of the sea as a density current. It also swirls in a circular fashion, because the rotation of Earth causes all currents to turn. A second current, flowing above and in the opposite direction of a density current, returns water, but turns it the other way.

RESOURCES

- Nye, Bill and Ian G. Saunders. *Bill Nye the Science Guy's Big Blue Ocean*. New York: Hyperion, 1999. (JUV/YA)
- Heiligman, Deborah. *The Mysterious Ocean Highway: Benjamin Franklin and the Gulf Stream*. Austin, TX: Raintree Steck-Vaughn, 1999. (JUV/YA)
- More about Ocean Currents.
  http://seawifs.gsfc.nasa.gov/OCEAN_PLANET/HTML/oceanography_currents_1.html
  http://www.whoi.edu/coastal-briefs/Coastal-Brief-94-05.html

Odum, Eugene P.

Ecologist: pioneered ecosystem ecology
Born: September 17, 1913, Lake Sunapee, New Hampshire

When Odum began his career in the late 1930s, **ecology** was studied on a small scale. Odum changed the focus to the large scale of ecosystems and in the process, changed people's thinking about the natural world.

An ecosystem, stressed Odum in his influential *Fundamentals of Ecology*, published in 1953, is the fundamental unit of ecology. Every ecosystem has six components: inorganic substances involved in **cycles of nature;** organic compounds (proteins, carbohydrates, etc.); climate; food producers (mostly green plants); macroconsumers (mostly animals); and microconsumers (mostly bacteria and fungi, which break down dead matter). Odum explored the interdependence among these components—how, for example, brook trout live in the colder, acidic upper reaches of a mountain

Pollution from runoff (below) can affect the health of an ecosystem, such as a trout stream (next page).

stream but are absent from the warmer, alkaline lower stretches.

Odum was also instrumental in integrating humans and their actions into ecological studies. He explained, for example, how pollution can spread through an ecosystem and how this can affect humans as well as other living things.

Odum has often collaborated with his brother, Howard T. Odum [American: 1924–]. Their study of a coral atoll in the Pacific Ocean during the 1950s was one of the first complete studies of an ecosystem.

See also conservation.

RESOURCES

- Odum, Eugene. *Ecological Vignettes: Ecological Approaches to Dealing with Human Predicaments*. Philadelphia: Harwood Academic, 1998.
- The History of the Ecosystem Concept: The Odum Brothers.

  http://www.acs.appstate.edu/dept/biology/Faculty&Staff/Neufeld/Ecosystems/OriginsPart3.htm

Oersted, Hans

Physicist: discovered electromagnetism
Born: August 14, 1777, Rudkjöbing, Denmark
Died: March 9, 1851, Copenhagen, Denmark

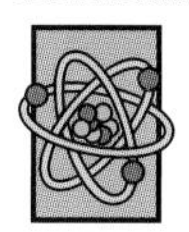

For centuries, an iron-bearing rock called lodestone was the only known source of **magnetism**. Then in 1820, Oersted discovered electromagnetism—magnetism produced by an electric current. It was probably the most important scientific discovery ever made in front of a class of students!

Oersted was giving a demonstration at the University of Copenhagen, using electric current to heat platinum wire. Either by chance or on purpose, a compass was underneath the wire and Oersted noticed that the compass needle moved as current passed through the wire. During the coming months he conducted numerous experiments to understand exactly what was happening. He concluded that an electric current flowing through a wire turns the wire temporarily into a magnet, and that a magnetic needle placed near the wire will move to a position perpendicular to the wire.

Oersted's discovery quickly led to other developments, including construction in the 1830s of the first electric generators.

YEARBOOK: 1820

- Oersted discovers electromagnetism.
- **André-Marie Ampère** explains how electromagnetism works.
- Johann Salomo Christoph Schweigger [German: 1779–1857] uses electromagnetism to invent the galvanometer, a device for measuring an electric current's intensity and direction.

RESOURCES

- Hans Oersted and the Discovery of Electromagnetism.
  http://www.clas.ufl.edu/users/fgregory/oersted.htm
- Understanding Electricity.
  http://www.duke-energy.com/kids-home/kids/understanding/basic/magnetism.html

Optical Telescopes

Lippershy (first optical telescope) ➤ **GALILEO** (astronomical telescope) ➤ **NEWTON** (first mirror telescope) ➤ **HERSCHEL** (large telescope) ➤ **Parsons** (improved mirrors) ➤ Construction of ever-larger mirrors

In ancient times people discovered that looking though curved transparent material makes objects appear larger. By the 13th century C.E. this effect was used to invent eyeglasses. Some glassmakers began to specialize in making curved glass, called a lens. In 1608, lens maker Hans Lippershy [Dutch: d. c. 1619] learned that combining two lenses could make distant objects appear closer, the first optical **telescope**. Optic can mean "visible"; an optical telescope modifies visible light. **Galileo** built the first optical telescope for astronomy in 1609.

Lenses bend light, but different colors bend at different angles, changing a point of starlight into a small rainbow. Telescopes that collect light with curved mirrors avoid this problem, although it is difficult to make a mirror that focuses incoming light on a point. Adding a correcting lens solves these problems, first accomplished in 1732.

Isaac Newton built the first mirror telescope (called a reflector) in 1668, but methods for making curved mirrors were still primitive. Lens telescopes (refractors)

Optical telescope

remained popular with astronomers until the end of the 19th century. The largest refractor, built in 1897 with a 40-inch (102-cm) lens, is still in use at Yerkes Observatory in Wisconsin.

A lens can only be supported at the edges, so large ones tend to bend, which distorts the image. Large mirrors do not have this defect since they are supported over the entire back surface. **William Herschel** in 1789 built a notable telescope with a mirror 48 inches (1.22 m) across — usually called "the 40-foot telescope," from the length of its tube. In 1845, William Parsons, the Earl of Rosse [Irish: 1800–1867], developed techniques for making better mirrors and built a reflector with a 72-inch (1.93-m) mirror, by far the largest of the 19th century. In the 20th century it was surpassed in 1917 by the 100-inch (2.54-m) Hooker telescope at Mount Wilson, in 1948 by the 200-inch (5.08-m) Hale at Palomar Mountain, and in 1993 by the 394-inch (10-m) Keck 1 at Mauna Kea (built in sections), as well as by several other telescopes larger than the Hale. Telescopes with mirrors as large as 33 feet (100 m) are planned for the 21st century. Meanwhile, optical telescopes have begun to work together as **interferometers**, producing significantly greater performance.

How It Works

Because light changes direction when it passes from air to glass (called refraction), a curved lens takes nearly parallel rays of light from distant objects and aims them toward a single focus. Although refracting telescopes make distant objects appear close, the main function of astronomical telescopes is to collect and concentrate light. Most astronomical telescopes use reflection instead of refraction to do this—a curved mirror sends light rays to a single point in front of the mirror.

RESOURCES

- More about Telescopes.

  http://library.thinkquest.org/C001429/waves/optical_telescopes.htm

  http://www.infoplease.com/ce6/sci/A0861466.html

  http://www.seds.org/billa/bigeyes.html

Organ Transplants

Carrel (method of connecting blood vessels) ➤ **Medawar** (impact of antibodies) ➤ **Murray** (first successful organ transplant) ➤ **Thomas** (bone marrow transplant) ➤ Development of cyclosporines

Replacing a damaged or diseased organ in one person with an organ —the transplant—from another person, living or dead, began with the work of Alexis Carrel [French-American: 1873–1944]. In 1902, Carrel published a method for sewing together blood vessels so that blood would circulate through the vessels. In 1910, he showed that blood vessels could be stored at low temperatures for future use. Using these and other techniques he devised, Carrel successfully removed and replaced animal organs.

Attempts to transplant organs from one organism to another, however, ended in failure. Work in the 1940s by Peter B. Medawar [British: 1915–1987] explained why: Unless a transplant comes from an identical twin, the body views it as foreign, much as it identifies germs as foreign. The donor and recipient have different antigens. Antibodies in the recipient's body fight and destroy the foreign antigens, and thus the transplant. Medawar's work led to numerous efforts to find drugs and other techniques that would control this rejection reaction.

Nobel Prize 1912

Alexis Carrel received the 1912 Nobel Prize in physiology or medicine for his work on uniting blood vessels and transplantation.

Meanwhile, surgeons realized that transplants are most likely to be successful if they involve a donor and recipient with closely matched antigens—a concept called tissue typing.

Nobel Prize 1960

Peter B. Medawar shared the 1960 Nobel Prize in physiology or medicine for his work on antigens.

The first successful transplant of an organ from one human to another took place at Peter Bent Brigham Hospital in Boston, Massachusetts, on December 24, 1954. A team of physicians headed by Joseph E. Murray [American: 1919–] transplanted a kidney from a young man into his identical twin. In 1956, E. Donnall Thomas [American: 1920–] performed the first successful bone marrow transplant, also between identical twins.

Famous First

Transplanting organs from animals to humans is called xenotransplantation ("xeno-" is Greek for "foreign"). The first systematic study of xenotransplants began in the 1960s, when chimpanzee and baboon kidneys were transplanted unsuccessfully into human patients. The procedure remains experimental, but it may someday become common.

These achievements were followed by successful transplants of various organs between non-related individuals. But

NOBEL PRIZE 1990

Joseph E. Murray and E. Donnall Thomas shared the 1990 Nobel Prize in physiology or medicine for their work on using transplants to cure patients with disease.

rejection remained a serious problem. Then, in the 1970s, researchers discovered that compounds from the soil fungus *Tolypocladium inflatum* block the activity of cells involved in the rejection reaction. Called cyclosporines, these compounds revolutionized organ transplantation.

Timeline of the First Successful Transplant Operations

1908	knee joint
1954	kidney (between identical twins)
1956	heart valves
1962	kidney (cadaver donor)
1966	pancreas
1967	liver
1967	heart
1981	heart-lung
1983	lung
1988	liver-small intestine
1990	small intestine

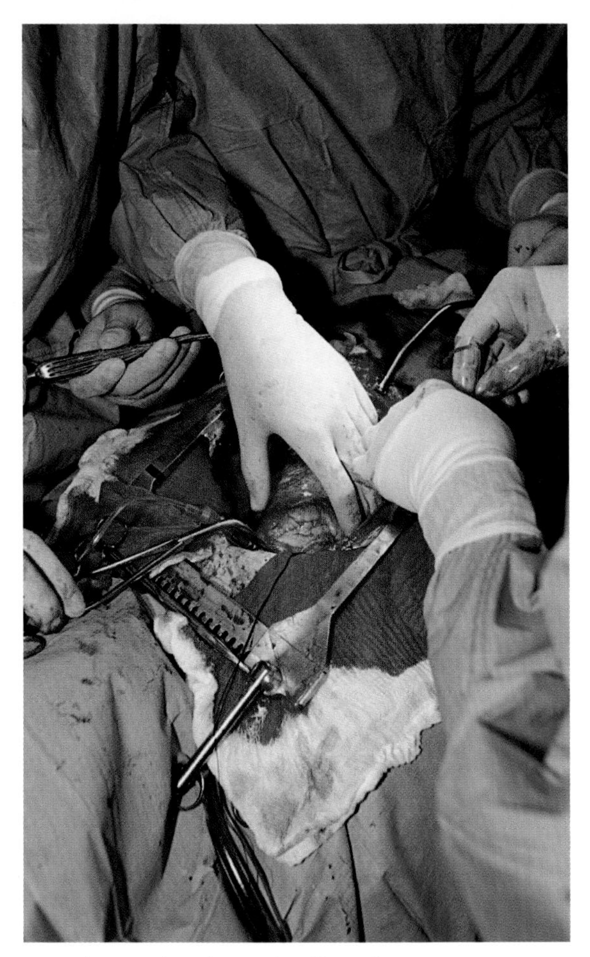

Transplants replace damaged or diseased organs.

Today, survival rates for patients receiving kidneys or pancreases are about 90 percent; for other organs, survival rates are between 55 and 80 percent.

See also immunity.

RESOURCES

- Hakim, Nadey S. *History of Organ and Cell Transplantation.* London: Imperial College, 2000.
- MODERN MIRACLES: ORGAN TRANSPLANTS. **http://library.thinkquest.org/28000/frames.html**

Otis, Elisha Graves

Inventor: designed the safety brake for elevators
Born: August 3, 1811, Halifax, Vermont
Died: April 8, 1861, Yonkers, New York

The first steam-powered lifting devices, or **elevators,** with a platform for freight, appeared early in the 19th century, but they were dangerous. If the lifting cable broke, the platform crashed to the ground. In 1852, Otis designed the first elevator with an automatic safety device to prevent a collapse if the lifting mechanism failed.

Otis set up a small elevator shop, but business was slow. People still were afraid to put freight on such devices—and they certainly wouldn't consider riding on elevators themselves. In 1854, Otis demonstrated his elevator at a fair, riding it high above a watching crowd, then

How It Works

An elevator moves up and down in a vertical passageway called a shaft. Otis equipped each side of the shaft with a notched rail. Any slackening of the lifting cables caused spring-operated "tongues" on the elevator to fall into the notches and support the elevator car.

Elevators made the construction of skyscrapers possible.

FAMOUS FIRST

Otis installed the first passenger elevator, in a New York City department store, in 1857. After his death, his sons continued the business, and in 1889 installed the world's first electrically powered elevator.

ordering the rope cut. Afterwards, sales slowly improved. Then, in the 1870s, builders realized that elevators enabled them to build tall buildings, and the age of skyscrapers began.

RESOURCES

- More about Elisha Graves Otis.
  http://web.mit.edu/invent/www/inventorsI-Q/otis.html

Paper

Mesopotamia (clay tablets) ➤ **Egypt** (papyrus) ➤ **Europe** (parchment) ➤ **China** (bark and rags) ➤ **Lun** (invented paper) ➤ **Japan** (paper clothing, houses, dishes) ➤ Availability of paper in Middle East, Spain, France, Germany ➤ **GUTENBERG** (printed books) ➤ **Réaumur** (paper from wood) ➤ **Fourdrinier** (continuous rolls)

The gradual evolution of writing from about 10,000 to 5000 B.C.E. also led to development of several useful materials on which to write. In Mesopotamia, writers turned to clay tablets, baked after symbols were pressed into the clay. In Egypt about 4000 B.C.E., writers began drawing symbols on thin sheets, called papyrus, made from pounded reed plants. Papyrus was a good writing material but not easily available away from the Nile where papyrus reeds grow. In Greece and other European civilizations, parchment, an expensive alternative based on thin, treated animal skins, was used for important documents. In the Americas, the common writing material was flattened tree bark.

In China, about 140 B.C.E., a combination of bark and rags in water was beaten and made into a paste. The paste, spread into thin sheets, dried into a flexible film, similar to papyrus. Scholars now think that rough versions of this material, a crude form of paper, were used for packing material and in other ways for over 200 years before anyone thought to write on it. Chinese tradition says that a court official named Ts'ai Lun invented paper in 105 C.E., and certainly paper made from rags— without bark— was used for writing about that time. The earliest preserved paper with writing on it is from 2nd-century China.

The method of manufacturing paper gradually spread from China. In Japan, where paper was made in about 610 C.E., many different uses were developed, including paper clothing, paper walls for houses, and heavily coated paper dishes. Arabs learned the skill from Chinese prisoners of war starting in 751. Soon after 1000, paper manufacturing was carried to Spain by Arabs, spreading to France in 1189, Italy in 1277, and Germany in 1411. Thus, paper was available for **Johannes Gutenberg** when he began printing books about 1450.

By the 18th century, so much paper was being used that not enough rags could be gathered. René de Réaumur [French: 1683–1758] experimented with other materials and proposed making paper from wood. Many inventors pursued this goal for the

IN CONGRESS, JULY 4, 1776.

A DECLARATION

BY THE REPRESENTATIVES OF THE

UNITED STATES OF AMERICA,

IN GENERAL CONGRESS ASSEMBLED.

WHEN in the Courſe of human Events, it becomes neceſſary for one People to diſſolve the Political Bands which have connected them with another, and to aſſume among the Powers of the Earth, the ſeparate and equal Station to which the Laws of Nature and of Nature's God entitle them, a decent Reſpect to the Opinions of Mankind requires that they ſhould declare the cauſes which impel them to the Separation.

WE hold theſe Truths to be ſelf-evident, that all Men are created equal, that they are endowed by their Creator with certain unalienable Rights, that among theſe are Life, Liberty, and the Purſuit of Happineſs—That to ſecure theſe Rights, Governments are inſtituted among Men, deriving their juſt Powers from the Conſent of the Governed, that whenever any Form of Government becomes deſtructive of theſe Ends, it is the Right of the People to alter or to aboliſh it, and to inſtitute new Government, laying its Foundation on ſuch Principles, and organizing its Powers in ſuch Form, as to them ſhall ſeem moſt likely to effect their Safety and Happineſs. Prudence, indeed, will dictate that Governments long eſtabliſhed ſhould not be changed for light and tranſient Cauſes; and accordingly all Experience hath ſhewn, that Mankind are more diſpoſed to ſuffer, while Evils are ſufferable, than to right themſelves by aboliſhing the Forms to which they are accuſtomed. But when a long Train of Abuſes and Uſurpations, purſuing invariably the ſame Object, evinces a Deſign to reduce them under abſolute Deſpotiſm, it is their Right, it is their Duty, to throw off ſuch Government, and to provide new Guards for their future Security. Such has been the patient Sufferance of theſe Colonies; and ſuch is now the Neceſſity which conſtrains them to alter their former Syſtems of Government. The Hiſtory of the preſent King of Great-Britain is a Hiſtory of repeated Injuries and Uſurpations, all having in direct Object the Eſtabliſhment of an abſolute Tyranny over theſe States. To prove this, let Facts be ſubmitted to a candid World.

HE has refuſed his Aſſent to Laws, the moſt wholeſome and neceſſary for the public Good.

HE has forbidden his Governors to paſs Laws of immediate and preſſing Importance, unleſs ſuſpended in their Operation till his Aſſent ſhould be obtained; and when ſo ſuſpended, he has utterly neglected to attend to them.

HE has refuſed to paſs other Laws for the Accommodation of large Diſtricts of People, unleſs thoſe People would relinquiſh the Right of Repreſentation in the Legiſlature, a Right ineſtimable to them, and formidable to Tyrants only.

HE has called together Legiſlative Bodies at Places unuſual, uncomfortable, and diſtant from the Depoſitory of their public Records, for the ſole Purpoſe of fatiguing them into Compliance with his Meaſures.

HE has diſſolved Repreſentative Houſes repeatedly, for oppoſing with manly Firmneſs his Invaſions on the Rights of the People.

HE has refuſed for a long Time, after ſuch Diſſolutions, to cauſe others to be elected; whereby the Legiſlative Powers, incapable of Annihilation, have returned to the People at large for their exerciſe; the State remaining in the mean time expoſed to all the Dangers of Invaſion from without, and Convulſions within.

HE has endeavoured to prevent the Population of theſe States; for that Purpoſe obſtructing the Laws for Naturalization of Foreigners; refuſing to paſs others to encourage their Migrations hither, and raiſing the Conditions of new Appropriations of Lands.

HE has obſtructed the Adminiſtration of Juſtice, by refuſing his Aſſent to Laws for eſtabliſhing Judiciary Powers.

HE has made Judges dependent on his Will alone, for the Tenure of their Offices, and the Amount and Payment of their Salaries.

HE has erected a Multitude of new Offices, and ſent hither Swarms of Officers to harraſs our People, and eat out their Subſtance.

HE has kept among us, in Times of Peace, Standing Armies, without the conſent of our Legiſlatures.

HE has affected to render the Military independent of and ſuperior to the Civil Power.

HE has combined with others to ſubject us to a Juriſdiction foreign to our Conſtitution, and unacknowledged by our Laws; giving his Aſſent to their Acts of pretended Legiſlation:

FOR quartering large Bodies of Armed Troops among us:

next 200 years, gradually finding chemical methods that remove undesirable parts of wood and leave **fibers** that can be pressed and dried into paper. Today, most paper is made from wood, although fiber from rags is added to better grades and the best grades are still made entirely from rags. Since 1807, most paper has been made in continuous rolls based on a process developed in England by Henry Fourdrinier [French-English: 1766–1854] and Sealy Fourdrinier [French-English: d. 1847], but some high-grade paper is still made in separate sheets.

Paper ranges from thin tissue paper used for sanitary purposes to heavy

Above and left: *paper has thousands of uses.*
Below: *making paper by hand is still practiced.*

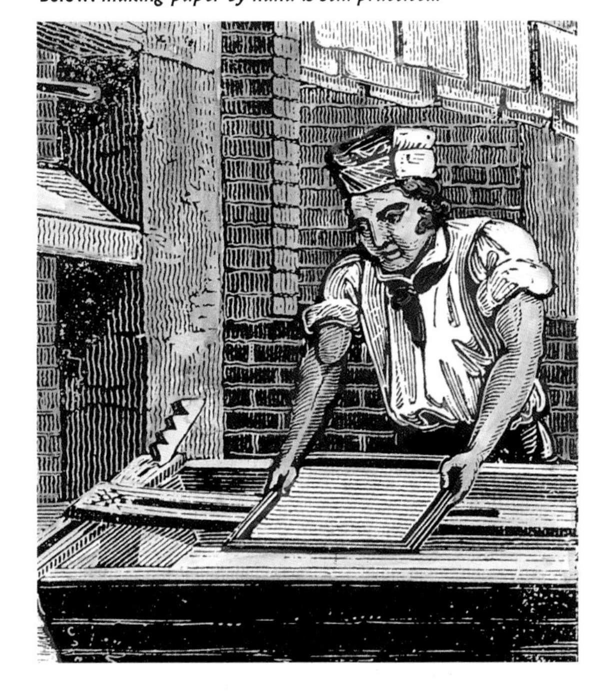

cardboard boxes. Paper that includes artificial fibers, such as nylon or polyester, is durable enough to be used for book covers and building materials.

RESOURCES

- Hunter, Dard. *Papermaking: The History and Technique of an Ancient Craft*. Mineola, NY: Dover, 1978.
- MORE ABOUT PAPER.

  http://www.mead.com/ml/docs/facts/history.html

  http://www.wipapercouncil.org/invention.htm

Paracelsus

Physician and alchemist: founded medical chemistry
Born: 1493, Einsiedeln, Switzerland
Died: September 24, 1541, Salzburg, Austria

About the time that Theophrastus Bombastus von Hohenheim began practicing medicine, he chose to call himself Paracelsus—Greek for "above Celsus." In other words, he considered himself superior to the famous first century Roman physician Celsus.

Paracelsus was a controversial figure because he criticized traditional medicine. For instance, he attacked the belief that **disease** results from internal disturbances of four bodily "humors." Rather, he said, external agents cause disease, and he pioneered the use of chemicals to fight such agents. He wrote that silicosis ("miner's disease") is caused by inhaling metallic dust, and that ingesting small doses of mercury compounds could treat syphilis. His work inspired other alchemists to prepare medicines, moving the focus of alchemy away from efforts to turn common metals into gold.

Paracelsus

Paracelsus also stressed the healing powers of nature. He disapproved of the then-common practice of covering wounds with dried dung or moss; "if you prevent infection, Nature will heal the wound all by herself," he insisted.

Notable Quotable

If you have been given a talent, exercise it freely and happily like the sun: give everyone from your splendor.

Paracelsus

RESOURCES

- Goodrick-Clarke, Nicholas (trans.). *Paracelsus: Essential Readings*. Berkeley, CA: North Atlantic, 1999.
- MORE ABOUT PARACELSUS.

  http://www.alchemylab.com/paracelsus.htm

  http://www.paracelsus-center.ch/e_Paracelsus-Alchemy.htm

Parsons, Charles Algernon

Engineer: invented the steam turbine
Born: June 13, 1854, Parsonstown, Ireland
Died: February 13, 1931, Newcastle upon Tyne, England

The modern **turbine** had its beginnings in the 1880s, when Parsons built the first steam turbine. This machine was powered by high-pressure steam that was allowed to lose pressure gradually as it moved past one set of moving blades after another. Parsons used the machine to power an electric generator, which he also designed. In 1888 he installed two of his steam turbines at Forth Banks Station in Newcastle—the first use of steam turbines in a public power station.

Parsons also realized the potential of steam turbines to power ships. In 1893 he and five associates formed a company that built the *Turbinia*, the first steamship to use turbines for power. It reached speeds of more than 34 knots, much faster than

YEARBOOK: 1884

- Parsons patents his steam turbine.
- **Hans Gram** develops a dye used to classify bacteria.
- **Telephone** wires connect New York and Boston.
- Lewis Waterman [American: 1837–1901] patents the first successful fountain **pen**.

A freighter powered by steam turbines

other ships of that time. By 1899 the Royal Navy had launched two ships powered by Parsons' turbines.

RESOURCES

- MORE ABOUT CHARLES PARSONS.

  http://www.birrcastle.com/birr/turbine/turbframetext.html

  http://www.history.rochester.edu/steam/parsons/

Particle Accelerators

Van de Graaff (first high-speed subatomic particles) ➤ **Cockcroft/Walton** (first working continuous accelerator) ➤ **LAWRENCE** (circular accelerator) ➤ Development of long linear accelerators

Particle accelerators, sometimes called "atom smashers," were invented to probe the inner working of **atoms** and **subatomic particles**. Later they were found useful in producing artificial elements and powerful **X-ray** beams. The high energy produced in some particle accelerators can create conditions similar to the centers of stars like those thought to have existed in the early **universe**.

The first high-speed subatomic particles were produced by Robert van de Graaff [American: 1901–1967] in 1929. His device, called a Van de Graaff generator, collects charged particles in one location until they leap as a giant spark to a region of opposite charge. All the acceleration, or speeding up, occurs in a short burst.

The first working continuous accelerator was developed in 1932 by John Cockcroft [English: 1897–1967] and Ernest Walton [Irish: 1903–1995]. It accelerated protons with a single high-voltage electric field. The final speed was limited by the strength of field that could be produced. As early as 1930, however, **Ernest Orlando Lawrence** had begun to develop circular accelerators that put particles through an electric field each time they reached that part of the circle. These "cyclotrons" gradually became larger and development of ways to synchronize many electric fields led to the

Van de Graaff generator

massive synchrotrons of today.

As circular accelerators became more powerful, physicists discovered that energy is lost by the changes in acceleration caused by following a curved path. This lost synchrotron radiation, in the form of high-energy X rays, is now deliberately produced for medical or other purposes. One way to rid the accelerator of energy lost through synchrotron radiation is to eliminate the curving path. A linear accelerator, or linac, must be very long to obtain useful energies. The longest is SLAC at Stanford University in California, which is 2 miles (3.2 km) long and began operations in 1965.

How It Works

Particles that carry a charge, such as electrons, protons, and ions, move in response to an electric field. Turning the field on makes the particle speed up (accelerate). Repeating this process over and over sends charged particles to speeds approaching the speed of light. They travel though a near vacuum to avoid collisions with molecules and are kept in their paths with magnets.

RESOURCES

- National Research Council. *Elementary Particle Physics: Revealing the Secrets of Energy and Matter.* Washington, DC: National Academy, 1998
- MORE ABOUT PARTICLE ACCELERATORS.

  http://www-elsa.physik.uni-bonn.de/accelerator_list.html

  http://www.hep.ucl.ac.uk/masterclass/EWuni/webpage/middleframe/particleaccellerate.htm

Pascal, Blaise

Physicist, mathematician: invented mechanical calculator
Born: June 19, 1623, Clermont Ferrand, France
Died: August 19, 1662, Paris, France

In 1640, Pascal began developing a machine that could help his father—a tax commissioner—calculate taxes. The first working model appeared in 1642. Known today as the Pascaline, it was the first mechanical **calculator** that used gears.

The Pascaline was a small brass box with, depending on the model, five to eight interlocking gears. The Pascaline efficiently added numbers and could also subtract, though less efficiently. Gottfried

The hydraulic jack is an application of Pascal's Law.

Leibniz [German: 1646–1716] later improved the Pascaline so it also could multiply and divide.

Pascal's scientific contributions also included the principle of hydrostatics, now known as Pascal's Law. This states that pressure applied to a fluid at rest in a closed container is transmitted equally in all directions. The law is the basis of the hydraulic press, which is used in hydraulic brakes and other applications. In mathematics, Pascal helped develop probability theory and did important work with infinite series and the geometry of curves.

RESOURCES

- More about Blaise Pascal.
  http://www.pascal-central.com/blaise.html
- Computers: History and Development.
  http://www.digitalcentury.com/encyclo/update/comp_hd.html

Pasteur, Louis

Chemist and microbiologist: developed germ theory
Born: December 27, 1822, Dôle, France
Died: September 28, 1895, Villeneuve l'Etang, France

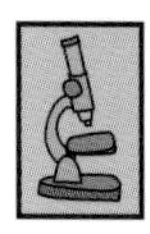

In the 1850s, Pasteur was asked to determine why products of **fermentation**, such as wine and beer, sometimes soured during production. He soon demonstrated that a specific microscopic organism causes each kind of fermentation, and that when other microorganisms get into the liquid, they can cause souring. He also showed that "germs" cause milk to sour and cause infectious **diseases**. "When we see beer and wine undergoing profound changes because these liquids have furnished a refuge for microscopic organisms, how can we avoid the thought that phenomena of the same order can and must be found sometimes in the case of men and animals," he wrote.

Louis Pasteur

YEARBOOK: 1885

- Pasteur uses his rabies vaccine to save a young boy who had been bitten by a rabid dog.
- Karl Benz [German: 1844–1929] builds a three-wheeled **automobile**.
- William Stanley [American: 1858–1916] invents the electric transformer.
- Clemens Alexander Winkler [German: 1838–1904] discovers germanium, an element whose existence was predicted by **Dmitri Ivanovich Mendeleyev**.

Pasteur developed a vaccine for anthrax, a disease that affects sheep and cattle.

While developing methods for culturing microorganisms in special liquid broths, Pasteur discovered that some microorganisms require air—specifically, oxygen—while others are active only in the absence of oxygen. He called these, respectively, aerobic and anaerobic organisms. He also found that he could improve the storage qualities of wine by heating and then rapidly cooling the wine—a process now called pasteurization.

In the 1870s, Pasteur studied anthrax, a disease affecting mainly of sheep and cattle. He used a weak strain of anthrax **bacteria** to develop a **vaccine**, and in 1881 vaccinated sheep against the disease. Pasteur developed a number of additional vaccines, the most famous of which was the first vaccine against rabies in humans.

Notable Quotable

In the fields of observation chance favors only the prepared mind.

Science knows no country, because knowledge belongs to humanity, and is the torch which illuminates the world.

Louis Pasteur

RESOURCES

- Smith, Linda W. *Louis Pasteur, Disease Fighter.* Springfield, NJ: Enslow, 1997. (JUV/YA)
- Pasteur, Louis. "On Spontaneous Generation." **http://guava.phil.lehigh.edu/spon.htm**
- Pasteur, Louis. "Physiological Theory of Fermentation." **http://www.fordham.edu/halsall/mod/1879pasteur-ferment.html**

Pauling, Linus

Chemist: explained chemical bonding
Born: February 28, 1901, Portland, Oregon
Died: August 19, 1994, Big Sur, California

While still in college in the early 1920s Pauling became interested in the influence of a chemical's molecular structure on its properties. Several years later he studied with **Niels Bohr** and other physicists working on **quantum theory,** which describes atomic structure in terms of electron clouds, rather than orbits. Pauling decided to apply quantum theory to his study of chemical bonds (the connections between atoms in a molecule). He showed that the distances between atoms and the angles of the chemical bonds influence the molecule's characteristics and determine its interaction with other molecules. His book *The Nature of the Chemical Bond* (1939) was extremely influential.

Pauling applied his understanding of chemical bonds to the study of highly complex **proteins** produced in living organisms. He found that hemoglobin, the protein that gives red blood cells their color, has a spiral structure. He also showed that sickle-cell anemia is caused by the change of a single amino acid in the hemoglobin molecule.

During the 1950s nations conducted

Linus Pauling

NOBEL PRIZE 1954

Pauling received the Nobel Prize in chemistry for his work on the nature of the chemical bond.

NOBEL PRIZE 1962

Pauling received the Nobel Peace Prize for his efforts to end atmospheric testing of nuclear weapons.

Notable Quotable

Science is the search for truth—it is not a game in which one tries to beat his opponent, to do harm to others.

Linus Pauling

atmospheric tests of **nuclear weapons**, a practice Pauling vehemently opposed because of the dangers of radioactive fallout. He organized a petition by 11,000 scientists against testing that was presented to the United Nations and wrote *No More War!* (1958).

• Biography of Linus Pauling.
http://www.nobel.se/chemistry/laureates/1954/pauling-bio.html

Pavlov, Ivan Petrovich

Physiologist: demonstrated conditioned reflex
Born: September 26, 1849, Ryazan, Russia
Died: February 27, 1936, Leningrad, Soviet Union (now St. Petersburg, Russia)

It is well known that the sight or smell of food causes salivary glands to release saliva. In experiments with dogs, Pavlov showed that the stimulus of seeing or smelling food also triggers secretion of digestive juices from glands in the walls of the stomach. He realized that this reflex, or automatic response to a stimulus, is controlled by the nervous system.

Pavlov noticed that dogs sometimes began salivating as soon as they heard the approach of laboratory assistants who fed them. This led Pavlov to demonstrate conditioned reflexes. In this case, that dogs can learn, or be conditioned, to salivate in response to nonfood stimuli. Each time he served food to the dogs, he rang a bell. After many

Nobel Prize 1904

Pavlov received the Nobel Prize in physiology or medicine for his research on the physiology of digestion.

Ivan Petrovich Pavlov

repetitions, the dogs salivated when the bell rang, even if they weren't given food.

Since Pavlov's time, other scientists have discovered that various kinds of conditioning are common in nature. For instance, a blue jay vomits if it eats a sawfly larva. The blue jay quickly learns to avoid sawfly larvae.

RESOURCES

- BIOGRAPHY OF IVAN PETROVICH PAVLOV.
  http://www.nobel.se/medicine/laureates/1904/pavlov-bio.html

Pens and Pencils

Early humans (pigments, charcoal) ➤ **Egypt** (reeds, dyes) ➤ **China** (fur brushes, carbon-based ink) ➤ **Greece/Rome** (reeds apply ink to parchment) ➤ Development of quill ➤ Development of wood-covered lead pencils ➤ **Scheele** lead (graphite) pencils ➤ **Waterman** (steel-nibbed pen) ➤ Development of ballpoint pen

Cave and rock art was created using pigments blown through hollow tubes along with smears from pieces of charcoal. Similar methods are used today. Pens lay down pigments in ink. Pencils use carbon from graphite instead of charcoal.

About 5,000 years ago, Egyptians frayed the ends of reeds and dipped them in dyes to make writing tools. Later, Chinese scribes made fur brushes to draw symbols with carbon-based India ink. Some 2,000 years ago, Greeks and Romans used hollow reeds to apply iron-based ink to prepared animal skins called parchment. During the Middle Ages, a goose feather, or quill, hollow like a reed and slightly harder, replaced the reeds. Quills and ink were used for most writing for the next thousand years.

In addition to ink, thin lead rods were used to make drawings. In 1564 C.E., a chance discovery in Borrowdale, England, revealed a soft mineral similar to lead, but darker. For over 200 years, British workers wrapped the Borrowdale mineral in wood to make pencils, thinking it a form of lead. After Carl Wilhelm Scheele [Swedish: 1742–1786] showed that it was pure carbon, its name was changed to graphite, which means "writing mineral." Soon, German manufacturers found ways to make good pencils by mixing graphite with clay.

Because quills had to be sharpened often, people began to fashion metal pens, which lasted longer. These became generally available after 1830, when good metal tips were mass-produced from steel. The metal tips, called nibs, still had to be repeatedly dipped in ink, however. In 1884, Lewis Waterman

Graphite pencils, ink and quill, and fountain pen

Timeline of Pens and Pencils

B.C.E.	
2000	Reed stylus used to mark clay tablets with cuneiform writing in Mesopotamia
	Reeds filled with dyes used on papyrus for hieroglyphics in Egypt
1200	Chinese use India ink and small brushes
600	Quill pen used with ink derived from iron salts and oak galls
C.E.	
1300	A drawing instrument of a rod of lead in a tube of wood is the original form of the lead pencil
1564	Pure graphite is discovered at one site in England and is mined to use for "lead" pencils
1662	Manufacturers in Nuremberg, Germany, develop alternative pencils using less pure graphite mixed with various binders
1765	Kaspar Faber in Germany begins to manufacture pencils of graphite mixed with fine clay
1830	James Perry in England develops the form of steel pen that replaces the quill pen
1858	Hyman Lipman in the United States conceives of attaching a rubber eraser to a pencil
1861	The first U.S. pencil factory is built in New York City by Eberhard Faber
1884	Lewis Waterman in the United States patents the fountain pen
1938	Ladislo Biró of Hungary invents the ball-point pen for writing on paper
1962	The modern fiber-tipped pen is invented by Yukio Horie in Tokyo, Japan

[American: 1837–1901] developed a successful steel-nibbed pen with a built-in ink reservoir. Such "fountain pens," once filled, are good for hours of writing.

The original ballpoint pen of 1888 was for marking on leather, but ballpoints for use on paper were invented in 1938. The ballpoint pen and the fiber-tipped pen, invented in 1962, are now the most common forms of pens.

RESOURCES

- Fishler, George and Stuart Schneider. *Fountain Pens and Pencils: The Golden Age of Writing Instruments.* 2nd rev. ed. Atglen, PA: Schiffler, 1998.
- Jaegers, Raymond G. and Beverly C. Jaegers. *The Write Stuff: A Collector's Guide to Inkwells, Fountain Pens, and Desk Accessories.* Iola, WI: Krause, 2000.
- Petroski, Henry. *The Pencil: A History of Design and Circumstance.* New York: Knopf, 1990.
- More about Pencils.

  http://www.generalpencil.com/history1.html

  http://www.pencils.co.uk/p_history.htm

  http://www.pencils.com/history.html
- History of the Fountain Pen.

  http://www.luttmanns.com/pens/intro.html
- History of Pens and Writing Instruments.

  http://inventors.about.com/science/inventors/library/inventors/blpen.htm?once=true&

Pesticides

Early humans (mud) ➤ Greece (burning sulfur) ➤ China (dried chrysanthemum) ➤ **MÜLLER** (DDT) ➤ **CARSON** (dangers of pesticides)

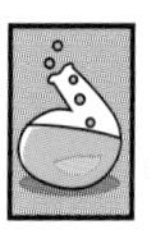

The earliest pesticide probably was mud, spread on the skin to repel biting insects. Around 900 B.C.E. the Greek poet Homer described using fumes from burning sulfur to destroy pests. About 100 C.E. the Chinese discovered that a powder of dried chrysanthemum flowers killed insects; the active ingredient, pyrethrum,

A "crop duster" plane can efficiently spray pesticide over broad areas.

is still used today. As the centuries passed, pepper, soapy water, fish oil, nicotine, petroleum oils, and many additional materials were used as pesticides, not always successfully. Many were as poisonous to humans and beneficial animals as they were to pests.

In the late 1930s, **Paul Müller** found that the synthetic organic chemical DDT was poisonous to insects but appeared not to harm other organisms. During World War II, DDT was used to kill insects that carry diseases such as typhus and malaria, saving the lives of many soldiers. Farmers soon began using DDT, greatly reducing losses to potato beetles and other crop pests. DDT's effectiveness led researchers to identify additional synthetic organic pesticides.

By 1946, however, there were indications that insects were developing resistance to DDT; getting rid of resistant forms required heavier applications of pesticides—or more potent pesticides. Fears of the effects of pesticides on the environment and human health were confirmed by **Rachel Carson's** *Silent Spring*, published in 1962. In 1972, the U.S. government ended use of DDT on crops.

Many modern pesticides are highly toxic, though designed to deteriorate quickly, making them less likely to spread through the environment. Alternatives to pesticides have gained wider use; these include improved **farming** and **irrigation** techniques, introduction of beneficial insects to attack pests, use of **microwaves** to kill weeds, use of **pheromones**, and **genetically engineered** pest-resistant seeds and plants.

RESOURCES

- Carson, Rachel. *Silent Spring*. Reprint. Boston: Houghton Mifflin, 1999.
- MORE ABOUT PESTICIDES.
  http://ipmworld.umn.edu/chapters/ware.htm
  http://chppm-www.apgea.army.mil/ento/timefram/DDT.htm

Peterson, Roger Tory

Ornithologist and artist: created the modern field guide
Born August 28, 1908, Jamestown, New York
Died July 28, 1996, Old Lyme, Connecticut

Peterson's fascination with birds began at age 11 when he paid a dime to join a Junior Audubon Club, was given a box of watercolors, and told to copy a picture of a blue jay. He never had any formal training in the study of birds, but developed his vast knowledge of these creatures through careful observation.

Notable Quotable

Birds have seemed to me the most vivid expression of life. They have dominated my daily thoughts, my reading and even my dreams. They have led me into the wider vistas of the natural world—and of awareness.

Roger Tory Peterson

In 1934, Peterson published his first book, *A Field Guide to the Birds.* It was radically different from traditional bird books. Instead of many details and

Peterson's interest in birds began when he was asked to paint a picture of blue jays.

measurements, Peterson offered simplified drawings and focused on birds' distinctive markings. He used little arrows to point out important things to look for. His text was brief and easy to remember. For example, he described the male common goldfinch as "the only small yellow bird with black wings."

The Field Guide was an immediate best seller, because it made bird-watching a hobby accessible to everyone. In the following years, Peterson wrote additional bird guides as well as other books on birds and nature.

RESOURCES

- Peterson, Roger Tory and Rudy Hoglund (eds.). *Roger Tory Peterson - The Art and Photography of the World's Most Foremost Birder.* New York: Rizzoli International, 1994.
- MORE ABOUT ROGER TORY PETERSON. **http://www.petersononline.com/tribute/bio.html**

Petroleum

Mesopotamia (used for cementing bricks) ➤ **China** (use in torches) ➤ **Canada/United States** (petroleum-burning lamps) ➤ **Silliman** (distillation) ➤ **Drake** (first oil well)

When ocean-dwelling creatures die, their bodies often become mixed with sand or mud. Gradually the remains become incorporated into rock. When the rock becomes buried in depths of Earth's crust, heat and pressure change the original carbohydrates, fats, and proteins into compounds called hydrocarbons. A liquid mixture of these hydrocarbons, usually with various impurities, is called petroleum (Greek for "rock oil"). Petroleum is a fossil fuel; another name for it is crude oil.

Petroleum often seeps from cracks in rocks. As such, it has long been gathered by humans and used for one purpose or another. In Mesopotamia, a thick petroleum—more like asphalt than like oil—was used to cement bricks together. The Chinese burned petroleum in torches at least as early as 980 C.E.

In the early 19th century, whale oil, made by melting blubber, was widely used in lamps. Sailors had to travel farther and farther in search of increasingly scarce whales. Inventors sought a cheaper and more abundant substitute. Several inventors in the U.S. and Canada developed lamps that would burn petroleum or petroleum products. Benjamin Silliman [American: 1779–1864] showed that petroleum could be distilled into tar, naphthalene, gasoline, and useful solvents. Petroleum, however, was scarce.

In 1859, Edwin L. Drake [American: 1819–1980] was hired by George H. Bissell [American: 1821–1884] to drill a well for petroleum in a region of Pennsylvania where oil seeps were common and oil often contaminated water wells. Drake's well was soon bringing in 22 barrels of oil a day, inspiring hundreds of others to enter the business. Today, about 9 million barrels a day are produced in the United States—and 80 million worldwide.

Petroleum products are still burned for energy, either to make electricity, as fuel for vehicles, or for heating. But petroleum is becoming increasingly more valuable as the base for **plastics** and other synthetic chemicals.

Top left: *gasoline is a petroleum product.* **Above left:** *a petroleum drilling rig.* **Right:** *an oil pipeline.*

RESOURCES

- More about Petroleum.

  http://www.ou.edu/special/ogs-pttc/earthsci/histpetr.htm

  http://looksmart.infoplease.com/ce6/sci/A0838640.html

Phases of Matter

Greeks (solid, liquid, gas, plasma) ➤ **Van Helmont** (recognized different gases) ➤ **Kaptiza** (fifth state of matter)

The ancient Greeks spoke of earth, water, and air as basic elements. These represented the three familiar phases (or states) of matter. Earth is a solid (which retains its shape); water is a liquid (which keeps its volume but takes the shape of its container); and air was the only gas (which completely fills the volume of a closed container) known until the 17th century when **Jan Baptista van Helmont** recognized several different gases. Steam, a mixture of water vapor, air, and tiny drops of liquid water, was thought by the Greeks to be a stage in water becoming air. Solid water (ice) showed water becoming more "earth-like" as it cooled. Water was the only substance then known that passed from one stage to

Solid (ice), liquid, and gas (steam) phases of water

another at low temperatures, but metals and even rocks were known to change from solid to liquid at high enough temperatures. Later, scientists learned that all matter changes from one phase to another at specific temperatures and pressures.

The fourth Greek element, fire, is actually hot gas, but it resembles the fourth known phase of matter, called plasma. Plasmas are so hot that **atoms** separate into electrons and atomic nuclei. Since stars and interstellar gases are plasmas, this phase is the most common in the universe, although present on Earth only in lightning or when produced by humans.

A fifth state of matter was first observed in 1937 when Pytor Kapitza [Russian: 1894–1984] studied very cold liquid helium. Some atoms in this form of helium have yielded their own identities and merged. In 1995, physicists at the U.S. National Institute of Standards and Technology produced a cold gas in which all the atoms huddle together this way. This phase of matter is called a Bose Einstein

Condensate (BEC) after Satyendra Bose [Indian: 1894–1974] and **Albert Einstein,** who in 1924 predicted this phase.

RESOURCES

- Cooper, Christopher. *Eyewitness: Matter*. New York: Dorling Kindersley, 2000. (JUV/YA)
- MORE ABOUT PHASES OF MATTER. **http://www.chem.uidaho.edu/honors/phases.html**

Pheromones

FABRE (suspected odor attractant) ➤ **Butenandt** (identified first pheromone) ➤ Identification of many additional pheromones ➤ Development of synthetic pheromones

Pheromones are complex chemical compounds secreted by animals to communicate with other animals, particularly others of their own species. For centuries, people have suspected that animals communicate with chemicals. In the 1870s, **Jean-Henri Fabre** noticed that male moths flew from great distances to visit a female moth caged in his lab. Fabre believed the males were lured by an odor emitted by the female, but couldn't prove it.

The first identification of a pheromone came in 1959. After dissecting many thousands of female silkworm moths (*Bombyx mori*), Adolf Butenandt [German: 1903–1995] identified the sex attractant, naming it bombycol. Butenandt's discovery energized pheromone research. Currently, pheromones of more than 1,000

Moths and rabbits secrete pheromones.

insect species plus other organisms–from protists to mammals– have been identified. Pheromones are not only used to attract mates. Rabbits use pheromones to mark territory and to disperse members of their group when a predator approaches.

Pheromones also appear to act as a "sixth sense" among humans, distinct from the well-known sense of smell. Research conducted since the 1960s suggests that the vomeronasal organ, a structure in the nasal cavity, detects human sexual pheromones. The organ connects directly to the part of the brain responsible for controlling emotions and behavior.

Synthetic pheromones used as bait in traps or as sprays can be very effective in eradicating insect pests, usually by disrupting their mating patterns. This reduces the need for synthetic **pesticides.**

RESOURCES

- Hughes, Howard C. *Sensory Exotica, A World Beyond Human Experience*. Cambridge, MA: MIT, 1999.
- Thomas, Lewis. *The Lives of a Cell.* New York: Viking, 1974.
- PHEROMONES IN THE CONTROL AND MONITORING OF PESTS. **http://www.roberth.u-net.com/Pheromones.htm**

Photoelectric Phenomena

Edmond Becquerel (connection between light and electricity) ➤ **Ireland** (photoconductive effect) ➤ **HERTZ** (photoemissive effect) ➤ **EINSTEIN** (particle and wave nature of light) ➤ **Anderson** (photons change into electron-positron pairs) ➤ Development of photovoltaic cells, xerography, fiber optics

Edmond Becquerel [French: 1820–1891], father of **Antoine Henri Becquerel,** the man who discovered **radioactivity,** was the first to make a direct connection between **light** and electricity. In 1839, he observed that in certain circumstances, exposure to light creates a small electric current (the photovoltaic effect). A few years later, in 1861, an Irish telegraph operator was the first to report that light increases conductivity in the metal selenium, an observation confirmed by experiment a dozen years later (the photoconductive effect). In 1887, while creating the apparatus used to make the first artificial radio waves, **Heinrich Hertz** observed that ultraviolet light lowers the voltage required for a spark to travel across a gap between electrodes. Later, researchers established that this occurs because energetic light knocks electrons off the electrodes' metal surfaces (the photoemissive effect—also called the photoelectric effect).

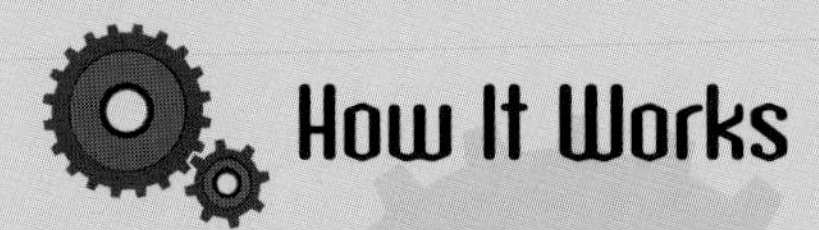

How It Works

When light strikes an electron, it gives up energy either by making the electron move faster or by increasing the energy state of the electron in other ways. The energy of the photon (light particle) is reduced by the same amount, so visible light that produces a photoelectric effect may become **infrared radiation** or even disappear if all its energy is given to the electron.

The theoretical explanation of these effects is primarily credited to **Albert Einstein.** In 1905, he showed that the photoemissive effect implies that light has a particle nature as well as a wave nature. In 1917 he theorized that atoms absorb and then re-emit light through changes

Solar energy panels—an application of photoelectric phenomena

in electron energy. Einstein's theory was extended and experimentally verified in 1926 by Arthur H. Compton [American: 1892–1962], whose Compton effect describes the energy exchange between a photon and an electron. In 1932, the discovery of a positively charged version of the electron—the positron by Carl David Anderson [American: 1905–1991]—included the observation that high-energy photons change into electron-positron pairs. Also, when an electron meets a positron, the particles disappear and are replaced by a photon.

Photoelectric effects are the basis of much existing technology and promise to lead to further developments. Solar power is produced by photovoltaic cells, xerography uses photoconductivity, fiber-optic networks use a form of the photoemissive effect to change optics into electronics, these, as well as lasers, are based on Einstein's 1917 theory of interactions between light and electrons in atoms. If optical computers become practical, they will also be based on photoelectric phenomena.

RESOURCES

- More about Photoelectric Phenomena.
  http://theory.uwinnipeg.ca/physics/quant/node3.html
  http://www.warren-wilson.edu/jekong/photoelectric/photoex.htm

Photography

Middle East (camera obscura) ➤ **DA VINCI** (camera obscura for sketching) ➤ Development of glass lens ➤ Discovery of properties of silver salts ➤ **Schulze** (light effects on silver salts) ➤ **Niepce** (first permanent photograph) ➤ **Daguerre** (improved methods) ➤ **TALBOT** (first negative to positive) ➤ **HERSCHEL** (hypo) ➤ Development of film ➤ **EASTMAN** (rolls of paper, plastic film) ➤ Development of digital technology, CCDs

The camera was invented hundreds of years before film. A camera is a device for creating an image, or picture, using light. As early as 1000 C.E., Arab inventors produced images on white paper when a tiny hole admitted sunlight reflected from external objects into a dark room; this was called a camera obscura (Latin for "dark chamber"). The image disappeared when the light was gone, however. About 1500, artists such as **Leonardo da Vinci**, used smaller versions of the camera obscura to help make sketches. In the 1500s, the camera was improved with a glass lens replacing the pinhole.

The key to making a permanent image was available in the 1500s, but no one realized it. Alchemists observed that salts made from silver start out white but soon turn black, but no one knew why until 1727, when Johann H. Schulze [German: 1687–1744] recognized that light was the cause. Coating the paper used in a camera obscura with silver salts captured the image.

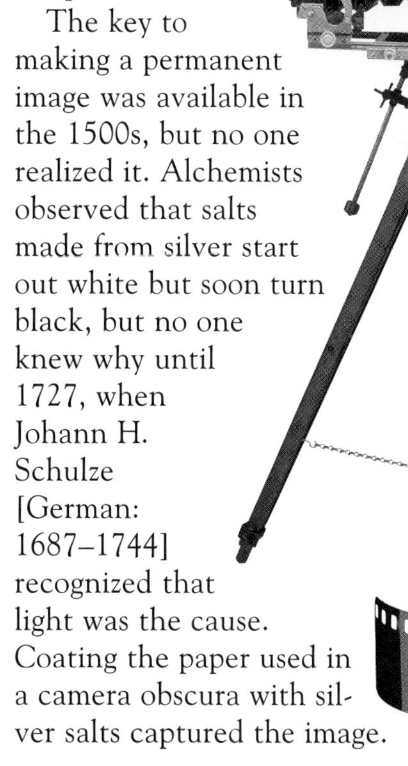

An early black-and-white photograph

FAMOUS FIRSTS

- Thomas Wedgwood [English: 1771–1805] in 1802 captured camera-obscura images of butterflies with silver salts.
- In 1840, John William Draper [English: 1811–1882] produced the first surviving photograph of a person, although an 1839 daguerreotype of a street scene reveals the silhouette of a person stopped to get a shoeshine.
- Also in 1840, John Benjamin Dancer [English: 1812–1887] made the first photograph of a magnified object.
- In 1861, **James Clerk Maxwell** demonstrated the first permanent color photograph.

The next problem, however, occurred when the image was placed in a lighted room—the light quickly turned the entire sheet black.

Joseph Nicéphore Niepce [French: 1765–1833] produced the first permanent photograph in 1822, using a metal plate coated with silver salts mixed with asphalt followed by oils to stop the change to blackness ("fix" the image). Niepce entered a partnership with painter Louis Daguerre [French: 1787–1851], who greatly improved the process. Daguerre's method, announced in January 1839, produced a sharp image (called a daguerreotype) on bright silver after an exposure to light of several minutes. Each daguerreotype is unique, since there is no way to make copies. Although the daguerreotype reverses black and white, at certain angles the silver underneath reflects as black, making it appear darker than the light-exposed salts, producing an image that resembles the original scene.

Simultaneously in England, competitor **William Henry Fox Talbot** was also experimenting with photography using paper soaked with silver salts and exposed in a camera obscura. The result was a grainy image with black and white reversed—a negative. Talbot then exposed a second sheet to light shined through the negative to obtain a positive print, the same process used today. Talbot was not able to fix images very well, but later, in 1839, John Herschel [English: 1792–1871] suggested developing images with sodium thiosulphate, known as hypo, which has remained in use ever since.

There have been many improvements, but chemical photography using a camera obscura—now a portable box instead of an entire room—and silver compounds has remained the dominant idea in picture reproduction since 1839. The biggest change came when silver plates or glass plates coated with silver compounds were replaced with film. The first Kodak cameras of 1888, produced by **George Eastman**, used a roll of paper, and were popular because the company developed and printed the pictures for the user. The

How It Works

In color photography, light from a scene projects through a lens to form an image on film coated with compounds that respond to different wavelengths of light. These colors must be fixed on the film, or negative, by developing the film in a chemical bath. The negative is used to make a positive image on light-sensitive paper, which is itself chemically developed into a permanent color print.

following year, Eastman switched to a transparent nitrate-based plastic film. Modern film is a different transparent plastic introduced in 1939.

Methods of converting light into digital information grew out of **television**. The digital system was first used successfully to image the Moon from a space probe in 1964. The actual chips that convert light into electronic form are called charged-couple devices, or CCDs. The rise of the **Internet** greatly increased interest in digital images. These were commonly produced with a **scanner**, but around 1995, manufacturers began to sell digital cameras based on CCDs. Such digital cameras have already replaced chemical-based ones for many purposes.

RESOURCES

- Czech, Ken. *Snapshot: America Discovers the Camera*. Minneapolis, MN: Lerner, 1996. (JUV/YA)
- Davenport, Alma. *The History of Photography: An Overview*. Albuquerque, NM: University of New Mexico, 1999.
- Farber, Richard. *Historic Photographic Processes.* New York: Allworth, 1998.
- Wallace, Joseph. *The Camera* (Turning Point Inventions). New York: Atheneum, 2000.
- HISTORIES OF PHOTOGRAPHY.

  http://genealogy.org/ajmorris/photo/history.htm

  http://www.spress.de/foto/history/

  http://www.kbnet.co.uk/rleggat/photo/

  http://www.rleggat.com/photohistory/
- MORE ABOUT PHOTOGRAPHIC PROCESSES.

  http://www.photographymuseum.com/primer.html

  http://www.digitalcentury.com/encyclo/update/photo_hd.html
- BIOGRAPHY OF DAGUERRE.

  http://genealogy.org/ajmorris/photo/history.htm

Photosynthesis

VAN HELMONT (plants absorb water) ➤ **Hales** (air source of nourishment) ➤ **INGENHOUZ** (importance of light) ➤ **Dutrochet** (chlorophyll) ➤ **Boussingault** (nitrogen from nitrates) ➤ **Engelmann** (red light most effective, green algae photosynthetic) ➤ **WARBURG** (chemical structure of chlorophyll)

Around 1640, **Jan Baptista van Helmont** demonstrated that plants absorb water from the soil. In 1727, Stephen Hales [English: 1677–1761] showed that plants "draw some part of their nourishment from the air" through their leaves. In the 1770s, **Jan Ingenhousz** established the importance of light to plants. But it wasn't until the following century that scientists followed up on this early work and began to study how plants make food, in a process now called photosynthesis.

> **FAMOUS FIRST**
>
> There are several kinds of chlorophyll. The most important is chlorophyll *a*, found in all organisms that carry out photosynthesis. Chlorophyll *a* was first synthesized in 1960 by Robert Burns Woodward [American: 1917–1979].

Understanding that plants take energy from sunlight and use it to turn carbon dioxide and water into food and oxygen required a series of discoveries that took more than a century. In 1837, Henri Dutrochet [French: 1776–1847] recognized that chlorophyll—the green pigment in leaves—helps plants absorb carbon dioxide and emit oxygen. In the 1850s, Jean-Baptiste Joseph Boussingault [French: 1801–1887] showed that plants require

Photosynthesis is a food-making process carried out in plant and algal cells that contain the green pigment chlorophyll.

nitrogen and obtain it from nitrates in the soil. In the 1880s, Wilhelm Theodor Engelmann [German: 1843–1909] demonstrated that red light is the most effective for photosynthesis. He also discovered that green algae have chlorophyll and carry out photosynthesis.

The chemical structure of chlorophyll was discovered in the early 1900s, and **Otto Warburg** measured the efficiency of photosynthesis under various conditions. Experiments conducted in the 1950s traced the complex pathway of food synthesis and indicated that photosynthesis involves two sets of reactions: light-dependent reactions, which must occur in light, and light-independent reactions, which can occur in darkness.

RESOURCES

- MORE ABOUT PHOTOSYNTHESIS.

  http://photoscience.la.asu.edu/photosyn/education/photointro.html

  http://photoscience.la.asu.edu/photosyn/education/learn.html

- CHLOROPHYLL.

  http://www.ch.ic.ac.uk/mim/life/html/chlorophyll_text.htm

- PHOTOSYNTHETIC PIGMENTS.

  http://www.ucmp.berkeley.edu/glossary/gloss3/pigments.html

Physiology

Herophilus (brain as center of nervous system) ➤ Erasistratus (epiglottis, trachea) ➤ **GALEN** (first physiological experiments, showed function of spinal cord) ➤ **Iatrochemists** (chemical processes as basis of body functions) ➤ **Iatrophysicists** (mechanical processes as basis of body functions) ➤ **Willis** (diabetes and sugar in urine) ➤ **Borelli** (mathematics and muscles) ➤ Development of microscope ➤ **MALPIGHI** (discovered capillaries) ➤ **VAN LEEUWENHOEK** (observed red blood cells) ➤ **Mayow** (blood absorbs oxygen from air) ➤ Discovery that organisms are composed of cells ➤ Discovery that bacteria can cause infectious diseases ➤ **Bernard** (glycogen in liver, pancreatic juices) ➤ **Cannon** (concept of homeostasis, X-ray studies of digestion) ➤ Development of powerful microscopes, radioactive isotopes, genetic engineering ➤ **KREBS** (chemistry of metabolism)

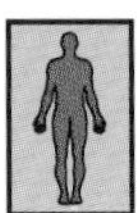

Physiology, the study of life processes, began more than 2,000 years ago. Herophilus [Greek: c. 335–c. 280 B.C.E.] showed that the **brain** is the center of the nervous system. Erasistratus [Greek: c. 300 B.C.E.] explained that the epiglottis prevents food from entering the trachea during swallowing. In Rome, in the second century C.E., **Claudius Galen** performed the earliest-known physiological experiments. For example, working with animals, he demonstrated that cutting the spinal cord causes paralysis in the part of the body below the cut.

For the next 1,200 years, the ideas of the ancient Greeks and Romans were considered infallible in Europe, and the study of natural phenomena was discouraged. With the arrival of the Renaissance in 1400, a renewed interest in **anatomy** developed, which resulted in new efforts to understand life processes. By the 17th century, two beliefs competed for acceptance. Iatrochemists said that chemical processes are the basis of body functions, while iatrophysicists believed that mechanical processes are primary. Both

Homeostasis—mechanisms within an organism that maintain an internal environment—is basic to physiology.

groups made useful discoveries. For example, Thomas Willis [English: 1621–1675] noted that people with diabetes mellitus have sugar in their urine. Giovanni Borelli [Italian: 1608–1679] used mathematics to calculate the pulling forces of various muscles.

The invention of the **microscope** resulted in major advances, such as **Marcello Malpighi's** discovery of capillaries and **Antoni van Leeuwenhoek's** observation of red blood cells. John Mayow [English: 1641–1679] demonstrated that blood absorbs a substance from the air as it passes through the lungs, making the blood bright red. Plant physiology also progressed, with the first important discoveries related to **photosynthesis.**

In the 19th century, scientists recognized that all organisms are composed of **cells**, leading to cell physiology. Introduction of the concept that infectious **diseases** are caused by bacteria and other germs led to increased research on germs' affect on life processes and how organisms develop **immunity** to disease.

Claude Bernard [French: 1813–1878] showed how glycogen is changed to sugar in the liver, and that pancreatic juice digests fats and starches. After discovering that the nervous system regulates blood flow, dilating and constricting vessels in response to external temperatures, he proposed that a stable internal environment is essential to an organism's survival. This stability was termed homeostasis in 1932 by Walter B. Cannon [American: 1871–1945], who expanded on Bernard's work and did pioneering **X-ray** studies on movements of the stomach and intestines.

Technological developments in the 20th century, including more powerful microscopes, radioactive **isotopes**, and **genetic engineering**, sped research. Scientists identified **enzymes**, **vitamins**, and **hormones** and determined their roles in the body. **Hans Adolf Krebs** and others discovered basic mechanisms of **metabolism**. Deciphering the **DNA** molecule led to an explanation of how **proteins** are synthesized. It became increasingly evident that, at every level within an organism—from molecules to organ systems—there is a high degree of organization and communication.

RESOURCES

- Alcamo, I. Edward. *Anatomy and Physiology the Easy Way.* Hauppauge, NY: Barrons Educational Series, 1996.

Piccard, Auguste

Physicist: made first stratosphere ascent
Born: January 28, 1884, Basel, Switzerland
Died: March 25, 1962, Lausanne, Switzerland

Piccard became famous for traveling high into the sky, then deep into the sea.

Unmanned **balloons** carrying instruments had relayed much information about the **atmosphere** during the early 1900s. But Piccard believed the only way to obtain large amounts of data about the stratosphere (upper atmosphere) was for humans to travel there. In 1930, he designed and built an airtight gondola containing air pressurized to sea-level pressure. The gondola was suspended from an enormous hydrogen-filled balloon. On May 27, 1931, Piccard and an assistant became the first people to enter the stratosphere, reaching an altitude of about 51,775 feet (15,800 m)—far higher

Auguste Piccard

than the previous record of approximately 29,000 feet (8,840 m).

Piccard also believed people should explore the ocean depths. He designed and built several **submersibles** called bathyscaphes that could withstand the great pressures of the deep ocean. In 1953, the submersible *Trieste*, carrying Piccard and his son Jacques [Swiss: 1922–], reached a record depth of 10,330 feet (3,150 m) in the Mediterranean Sea. Then in 1960, Jacques and U.S. Navy scientist Don Walsh took *Trieste* 35,800 feet (10,912 m) to the bottom of the Challenger Deep in the Pacific—the deepest part of Earth's ocean floor.

- More about Auguste Piccard.

http://www.execpc.com/shepler/piccard.html

http://www.diveweb.com/maritech/features/uw-wi99.02.htm

Piezoelectricity

Curie brothers (discovered piezoelectricity) ➤ Development of quartz-crystal clock ➤ Use of piezoelectricity in scanning tunneling microscope ➤ Applications of piezoelectric ceramics

Although his work with his wife **Marie Curie** is more famous, Pierre Curie [French: 1859–1906], working with his brother Jacques [French: 1855–1941], had made a major discovery well before meeting Marie. In 1880, the brothers observed that when pressure is applied, certain crystals, such as quartz, produce electric current. They named this piezoelectricity ("electricity from pressing"). They soon found that, like many effects in physics, the reverse process also occurs. Current in one direction makes a crystal lengthen and in the other shortens it. AC (alternating current), the kind transmitted by power plants, changes direction rapidly, causing a piezoelectric crystal to vibrate at the rate of change of the electric source.

Piezoelectricity has important applications. Vibrating crystals are used in **sound amplification**. The quartz-crystal clock, invented in 1928, is a piezoelectric device. Crystals that respond to pressure are the basis of some microphones and

Quartz crystal

methods of **sound recording.** The scanning tunneling **microscope** of 1981 requires a piezoelectric device to move its tip over a surface.

Recently, Japanese inventors have worked with piezoelectric **ceramics** to develop coatings that produce small electric currents in response to bending.

Planetary Rings

GALILEO (discovered Saturn's rings) ➤ **HUYGENS** (more detailed Saturn observations) ➤ **Cassini** (gap between Saturn's rings) ➤ **MAXWELL** (rings as satellites) ➤ Discovery of Uranus rings ➤ Discovery of rings around Jupiter ➤ Discovery of rings around Neptune

Galileo was the first to discover the rings around the **planet** Saturn in 1610, but could not see them well enough to know what they were. At first, he thought they were ears. In 1655, **Christiaan Huygens** began observing Saturn with a better **telescope** and, by 1656, had correctly concluded that the planet is circled by "a thin, flat ring, nowhere touching." But he assumed that the ring was as solid as it appears through a good telescope. Others doubted that assumption, especially after Giovanni Cassini [Italian-French: 1625–1712] in 1675 observed a gap between rings. Other evidence began to accumulate in favor of the rings being formed of many small bodies, each in its own orbit about the planet. **James Clerk Maxwell,** in 1860, developed the theoretical proof that the rings are composed of many small satellites, and, in 1895, observations

Saturn's rings, discovered following the invention of the telescope, were long believed to be unique in the solar system.

confirmed Maxwell's theory.

Until 1977, astronomers assumed that only Saturn had a ring system. That year, observations from a telescope in a high-flying airplane detected rings around Uranus, the planet beyond Saturn. Like Saturn, Uranus was also a giant ball of gas. Two years later, the space probe *Voyager 1* transmitted pictures of a ring around Saturn's other neighbor, gas-giant Jupiter. The rings around these planets are much narrower than Saturn's—more like wedding bands than like a disk with a hole for the planet—but also composed of many bodies. Astronomers searched for rings around the remaining gas-giant, Neptune. In 1984, they found rings but with a difference. At first they thought that the rings had gaps, but a visit by *Voyager 2* in 1989 showed that instead of gaps the outer ring contains four places where the small bodies form clumps.

Since 1979, several space probes have observed Saturn's rings. The visits revealed that there are thousands of individual rings. The ring bodies are ice and rock. Although Saturn's ring system is thousands of miles wide, it is less than 400 feet (120 m) thick.

RESOURCES

- Editors of Time-Life Books. *Moons and Rings* (Voyage through the Universe). Alexandria, VA: Time-Life, 1991.
- MORE ABOUT PLANETARY RINGS.

  http://ringmaster.arc.nasa.gov/

  http://www.agu.org/revgeophys/porc001/porc001.html

  http://imagine.gsfc.nasa.gov/docs/ask_astro/answers/981027a.html

Planets

Greece (Earth as sphere in space) ➤ **COPERNICUS** (sun at center of solar system) ➤ **GALILEO** (observed planets with telescope) ➤ **HERSCHEL** (discovered Uranus) ➤ **Adams/Leverrier** (predicted existence of Neptume) ➤ **Galle** (discovered Neptune) ➤ **Tombaugh** (discovered Pluto) ➤ Development of high-powered telescopes ➤ Discovery of extrasolar planets

The earliest known civilizations recognized that, although all other **stars** keep the same positions with respect to each other, five bodies that look like stars move among the rest. These five are not stars, but planets ("wanderers"). When the early sky-watchers described the **universe**, they included Earth, its Moon, the Sun, all the stars, and the five planets—Mercury, Venus, Mars, Jupiter, and Saturn. The ancient Greeks established that Earth is a sphere suspended in space. But their theories led them to explain the universe in terms of all bodies circling Earth. Starting with Earth, they counted the Moon, Mercury, Venus, the Sun, Mars, Jupiter, Saturn, and the stars. In 1543, however, **Nicolaus Copernicus** correctly placed the Sun at the center, and Earth, with its orbiting Moon, between Venus and Mars.

With his telescope in 1610, **Galileo** was able to see planets appear as "exactly circular globes that appear as little moons" instead of as twinkling points of light like stars. Astronomers soon concluded that the five planets and Earth are similar bodies, making six planets in all.

In 1781, **William Herschel** surprised the world by noticing a seventh planet that had been overlooked. Uranus, in orbit beyond Saturn, was just barely visible without a telescope. As astronomers studied Uranus over the next few decades, they recognized that its observed orbit does not match the orbit predicted by **Isaac Newton's** laws. In 1845, John Couch Adams [English: 1819–1892] and, independently in 1846, Urbain Leverrier [French: 1811–1877] calculated that another planet the size of Uranus orbiting beyond it could be the explanation. Each suggested to astronomers that they search the same region of the sky for this eighth planet, but only Leverrier found a cooperative astronomer. Johann Galle [German: 1812–1910] led the search, which found the planet Neptune in 1846, almost exactly where predicted.

It seemed likely that there might be a ninth planet beyond Neptune. An intensive search was mounted at the Lowell Observatory starting soon after it began operations in 1893. In 1929, Clyde Tombaugh [American: 1906–1997] joined the search team at Lowell, inventing a technique for comparing two sky photographs from consecutive days to see if any bodies wandered. On February 18, 1930, he found his wanderer. After following it for a few weeks, he announced the ninth planet, Pluto. Many astronomers still accept Pluto as the ninth planet—its very long orbit

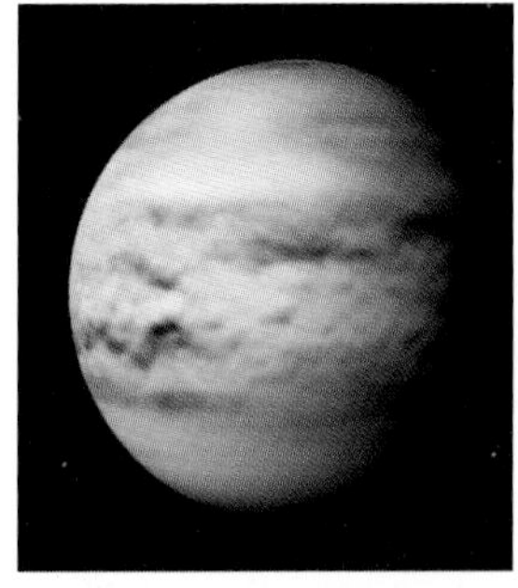

Earth (below), Venus (near right), and Mercury (far right)

takes it for part of the time inside Neptune's orbit, making it the eighth planet from the Sun about 10 percent of its 248-year trip around the Sun. But other astronomers have concluded that Pluto is too small to be a planet and is instead a giant frozen comet that never comes near enough to the Sun to develop a tail.

Starting in 1991, astronomers developed telescopes sensitive enough to detect dozens of planets that orbit stars (or star remnants called pulsars) other than our Sun. These are termed **extrasolar planets**.

RESOURCES

- Lauber, Patricia. *Journey to the Planets*. 4th ed. New York: Crown, 1993. (JUV/YA)
- Morrison, David. *Exploring Planetary Worlds*. New York: W.H. Freeman, 1993.
- Pasachoff, Jay M. *A Field Guide to the Stars and Planets*. 4th ed. Boston: Houghton-Mifflin, 1999.
- MORE ABOUT THE PLANETS.
  http://pds.jpl.nasa.gov/planets/welcome.htm
  http://www.seds.org/nineplanets/nineplanets/nineplanets.html
  http://www.bbc.co.uk/planets/
  http://nssdc.gsfc.nasa.gov/planetary/

Plastics

Parkes (first plastic) ➤ **Hyatt** (celluloid) ➤ **BAEKELAND** (first thermoplastic) ➤ **Staudiner** (theory of polymers) ➤ Germany (polystyrene) ➤ United States (polyvinyl chloride) ➤ Great Britain (polyethylene) ➤ **CAROTHERS** (first nylon) ➤ **PLUNKETT** (invented Teflon) ➤ Development of polyurethane ➤ Development of first electrically conducting plastic ➤ **Kwolek** (invented Kevlar)

The definition of the word "plastic" as anything that can be molded or shaped is broad enough to include such natural materials as rubber, wax, and even clay, but plastics today are always artificial. They can be molded and shaped, of course, but typically, plastics are made up of polymers, elements that repeat a specific chemical structure many times over.

The first material recognized as a plastic was a polymer made from wood cellulose that Alexander Parkes [English: 1813–1890] introduced to the world in 1862, although he had patented versions of the material he called parkesine as early as 1855. Parkesine was made by treating nitrocellulose, a powerful explosive, with wood alcohol to make it more stable. Other inventors also worked with nitrocellulose, trying to keep the plastic qualities while reducing the nitrogen content that makes it so explosive. The best known version is Celluloid, created by John Hyatt [American: 1837–1920] in 1868 to win a contest for a substance to replace ivory in billiard balls. In addition to reducing nitrogen, Hyatt added camphor to the mixture. By 1888, it had become the basis of photographic film and a commercial success. Later inventors removed all the nitrogen and replaced it with acetate. Cellulose acetate is less flammable and more stable in other ways also. **Fibers** based on cellulose plastics are known as rayons.

Cellulose plastics are called thermoplastics because they melt when heated. Thermosetting plastics are more useful in many applications because after they are shaped by molding, they no longer melt, even at high temperatures. The first thermosetting plastic is Bakelite, invented by **Leo Hendrik Baekeland** in 1906 and put on sale in 1917. The great success of Bakelite, made from phenol and formaldehyde, marks the beginning of what some

Plastics have numerous applications in today's world.

have called "the age of plastics." As with the cellulose nitrate plastics, many inventors created similar plastics by substituting for one of the ingredients.

Hermann Staudiner [German: 1881–1965] developed the theory of polymers, starting in 1926. Several familiar plastics were invented in 1930, including polystyrene in Germany and polyvinyl chloride (PVC) in the U.S. Polyethylene was created in Great Britain in 1933. In 1935, **Wallace Hume Carothers** invented the first of the nylons, a tough plastic most familiar as a fiber. **Roy J. Plunkett** invented Teflon in 1938. Polyurethane was patented in the U.S. in 1942. With some variants, such as biodegradable plastics made by adding starch molecules, the plastics of the 1930s and 1940s are still among the most popular today.

Although plastics have often replaced wood or metal, recent developments suggest even wider uses. In 1972, the first electrically conducting plastic, a form of polyacetylene, was accidentally found; since then, several improved versions have been invented. Kevlar, invented in 1976 by Stephanie L. Kwolek [American: 1923–], is lightweight but as strong as steel. Japanese researchers in 1987 developed a plastic that remembers a shape, which, in improved versions, may be used for chairs that remember the shapes of their owners, or for similar products. Also under development are light-emitting polymers and plastics that can replace silicon in transistors.

RESOURCES

- Meikle, Jeffrey L. *American Plastic: A Cultural History.* Piscataway, NJ: Rutgers University, 1995.
- History of Plastics.
  http://www.americanplasticscouncil.org/benefits/about_plastics/history.html

Plate Tectonics

WEGENER (theory of continental drift) ➤ Development of improved ocean mapping ➤ **Atlantis** (ocean floor comparatively thin) ➤ Development of fossil magnetism maps ➤ **Dietz** (concept of sea-floor spreading) ➤ **Hess** (expanded continental drift ideas) ➤ Development of plate tectonic theory

Plate tectonics is a theory about **Earth's structure** that is based on the idea that the crust of Earth is broken into more than a dozen rigid pieces called plates. These giant plates move in relation to one another, rising out of the depths of the Earth at one edge and plunging back at the other.

An earlier theory called "continental drift" led to the plate tectonics theory. The main proponent of this idea was **Alfred Wegener**, who initially described the theory in 1912. Wegener—and several other scientists, both before and after him—argued that the apparent matches of continental edges (such as fitting Brazil into the west African coastline) and of geological and paleontological features that pass from continent to continent prove that continents now separated by oceans were once joined. Geologists who opposed continental drift argued that no force could move the continents through the rock floor of the oceans. Until about 1950, most geologists opposed continental drift, although it continued as an alternative to theories based on all crustal motion being either up or down.

The change in attitude in the 1950s began in part because of better maps of the ocean floor from such expeditions as the ***Meteor* expedition** of the 1920s and **sonar** maps developed during World War II. These maps revealed giant mountain chains in mid-ocean with twists and curves that mirrored the zigzags of the nearest continents' coastlines—hundreds of miles away. Also in 1947, the U.S. *Atlantis* research ship demonstrated that the ocean floor is much thinner than the continental crust. The prevailing up-and-down theory

Collapsed highway caused by an earthquake.

Plate tectonics explains how volcanoes and mountain ranges form.

was based on the ocean crust's being much thicker than continental crust.

Also during the 1950s, the first maps of fossil **magnetism** trapped in rock began to be made. These confirmed that the continents had been in a different relation to one another in the past. The past locations of continents revealed by fossil magnetism are consistent with locations described in continental drift theory. In 1961, Robert S. Dietz [American: 1914–1995], a proponent of continental drift, coined the term "sea-floor spreading" to describe how the growth of ocean floor could move continents. Similar ideas were proposed in 1962 by Harry H. Hess [American: 1906–1969] and worked out in more detail. When studies of fossil magnetism in 1963 demonstrated that sea-floor spreading was occurring, the idea came to be accepted by orthodox geol-

ogists. There were still several objections to the theory, but studies in the next three years resolved all in favor of a broad theory that combined continental drift, sea-floor spreading, and the origins of earthquakes, **volcanoes**, and **mountains** into the single concept labeled plate tectonics. The ***Glomar Challenger* mission** that began in 1968, and the 1974 discovery of new seafloor being created at deep ocean rifts, confirmed plate tectonics.

RESOURCES

- Gallant, Roy A. *Dance of the Continents* (The History of Science Series). Tarrytown, NY: Benchmark, 2000. (JUV/YA)
- More about Plate Tectonics.

  http://www.seismo.unr.edu/ftp/pub/louie/class/100/plate-tectonics.html

  http://pubs.usgs.gov/publications/text/dynamic.html - anchor19309449

  http://www.ucmp.berkeley.edu/geology/tectonics.html

  http://wwwneic.cr.usgs.gov/neis/plate_tectonics/rift_man.html

Plunkett, Roy J.

Chemist: discovered Teflon
Born: June 26, 1910, New Carlisle, Ohio
Died: May 12, 1994, Corpus Christi, Texas

In 1938, while trying to develop an improved refrigerant (cooling gas), Plunkett discovered polytetrafluoroethylene (PTFE), better known under its trademarked name, Teflon. Teflon is a polymer **plastic**, with a surface so slippery that almost nothing sticks to it or is absorbed by it. It doesn't react with other chemicals and isn't affected by heat or cold. These characteristics make Teflon useful in numerous applications, including kitchenware for easy cleaning and outdoor clothing for water repellence.

YEARBOOK: 1938

- Plunkett discovers Teflon.
- Hungarian inventor Lazlo Biró invents the first ballpoint **pen** for writing on paper.
- The Nestlé Corporation introduces the first successful instant coffee.
- Fluorescent **lighting** is introduced.

Teflon was discovered accidentally. One day Plunkett and an associate filled some cylinders with tetrafluoroethylene (TFE) gas and placed them in cold storage. The next day, when they opened the valve at the top of one cylinder, they found that the gas was gone. Curious, they sawed open the cylinder and found a slippery white powder on its inner walls. As Plunkett studied the powder, he realized that the TFE had spontaneously polymerized (formed huge chain molecules).

RESOURCES

- More about Roy J. Plunkett.

  http://www.chemheritage.org/HistoricalServices/Abstract/plunkett.htm
- History of Teflon.

  http://www.dupont.com/teflon/newsroom/history.html
- History of Plastics.

  http://www.americanplasticscouncil.org/benefits/about_plastics/history.html

Polarization

Bartholin (first to observe polarized light) ➤ **Malus** (developed many rules of polarization) ➤ **Biot** (polarized light exists in a single plane, circular polarization) ➤ **Fresnel** (wave theory of polarization) ➤ **PASTEUR** (left and right handed forms of compounds) ➤ **LAND** (invented polarizing sunglasses)

Light waves act like water waves, but they fill space instead of being confined to a surface. Certain transparent materials, reflections from surfaces other than metals and mirrors, or diffusion by tiny particles, eliminate part of the wave parallel to one plane, leaving for example, only the vertical part or the horizontal part. Light transmitted by such partial waves is polarized. Polarized light (or other electromagnetic radiation) explains many phenomena and also has useful applications.

Although birds and bees are able to recognize polarization of sunlight by dust and use it for navigation, credit for the first scientist to observe polarized light usually goes to Erasmus Bartholin [Danish: 1625–1698], who in 1669 described how a transparent form of the mineral calcite, called Iceland spar, splits light into two different images. In 1808, Etienne Malus [French: 1775–1812] accidentally discovered that reflected light varies in intensity when seen through Iceland spar as the mineral is rotated. He worked out many of the rules of polarization and coined its name, based on an incorrect theory that particles of light have two poles. The correct theory, based on waves, was developed in 1821 by Augustin Fresnel [French: 1788–1827]. The two images of Iceland spar are each polarized along different planes, which causes them to refract at different angles.

A few years before Fresnel's theory, Jean Biot [French: 1774–1862] discovered another aspect of polarization. Polarized light consists of waves in a single plane, as if the light had passed though a filter that removes waves perpendicular to that plane. Biot, in 1812, found crystals that rotated the plane of polarization, some clockwise and others counterclockwise. In 1815, he also discovered liquids that rotated the polarization. This phenomenon is called circular polarization. It led to the discovery by **Louis Pasteur** in 1848 that some compounds occur in both left-handed and right-handed forms.

Perhaps the most common application of polarization today is polarizing sunglasses, based on an invention of **Edwin Herbert Land** in the 1920s. These eliminate polarized glare reflected from surfaces such as water or sand. Polarization of electromagnetic waves, from radio to gamma rays, is used as part of many devices, including liquid crystal **displays** for computers.

• More about Polarization.

http://www.glenbrook.k12.il.us/gbssci/phys/Class/light/u12l1e.html

http://www.polarization.com/

Pollution Controls

Introduction of harmful or unpleasant substances into the environment is termed pollution. Pollution can occur naturally when volcanic eruptions dirty the air, or minerals leaching from soil contaminate water; but most pollution today is caused by human activities. The best way to limit pollution is to stop the activity that causes it, just as coal

Smog is a form of air pollution.

A catalytic converter uses a catalyst (a substance that speeds a chemical reaction) to remove poisonous carbon monoxide from automobile exhaust along with nitrogen oxides and unburned fuel that together cause smog and ozone. Heavy metals, especially platinum, rhodium, and palladium, absorb nitrogen oxides and encourage them to break into harmless nitrogen and oxygen. The unburned fuel and carbon monoxide are similarly encouraged to combine with oxygen, producing carbon dioxide and water vapor.

burning was banned in London in 1307 (although it resumed later), or as nations banned chlorofluorocarbons (CFCs) in 1989 when it became clear that they damage the ozone layer of the atmosphere.

When a polluting activity is deemed essential, such as producing electric power or driving in **automobiles**, pollution is reduced by removing harmful substances before they enter the environment. Two devices for reducing air pollution are important examples. In 1908, Frederick G. Cottrell [American: 1877–1948] invented the electrostatic precipitator, which uses **static electricity** to remove soot from smokestack emissions. Similarly, in the 1970s, automobile manufacturers, faced with new U.S. requirements for reducing pollution produced by automobiles, began to install catalytic converters in automobiles. The catalytic converter was invented in 1962 by Eugene J. Houdry [French: 1892–1962], who had also invented the main process used for obtaining gasoline from **petroleum.**

- BIOGRAPHY OF EUGENE J. HOUDRY.

  http://www.invent.org/book/book-text/59.html

- MORE ABOUT CATALYTIC CONVERTERS.

  http://www.howstuffworks.com/catalytic-converter.htm

Priestley, Joseph B.

Chemist: discovered oxygen
Born March 13, 1733, Birstall Fieldhead, England
Died February 6, 1804, Northumberland, Pennsylvania

Oxygen was discovered twice. In 1774, Priestley heated red mercuric oxide and noticed it produced a colorless gas that made a candle burn "with a remarkably vigorous flame." Later that

Joseph B. Priestley

YEARBOOK: 1775

- Priestley discovers hydrochloric acid and sulfuric acid.
- **James Watt** patents his **steam engine**.
- **Alessandro Volta** describes his electrophorus, the first practical device to generate static electricity.

year, he traveled to France and told **Antoine-Laurent Lavoisier** about this new kind of "air." After doing his own experiments in 1777, Lavoisier gave Priestley's discovery the name oxygen. That same year Carl Wilhelm Scheele [Swedish: 1742–1786] published results of his discovery of the gas, which had occurred at least a year prior to Priestley's discovery.

Using equipment he designed himself, Priestley discovered a number of other gases, including ammonia, nitric oxide, and carbon monoxide. He recognized that green plants need light to grow and that they give off oxygen—observations that led to the work of **Jan Ingenhousz**.

In the 1760s, Priestley conducted electrical experiments. He met **Benjamin Franklin**, who encouraged Priestley to write a summary of knowledge of electricity up to that time. Priestley published *The History and Present State of Electricity* in 1767.

RESOURCES

- Gray, Dulcie. *J.B. Priestley*. New York: Sutton, 2000.
- More about Joseph Priestley.

  http://www.spaceship-earth.de/Biograph/Priestley.htm

Printing and Type

China (invention of paper, wood block carving) ➤ **Bi Sheng** (ceramic characters, movable type) ➤ Europe (paper manufacturing, wood block printing) ➤ **GUTENBERG** (first printing based on letters, better ink) ➤ Development of stereotype ➤ **SENEFELDER** (lithography) ➤ Development of steam engines to power presses ➤ **Hoe** (printing on curved plates) ➤ **Mergenthaler** (Linotype) ➤ Composition of type directly onto film ➤ Development of digital composition ➤ Development of laser character formation, ink-jet technology

Printing is a process of reproducing images from an original. Type composition, or typesetting, is the creation of arrangements of strings of words, letters, or numbers to be used in printing. Text that has been composed is often arranged on pages, perhaps with illustrations, a process sometimes called formatting. All three processes are closely connected.

The invention of **paper** in China made printing practical. For the first time, there was an abundant material on which to print. Printing came before type. The Chinese about 600 C.E. carved characters

From earlier times, a composition stick and typecase

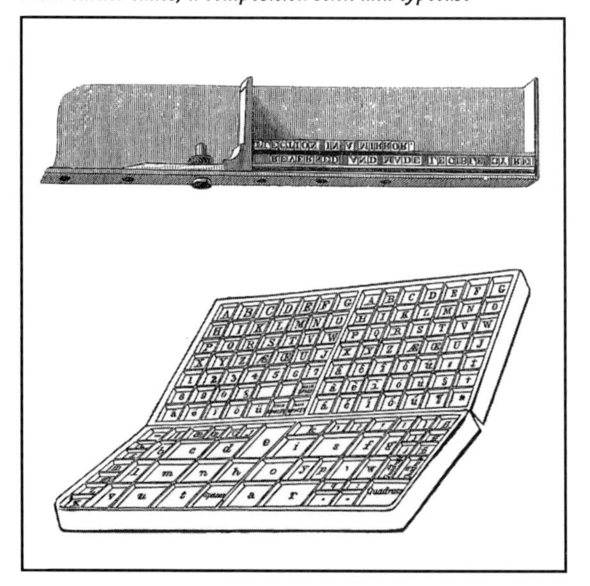

An early printing press

and illustrations on flat blocks of wood, which were coated with ink and pressed onto paper. The earliest surviving book, however, comes from 870. About 1045, a Chinese inventor named Bi Sheng, about whom little is known, began to make separate ceramic characters for each word and placed them in wooden frames to make running text. This is called movable type, since the separate pieces, or type, can be rearranged and reused.

About the time of the invention of movable type in China, paper manufacture began in Europe, followed rapidly by printing with wood blocks. About 1450, **Johannes Gutenberg** combined several technologies to create the first printing based on letters instead of characters for whole words. He created a better ink and adapted a wine press to make multiple copies of pages. Soon after this, the stereotype was developed, a mold of a movable type page. While it was not used for the first printing, the stereotype could be used for reprints, so the original type could be separated and reused. Gutenberg's invention quickly spread from Germany throughout Europe—by 1500 about 35,000 different books had been printed along with countless other materials.

Printing and composition methods did not change much from Gutenberg's time until the **Industrial Revolution**. Stereotyping was improved enough that stereotype plates were often used for printing first runs in place of the original page

A pressman supervises a modern printing press.

set in movable type. In 1798, **Aloys Senefelder** invented lithography, a method of copying type onto a stone plate that could then be used for printing. In the early 1800s, steam engines began to be used to power presses. To get paper through the presses faster, printing on rolls of paper using rotating curved plates replaced printing on separate sheets, starting with the inventions of Richard March Hoe [American: 1812–1886] in 1847.

Type was still set by hand before making plates, but that changed in 1884, when Ottmar Mergenthaler [German-American: 1854–1899] invented the Linotype, a machine that cast a single line of type at a time following keyboarding. Other methods of mechanical typesetting soon followed. Gradually, photographic methods were introduced to plate making. The first commercial device that composed type directly onto film went on the market in 1948. In 1985, the process advanced one step farther as software was introduced for composing and formatting in digital form, which then could be directly scanned onto film.

The advent of the personal computer led to a new form of printing—single copies that duplicate material viewed on a computer monitor. Although this form of printing began with metal type used by devices similar to a **typewriter**, it has evolved into several forms. In one, characters are formed by lasers in a system based on xerography, which is fast, but most suitable for black type. Another system, called ink-jet printing, forms letters in black or in color by spraying small drops of ink onto the paper.

How It Works

In the most popular commercial printing method today, letters, illustrations, and formats are first stored as digital information. This is converted to images on film. The film is used to make curved plates that have raised surfaces for the material that is to appear printed on paper. As rolls of paper are fed to the printing press, the plates are inked and the ink is transferred to a rubber roller, which then rolls the ink onto the paper, a process called offset lithography.

RESOURCES

- Needham, Paul and Michael Joseph (eds.). *Adventure and Art: The First Hundred Years of Printing.* Piscataway, NJ: Rutgers University, 1999.
- More about Printing.

  http://www.digitalcentury.com/encyclo/update/print.html

  http://www.hotlinecy.com/prthistory.htm

Prions

In 1982, Stanley B. Prusiner [American: 1942–] isolated very tiny particles called prions from brains. He proposed that prions cause infectious diseases known as spongiform encephalopathies. Prions consist solely of a protein, lacking cell structure and the nucleic acids DNA and RNA. Normal prions form part of the surface of nerve cells. For reasons not yet understood, normal prions can be transformed into abnormal prions capable of destroying cells.

Spongiform encephalopathies are fatal diseases characterized by the breakdown of brain tissue, leaving holes and giving it a spongelike consistency. The diseases include bovine spongiform encephalopathy (BSE), popularly called "mad cow disease," and Creutzfeldt-Jakob disease in humans. In 1996, it was announced that the infectious agents causing BSE probably could spread to humans who ate contaminated beef, causing a variant of Creutzfeldt-Jakob disease. This was proved beyond a doubt in 1999.

RESOURCES

- Rhodes, Richard. Deadly Feasts: *The 'Prion' Controversy and the Public's Health.* New York: Touchstone, 1998.
- PRUSINER, STANLEY B. "THE PRION DISEASES." **http://www.nmia.com/mdibble/prion.html**

Humans can obtain proteins by eating beef and other meat.

Proteins

Vauquelin/Robiquet (isolated first amino acid) ➤ **Rose** (isolated threonine) ➤ **Fischer** (amino acids linked by peptide bonds, first synthesized polypeptide)

Proteins are large, complex organic chemicals essential for life. Some are major structural materials, some are **enzymes**, and some function as carriers or storage molecules.

Despite the great variety of proteins—a typical human cell contains about 10,000 different proteins—all proteins are composed of the same sub-units called amino acids. Organisms use 20 different amino acids to build proteins. The first amino acid to be isolated was asparagine, by Louis Nicolas Vauquelin [French: 1763–1829] and Pierre Jean Robiquet [French: 1780–1840] in 1806. The last to be recognized was threonine, by William Cumming Rose [American: 1887–1985] in 1935.

At the beginning of the 1900s, Emil Fischer [German: 1852–1919] found that amino acids are linked together in chains by peptide bonds, which connect the carboxyl group of one amino acid to the amino group of the next. A protein is called a polypeptide because it consists of a long chain of amino acids. In 1907, Fischer synthesized a polypeptide by uniting 18 amino acids.

> **FAMOUS FIRST**
>
> During the 1950s, Paul Zamecnik [American: 1912–] and Mahlon Hoagland [American: 1921–] demonstrated that protein synthesis takes place in ribosomes. Ribosomes are tiny structures found in all cells.

Initially, each protein was believed to have a unique structure. But, beginning in the 1950s, scientists determined that there is an organization common to protein molecules. The primary structure is the specific sequence of amino acids in a polypeptide chain. The secondary structure is the way the chain is twisted or pleated. The tertiary structure is the folding of the chain. A quaternary structure results from the bonding of two or more polypeptides.

RESOURCES

- More about Amino Acids.

  http://ntri.tamuk.edu/cell/chapter3/amino-acids.html

  http://www.ann.com.au/MedSci/amino.htm

- More about Proteins.

  http://synapseman.norulez.com/bioinformatics/backgrnd.htm

Ptolemy, Claudius

Astronomer, geographer: developed theory of planetary motion
Born: c. 100, Egypt
Died: c. 170, Alexandria, Egypt

Building on work by **Hipparchus**, Ptolemy constructed the best model up to his time of how **planets** move. Ptolemy accepted the contemporary belief that Earth is at the center of the **universe**. He showed the planets and Sun orbiting Earth in circular paths. At the same time, he said, these objects move in smaller circles called epicycles—similar to advancing around a circular track in smaller circles. Though Ptolemy's model more or less matched observed planetary movements, it was incorrect. Nonetheless, it was widely

Claudius Ptolemy

accepted until contradicted by **Nicolaus Copernicus** in the 1500s.

Based on his astronomical observations, Ptolemy expanded a catalog of star positions developed by Hipparchus to include 48 constellations and 1,022 stars.

Ptolemy's eight-volume *Geography* included **maps** of the known world and extensive use of coordinates now called longitude and latitude. *Geography* had many errors, but influenced Europeans for centuries. In the 1400s, it strengthened Christopher Columbus's belief that he could reach Asia by sailing west across the Atlantic Ocean.

RESOURCES

- MORE ABOUT CLAUDIUS PTOLEMY.
  http://www.janusgroup.org/ptolemy.htm
  http://www.norfacad.pvt.k12.va.us/project/ptolemy/ptolemy.htm

Pumps

Development of first bellows ➤ China (double-acting bellows) ➤ **Ctesibius** (stream of water pump) ➤ Italy (pump for removing fluids) ➤ **GUERICKE** (air pump to create vacuum) ➤ **HOOKE/BOYLE/Sprengel** (better vacuum pumps) ➤ Development of steam engines to lift water to new heights ➤ **Savery** ("miner's friend") ➤ **NEWCOMEN** (improved steam engine)

Some pumps are designed to push a fluid out of a reservoir so that the fluid can be used, while others are designed to empty a reservoir of a fluid. The simple and ancient bellows is a pump that pushes air. About 300 B.C.E. the Chinese developed a double-acting bellows that pumped a continuous stream of air. A similar early pump, dating from about 200 B.C.E. was designed by Ctesibius [Greek: b. c. 250 B.C.E.] to make a stream of water to put out fires. The same idea was used well into the 19th century. The water in each of two cylinders is pushed alternatively by pistons into a central space from which it streams forth continuously.

The earliest known pump for removing a fluid was built about 50 C.E. by Roman engineers to empty water that leaked into a ship. It operated with a crank handle, the first known use of a crank outside of China. Miners and construction workers in the Middle Ages developed suction pumps that created a partial vacuum to clear mines and ditches. About 1645, **Otto von Guericke** developed a small air pump that could produce a good vacuum; improvements on this idea by **Robert Hooke** and **Robert Boyle** made several advances in science possible. In 1865, Herman

Water pump

Sprengel [German-English: 1834–1906] invented an improved vacuum pump based on using the weight of mercury to create the vacuum; Sprengel's pump made incandescent electric lights and vacuum tubes possible.

Suction pumps to lift water are limited by the force of air pressure, which is strong enough to push a column of water up about 30 feet (10 m) but no more. **Steam engines** were invented to remedy this problem. "The Miner's Friend" of Thomas Savery [English: c. 1650–1751] in 1698 simply added steam pressure to atmospheric pressure to make a more effective suction pump, but **Thomas Newcomen's** steam engine of 1712 pushed water out of the mine; even the earliest model raised 120 gallons (540 L) of water 153 feet (46 m) each minute.

Purkinje, Jan Evangelista

Physiologist: discovered a visual phenomenon
Born: December 17, 1787, Libochovice, Bohemia (now Czech Republic)
Died: July 28, 1869, Prague, Bohemia (now Czech Republic)

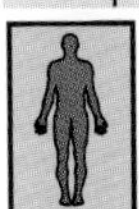

As a university student Purkinje (sometimes spelled Purkyne) studied vision and discovered a phenomenon now known as the Purkinje effect. As light intensity decreases, objects of equal brightness but different colors appear to fade at different rates. For instance, the eye perceives that red objects fade faster than blue objects.

Purkinje recognized that fingerprints are unique.

In 1832, Purkinje acquired a compound microscope and became a pioneer in the study of **cells**. In the brain's cerebellum he discovered large nerve cells with numerous extensions (Purkinje cells); in the heart he found fibers that carry stimuli from the pacemaker to other parts of the heart (Purkinje fibers). He was the first to recognize that each person has unique fingerprints and, therefore, that fingerprints can be used for identification.

Purkinje introduced several improvements to the study of cells. He was the first to use a microtome, a mechanical device for

YEARBOOK: 1833

- Purkinje discovers sweat glands.
- The first **enzyme** is discovered.
- William Whewell [English: 1794–1866] introduces the terms **electrolysis**, anode, cathode, and ion.
- Marshall Hall [English: 1790–1857] coins the term "reflex" to describe an automatic response to a stimulus.

cutting tissue into thin sections for microscopic examination. Previously, people sliced tissue freehand with a razor.

RESOURCES

- More about Jan Evangelista Purkinje.
  http://neurolab.jsc.nasa.gov/purkinje.htm
  http://www.medicalpost.com/mdlink/english/members/medpost/data/3321/51.HTM

Quantum Theory

Planck (energy in packets) ➤ **EINSTEIN** (light can behave as particles) ➤ **BOHR** (electrons can change orbits) ➤ **DE BROGLIE** (electrons can behave as waves) ➤ **Heisenberg/Schrodinger/Dirac** (quantum mechanics) ➤ Development of quantum electrodynamics ➤ **GELL-MANN** (quarks)

Quantum theory is that part of modern physics that deals with very small objects, especially **subatomic particles** and **atoms**. It also studies effects that occur because these objects follow mathematical rules different from those used to describe larger objects. The first example of this was the discovery in 1900 by Max Planck [German: 1858–1947] that energy comes in small packets, which he called quanta (Latin, loosely, for "just so big"). Before this, most scientists thought that energy was a continuous quantity. **Albert Einstein** used the quantum idea in 1905 to show that light sometimes behaves as particles, although there was much convincing evidence of light also behaving as waves. Similarly, **Niels Bohr,** in 1913, used the idea to show that an electron jumps instantly from one orbit to another in a hydrogen atom.

In 1924, **Louis-Victor De Broglie** proposed that electrons and, indeed, all particles can also behave as waves. His idea led to quantum mechanics—methods of calculating the behavior of electrons developed in 1925 by Werner Heisenberg [German: 1901–1976], in 1926 by Erwin Schrödinger [Austrian: 1887–1961], and, in 1928, by Paul A. M. Dirac [English-American: 1902–1984]. This work enabled physicists and chemists to understand the physical basis of most phenomena and to predict new ones. Since then, these ideas have become the basis of modern **microprocessors** and other advanced technology.

Quantum theory was extended again starting in 1947 when the combined ideas of several scientists became a new theory of electrons and other charged particles in motion, known as quantum electrodynamics. After **Murray Gell-Mann** introduced quarks in 1964, the theory came to be called quantum chromodynamics. In all versions of quantum theory, highly mathematical ideas are used to predict the behavior of particles or waves with unprecedented accuracy.

RESOURCES

- Gallant, Roy A. *The Ever-Changing Atom*. Tarrytown, NY: Benchmark, 2000. (JUV/YA)
- Pauling, Linus and E. Bright Wilson. *Introduction to Quantum Mechanics.* Mineola, NY: Dover, 1985.
- Rudiments of Quantum Theory.
  http://www.chembio.uoguelph.ca/educmat/chm386/rudiment/rudiment.htm

Quasars

In the 1950s, astronomers began to survey the sky with **radiotelescopes**. At first, they could not determine which radio sources matched

FAMOUS FIRST

In 1963, Maarten Schmidt [Dutch-American: 1929–] became the first to recognize that a quasar is a distant, powerful energy source. He determined that 3C273 is moving away at a speed of 29,400 miles (47,400 km) per second—a sixth the speed of light. This great speed is explained by the effect that the expansion of the universe has on very distant objects.

visible objects. In 1960, Allan Sandage [American: 1926–] matched a dim "star" to radio source 3C48. But light from 3C48 does not resemble light from a star, so the object was named a quasi-stellar ("star-like") radio source, or quasar for short. Soon, other quasars were seen. These mysterious objects were found to be very far away. A quasar observed in 2000, for example, is nearly 12,000,000,000 light years away.

How can something that far away be seen? A quasar is a cloud of gas and dust being pulled so fast into a black hole that the cloud releases energy in massive amounts. As quasars age, matter nearby has vanished into the black hole, so energy production slows. We only see young quasars, whose light started toward us billions of years ago.

RESOURCES

- Englebert, Phillis (ed.). *Astronomy and Space: From the Big Bang to the Big Crunch.* Detroit, MI: U*X*L, 1996. (JUV/YA)
- Kerrod, Robin. *Astronomy* (Learn About Series). London: Lorenz, 1998. (JUV/YA)
- More about Quasars.

  http://starchild.gsfc.nasa.gov/docs/StarChild/universe_level2/quasars.html

  http://chandra.harvard.edu/xray_sources/quasars.html

  http://www.phys.vt.edu/jhs/faq/quasars.html

Pictures of quasars taken by the Chandra X-ray Observatory, left, and the Hubble Space Telescope, right.

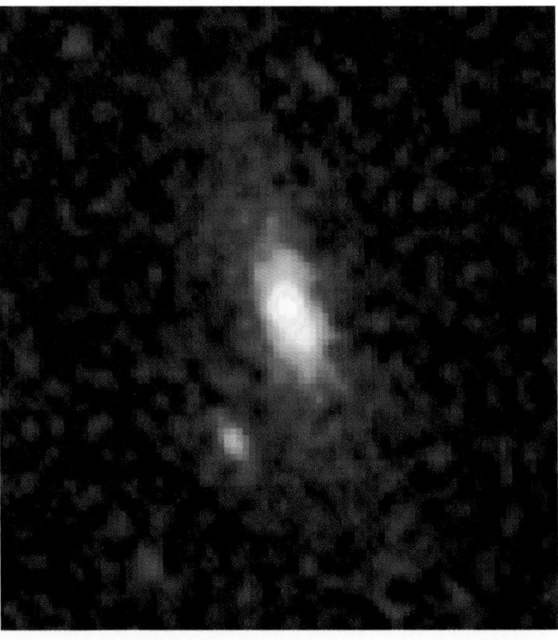